# From the Ashes

CANDICE WRIGHT

This is a work of fiction. Names, characters, places, and incidents either are the products of the author's imagination or are used fictitiously.
Any resemblance to actual persons, living or dead, businesses, companies, events, or locales is entirely coincidental.

# CONTENTS

## ALSO BY CANDICE WRIGHT

### THE INHERITANCE SERIES

Rewriting yesterday

https://books2read.com/u/3JVj6v

In This Moment

https://books2read.com/u/bxvnJd

The Promise of tomorrow

https://books2read.com/u/bowEy1

The Complete Inheritance Series Box Set

https://books2read.com/u/mBO7ev...

### THE UNDERESTIMATED SERIES

The Queen of Carnage

https://books2read.com/u/47EMrj

The Princess of Chaos

https://books2read.com/u/mBOX9Z

THE FOUR HORSEWOMEN OF THE APOCALYSE SERIES

The Pures

https://books2read.com/u/3np7N9

*For Phoebe*

*You are strength, beauty and grace personified.*

# ONE

*I'll die here; we all will.*

That's the thought that flashes through my mind as I take in the town before me. The cool, crisp air feels refreshing against my skin as I step off the stuffy bus that was overfilled and smelled like sickness and despair. Everyone surrounding me is more dead than alive, but then, that's something we all have in common.

I inhale and let the clean fresh air fill my lungs before moving aside and making space for the rest of the passengers to exit and drift towards the growing crowd. From the size of it, I would say we are one of the last buses to arrive, bringing the total of people marked for death to 6,472 in total. Six thousand four hundred and seventy-two people all diagnosed with some kind of terminal illness, but we didn't come here to live out the rest of our days in peace, we came here to die.

Every single one of us had signed on the dotted line, giving away control of our lives—or what was left of them—to a clandestine government-run operation known only as the Phoenix Project. None of us really knew for sure what we had signed up for, only that we would be test subjects for some type of new biological agent. Reading between the lines, it's easy to guess what the government's interest in that would be. Nothing makes a more effective weapon than a bigger and badder biological agent than the one your enemies have. But that isn't for us to worry about. We had all decided to push aside whatever morals we had left in order to leave something behind for our families. We were here for our brothers and sisters, our mothers, fathers, and our children. The Phoenix Project offered a one-off payment of one million dollars to the person or persons of our choice as compensation, giving them financial security long after we were gone. My family, crippled over the years with my continuous medical bills and expenses, would be able to breathe again. My funeral costs would be covered and all my medical bills would be wiped clean. My death was inevitable; anything I might have to endure here would be worth it to know they would be looked after. Peace of mind is all I can ask for right now, which is how I find myself standing on the side of an old-fashioned cobbled road, staring up at their so-called facility. This is the place I'm going to be calling home from now on, however temporary that may be.

Some of the information provided was incredibly detailed, explaining exactly what was expected from us and for us. Some of the details, however, had been purposely vague. One of those vague details I didn't dwell too much on was the word "facility," which turned out to be just that—a word. I had conjured up an image of a private hospital or even a laboratory of some kind but nothing like this. Instead, I'm moving here, to a privately funded town with thousands of other people who found themselves in the same boat as me.

The town itself is beautiful, a mix of old and new with a modern twist. Small timber buildings with wraparound porches give way to neat little lawns with pretty flower borders. It gives off a charming, homey kind of vibe. Everything is well kept, tidy, and unspoiled. It's also eerie as fuck. All that's missing are people sitting on porch swings sipping lemonade and waving at passing neighbors as they drive at a leisurely pace through town.

Instead of feeling inviting, it just feels lonely. Probably because before our mass arrival, it had been deserted. Like a place that time forgot. In fact, I'm willing to bet everything I have that you won't find this town marked on any map, not out here in the middle of bumfuck nowhere.

I'm jerked out of my thoughts as someone knocks into me, sending me sprawling across the uneven ground. I land hard on my hands and knees in the dust and wince. Checking my hands, which are now embedded with tiny pieces of gravel, I sigh in resignation.

Looking up, I find myself staring at the back of a seriously built guy with tattoos running up the back of his neck and hands, which is the only skin I can see from here. He's dressed from head to toe in black, from his jeans and T-shirt to the duffel bag tossed over his shoulder. Guess the color suits him because nothing about this guy's demeanor screams sunshine.

I'm assuming that's the dickhead that just pushed me over, the arrogant ass.

"You all right?" A hand appears in front of me, so I snag it, ignoring the stinging of my palms, and use it to hoist myself up.

"Thanks. I'm fine. Figures that even here there would be at least one asshole. I'm Cam, by the way."

"I'm Jack." He smiles. "And you're right about Fox, the guy is an asshole." He laughs.

Jack is, in a word, hot. Shoulder length dirty blonde hair, eyes so green they remind me of grass in the springtime, and twin dimples that I'm sure make the ladies swoon. He's a little too pretty for my brain to process, making my nerves kick in. I gently pull my hand from his, feeling my palm getting a little sweaty. I try to discreetly wipe my hand on the leg of my jeans before he notices and I embarrass myself any further.

I pull up a mental snapshot of what I look like and sigh. It figures. Why is it the way of the world that whenever you look like shit, you'll either run into your ex or meet a guy who is hotter than hell?

I mean, from where I'm standing, Jack looks healthy as fuck to me.

Obviously that isn't the case, otherwise he wouldn't be here, but still, this boy is fine. I look away and sigh. It's not like he would be interested in me anyway and even if he was, who wants to make connections with someone who could be dead the next day?

I try to memorize the faces of the people pouring out of the remaining buses, but my effort is in vain. I know that maybe not today or even tomorrow, but soon, these people will be gone. They will fade from existence, leaving this town as desolate as before. All that will remain will be the memories of the people that once loved them, the people they left behind.

"Hey, where'd you go?"

I turn back to Jack. "Sorry, I zoned out a little. I'm just trying to take it all in," I tell him.

"It's a lot, huh?" he asks, stealing the thoughts from my head.

I nod, scanning the sea of people surrounding us. All are aged between eighteen and sixty; that was one of the requirements. Each and every one of us is suffering from a variety of terminal illnesses. There are some that you can see are sick straight away. I guess I fall into that category. Thanks to intense rounds of chemo and radiation, I'm down to around eighty-five pounds and I lost all my hair in the process. I look like a walking toothpick with a head as smooth as a billiard ball. In fact, my whole appearance screams *I have cancer* and I fucking hate it.

Believe it or not, there are some people here that look worse than me. I'll be surprised if they make it through the night. I find myself respecting them for hanging on by the skin of their teeth so their families will be provided for. It's a great way of sticking your middle fingers up at your weakening body and saying fuck you.

Then there are others who look like Jack. They almost appear as if they just got off at the wrong stop.

"It's just sad. All these people are leaving behind someone they care about. People who will love and miss them. All of us are going to die here alone, thousands of miles from home. I guess a part of me feels a little like I sold my soul to the devil," I tell him.

"I get that, but the truth is, Cam, everyone dies. There's no point in sugarcoating it. It is what it is. At least you're leaving your family with something to help them when you're gone. It's more than a lot of people get. Most are left with broken hearts and forgotten dreams, not a million-dollar legacy." Wow, and I thought I was jaded.

The unmistakable sound of a megaphone crackles before a loud voice booms out across the crowd.

"All right everyone, gather around. Your housing has been designated based on your needs and your health. Everything you could possibly want or need will be provided for you."

"Yeah, except a cure," I mumble under my breath.

"You were all given a pack when you boarded your bus. Your apartment number and key will be in there with a map of all the facilities. We want you to live as much of a normal life as possible. You will notice the town is outfitted with state-of-the-art cameras. They are there for us to observe you, but also for your safety. By now, you should have already studied the rules. You must abide by each of them, including the curfew. If you break them, your family will forfeit any payments from us when you pass."

What? I don't remember that being in the small print. It's not that I'm a rule breaker by nature but I'm not good with curfews and confinement, especially after spending so much time stuck in hospital beds and isolated away from my friends and family.

"I don't remember reading that part," I whisper to Jack.

"That's because it wasn't in there." I look up at him sharply. How can he be so sure?

"I have an eidetic memory. Unfortunately, I can't forget anything even if I want to," Jack answers glumly. I don't question him on this, sensing it's a hot topic for him.

"Guess there isn't much we can do about it now. What would I even say? Hey, I was planning on breaking some rules but I'm not comfortable with being punished for it?" I shake my head, imagining how that would go down.

He offers me a small smile before opening his pack.

Looks like I'm just going to have to suck it up.

"If everyone would like to make their way to their designated accommodation now, someone will be along shortly to answer any questions you might have. It is important that you ask everything you need to know because, after today, the city will be on lockdown. Only medical personnel will be permitted to come and go freely."

That part was in the information pack. Something about having a controlled environment while they run their tests and dose us. Let's not forget that the last thing these guys want is for one of us to end up back in the general population contaminating them. Plus, it kind of messes with the whole top secret thing they have going on. I pull the welcome pack from my backpack and search for my apartment number. Apartment 8823, room 4, building G grid number 6. Grid number? Jesus, could they have made this any more difficult? With my sense of direction, chances are I'll be breaking the imposed ten o'clock curfew before I ever find my apartment.

"Any idea where you're going? I'll be honest, I haven't got a clue," I tell Jack, who is studying his own information.

He smiles that freaking dimpled smile at me before grabbing the sheet from my hand.

"Ah, cool. You're in the same apartment building as me." Huh, what are the odds? Everyone starts to shuffle forward, so I follow along with Jack by my side as we move within the sea of people. Turns out our apartment is one of the new modern structures set farthest from the drop-off point. I don't mind this one little bit though, because the building backs up against a pretty wooded area. As it's autumn right now, all the trees are at various stages of turning red and yellow, providing us with a picturesque foliage canopy.

Jack and I walk over to the group of people already there. It seems we are the last two to arrive, everyone else has already gathered around outside our new home listening to the designated spokesperson talk about the amenities and what the daily routine will look like.

I glance around at my new neighbors, checking to see who else I will be sharing the building with. There are maybe thirty of us in total and all of us, at a rough guess, appear to be between twenty and thirty years old. Unfortunately, that's not the only thing I notice. I take another quick glance around just to be sure then silently curse my luck.

I seem to be the only female here. Fuck. I'm utterly exhausted. The thought of having to traipse myself back through town to find the correct accommodation makes my head hurt. I wait until everyone makes their way inside before approaching the speaker.

"Um... hi. I was just wondering, erm... I seem to be the only girl?" Her head pops up sharply from her clipboard. Huh. I didn't think she was even listening to me.

"The girls within your age group are all housed in apartments B to F, grid number 3. You need to go back the way you came." I pull my pack out and glance down at it one more time, even though I know the information won't magically change. I offer it to her, which she takes reluctantly with an eye roll. *Wow, excuse me for being such an inconvenience.*

"This is the apartment they assigned me to, though," I tell her, frustrated and quite frankly pissed off at her whole attitude toward me.

"Cameron James Miller, twenty-four years old, stage four breast cancer, female. Dammit" She looks me up and down unhappily like it's my freaking fault they messed up.

"Your name is Cameron James." Is that supposed to be a question or a statement?

"Yes," I say slowly. I am well aware what my name is, thanks.

"That is a boy's name," she snaps at me. I roll my eyes; I can't help it. Seriously? In this day and age, I'm just glad I wasn't named something ridiculous like Apple or Thursday.

"It was my grandfather's name. He died before I was born. My father wanted to honor his memory." Why I'm explaining this to the uppity bitch, I don't know.

"Right, well, it's too late now to make other arrangements." I frown at her. The town is half empty; I'm pretty sure I could throw a stone and hit an empty apartment.

"I'm sure you will... blend in just fine." She glances down at my breastless chest thanks to the double mastectomy, making her point clear. Is she fucking kidding? Her words scrape over my skin like a knife, dragging against my already tattered self-esteem.

"It will be, how shall I say this? Safer if they think you are just a boy. We don't know yet how these new drugs will affect you on an emotional or physical level. Until we have had the chance to observe you, we cannot possibly make any assumptions, but it would be foolish to rule out rage and increases or decreases in libido." This woman is fucking insane. She eyes me up and down, a sly smile creeping over her thin-lipped mouth.

"I doubt it will be an issue. It's hardly likely anyone is planning on stripping you naked to investigate, is it? Now, please hurry along, the gates will be closing soon." She walks away before I can say anything else. I just stand there like a fool, gaping at her retreating back in disbelief.

I turn to the door, every muscle coiled tight as my brain tries to figure out what to do. I slip my shaking hands into my pocket and try to slow my breathing as the panic starts to claw at me. The urge to run, to flee this whole fucked-up situation is all-consuming but I know I can't.

"Hey, Cam, you coming up or what?" I look up and see Jack leaning out of one of the windows a couple of stories up.

I nod slowly and make my way inside, suddenly knowing with absolute clarity that I've fucked up. I've made the single biggest mistake of my life by being here, and now it's too late to do a damn thing about it. Checking the apartment number on my sheet of paper again, even though it's embedded in my brain, I reluctantly make my way up the stairs, bypassing the elevator despite my aching body crying out for a reprieve. I'm in no rush however, to get there any quicker than necessary.

By the time I make it to the top floor, my legs are shaking in protest and I'm a hot sweaty mess.

I open the door and walk into what appears to be a communal room. Decorated in an off-white color, the smell of fresh paint still permeates the air.

White distressed wood floors run all the way through to the kitchen, the starkness broken sporadically with abstract rugs. There are three large comfy-looking gray cord sofas set up so no matter where you sit you'll still see the ridiculously large flat screen television mounted on the wall. A white wooden coffee table, with the same distressed effect as the floor, and a couple of chrome floor lamps make up the rest of the furniture. It's like everything else in this place, clean and tidy, for now at least. But despite the pop of color provided by the rugs, there is no escaping the stark coldness of the room. The far end of the room opens into the kitchen area, which houses a large table big enough to seat eight, also in the damn white distressed wood. I'm starting to feel distressed just looking at it. Surrounding the table are eight high-backed chairs, thankfully in a black and gray check velvet-looking material.

The kitchen itself is made up of glossy white cabinets and dark gray countertops with what looks like an integrated stove, dishwasher, and fridge. I continue looking around and notice four doors leading off the sitting area, two on each side. I head to the one with number four on it, open it, only to quickly close it again.

Why is there a naked man in my room? I crack the door

open and peek through the crack. Yep, there is definitely a naked man, tattooed from head to toe, standing in my room. I try not to check him out but it's impossible to not take a second look at that ass. He slips on a pair of boxers and turns to face me. Oh, no. Busted.

"Want to take a picture? It lasts longer." He slips his hand into the front of his boxers and grips his... Oh, my god. He's hard and big and...hard.

"Jesus, are you mute?" he mocks me, but I can't tear my eyes away.

I stand there gaping as he pulls his cock out and starts slowly stroking it up and down in front of me.

"You're kind of scrawny, chemo boy, but I guess that's to be expected, huh? Want to taste it?" he offers, a devilish glimmer in his eye.

I do the only thing I can think of. I turn and run out the door, through the sitting area, and down the stairs. When I get to the bottom, I collapse to the dusty floor in a heap, knowing damn well I've pushed my already sick body too far. I didn't sign up for this, any of this. Jesus, what the hell am I doing here?

"Hey, Cam, you all right?" A hand on my shoulder has me looking up into Jack's worried eyes.

"Negative, ghost rider. I am about as far from all right as you can possibly get." He sits on the bottom step next to me.

"Don't let Fox get to you. I told you he's an asshole. He's like that with everyone." He looks away with an almost sad smile on his face but it's fleeting and before I blink, it's gone, making me wonder if I imagined it.

"You know him? Shit, that's the guy who knocked me over earlier. I'm surprised, I guess I figured we would all be strangers."

"Eh... yeah. I know all the guys in our apartment. We were all in the medical wing of Talson's Correctional Center." He shrugs. He fucking shrugs like he's talking about the weather.

"Correction center? You mean you guys were all in fucking prison? Oh god, I'm going to die." And queue hysterical laughing. You know, because having cancer isn't enough, I had to throw myself into the middle of a bunch of convicted felons. Oh, and let's not forget the fact that I need to pretend I'm a guy.

"Dramatic much? Besides, isn't that why you're here to begin with, because you're dying? Look, my advice, don't show them any weakness because they will take full advantage of it. None of us are plotting to kill you in the middle of the night, Cam, just chill." I can't tell him all the reasons I'm freaking out, but he's right. If I don't pull myself together, they will circle me like sharks hunting their next meal.

"Right. I'll give you a quick rundown. As you know, you're sharing a room with Fox." What the fuck? Sharing a room? Oh, this is just getting better and better.

"His real name is Valentine, Valentine Fox, but I would *not* recommend you calling him that. He used to be a gang member or, should I say, he was the leader of the gang, but whatever, none of that matters anymore. Before you ask, no, I don't know the ins and outs of what he has or hasn't done, but look at it this way. If he was a mass murderer of some kind, he wouldn't be in here with us, now, would he?" Yeah, Jack, you keep telling yourself that, buddy. I don't think this stupid fucking project is going to be anything like the idea they pitched to us.

"Then you have AJ Black and Levi Adams sharing the room next to yours. AJ got busted for dealing and Levi got sent down for robbery." Not great but I can handle that.

"Although, in the spirit of full disclosure, I should probably mention that AJ was an arms dealer and Levi got ten years for armed robbery." Perfect. At this rate, I won't have to wait for the cancer to kill me because I'm going to have a goddamn heart attack.

"I'm in the room opposite you with Dylan Gibbs. You ever need a fake ID, he's the guy you look for."

"What about you? What did you do?" Dread has my stomach twisted and my jaw locked tight.

"Ah, I like to play around on computers," he answers, somewhat bashfully.

"You're a hacker?" I ask, somewhat relieved that he isn't a trafficker or something worse like a freaking serial killer.

"I was. I am now a changed man." He winks at me. *Liar*. He's a dying man. That's a whole different thing.

"The last room is home to Nathan Adler and John Davis. Nathan is an odd one. Quiet, always watching, but doesn't really interact much. He was in for assault with a deadly weapon.

"John is the one to watch out for. There is something not right about him at all. He was sent down on some kind of trumped up tax evasion charge, but rumor has it he has a penchant for the ladies. In particular, the ones that have no interest in him."

A rapist and my nightmare is complete.

I have hated my body for years. It has done nothing but hold me hostage and mock me but, at this moment, I have never been so grateful to have the figure I do now. I really do look like a prepubescent boy. Sure, it might make me a target for bullying, but I can take a punch. What I can't take is having someone take something from me that is not theirs to have. I have my first meeting with the medical team tomorrow down at the town clinic. I'll just have to make them aware of the situation. Once they realize the danger they have inadvertently placed me in, they will be forced to move me. They have to, right?

# TWO

After I manage to get some strength back, I wander around the town aimlessly for a while, trying to figure out my surroundings. After all that had happened, I was now observing everything with new eyes. I don't know what it is, some sixth sense I never knew I had or needed, but tonight something is screaming out to me that I should prepare myself. I make a mental note of all the cameras I see, look for the best places to hide and weak spots that might lead to an escape. My brain is one fucked-up mess at the moment, one half arguing at the other over the futility of the situation I placed myself in. I came here to die but every single natural born instinct is willing me to fight, to live. I look down when the alarm on my watch lets me know it's 9:45—and I'm almost reaching the curfew. Not willing to test the boundaries just yet, I head back and pray for a fucking miracle.

Someone must have been listening. The apartment is silent when I creep back inside. As I approach my room, I hear a shower running from one of the rooms adjacent to mine but otherwise it appears as if everyone else has gone to bed. The door to my room opens soundlessly, thank god, letting me slink in without disturbing the softly snoring gangbanger in the bed closest to me. I walk to the empty bed on the opposite side of the room and quietly slide my backpack to the floor, tucking it under the edge of the bed frame. I slip off my jacket, but that's all I'm taking off. If I have to run in the middle of the night, I need to be prepared. I pull back the patchwork comforter and lie down, drawing it up over my shoes, jeans, and hoodie, tucking it up under my chin.

I'm exhausted. Not just tired, but weary down to my core. I don't know if I have the strength to face what's to come. Maybe the key is not to fight it at all, just take whatever they throw at me and hope my death comes quickly. That's the ultimate freedom, right? I try to relax but my brain refuses to switch off, spinning the day's events over and over in my mind until, finally, everything fades into darkness.

"CAMERON." I feel a hand on my wrist, but my eyes refuse to open.

"I can't find it. You try. I can't even tell if he's fucking breathing."

"For fuck's sake, move." I vaguely recognize the voices arguing, but I can't place faces to them. My arm is snagged again and my sleeve is yanked up hard. This person is much rougher, gripping my wrist so tightly I know there will be bruises. I can feel their fingers moving around and hear more cursing before the top of my hoodie is pulled over and a couple of fingers press against my neck. Something tickles against my nose and cheek. Hair, maybe? I finally will my eyes open and find a mop of messy black hair.

"What the fuck?" I croak out.

The head attached to the hair lifts and turns around at my words. Fuck. I remember where I am now that I find myself face to face with Fox.

"He's alive, Jack. You can stop your whining now. It's too early to have to deal with this shit," he grumbles as he pushes himself off me, glaring at me in the process.

"You look like shit, Nemo."

I feel like shit, dickhead. "Nemo?" I question. He stares at me with annoyance.

"If I call out 'chemo boy' in this place, ten people will come running. Nemo works. You look like a scared little boy that can't find his way home." Well, he's not wrong about that for the most part. Minus the whole boy thing of course.

"Or you could just call me Cam." He turns his back on me, dismissing me completely. Or not. Jack plonks down on the side of the bed next to me.

"Guess I better get used to finding corpses in the morning, huh?" he tells me wryly.

"You realize I'm not dead, right?"

"Tell me that after you've had a look in the mirror. If I had to describe your appearance this morning in one word, it would be 'reanimated.'"

I close my eyes and sigh.

"First night without my meds was always going to be hard," I tell him quietly. "Honestly, I doubt my body will cope with much more so if you don't want to find my dead body one of these mornings, don't fucking come in here," I finish, my voice a few octaves higher than when I started speaking.

"Well, someone's grumpy in the morning," he grumbles. "Come on, get up. I'll make you a coffee. We all have to get our asses down to the clinic in an hour."

He heads to the living room, so I sit up slowly, feeling my stomach revolt as the room spins. I take a deep breath and stand up before sitting back down quickly. Yeah, I'm in trouble here.

"Fucking pain in my motherfucking ass." I hear Fox complain before a thick muscular arm slides around my back and under my armpit, pulling me up and supporting my feeble body. I don't bother telling him I can do it alone because we both know I'd be lying. He takes most of my weight as he half walks, half drags me out into the sitting area. He's wearing nothing but a pair of black boxers, giving me complete access to his art-covered body. Every inch of him, from his ankles to his jaw, is covered in tattoos. He's a walking, talking piece of artwork, all prettied up in various shades of black and gray. If I didn't think he might kill me for it, I'd have stared at his body quite happily for days. He maneuvers me to one of the sofas, plonks me down without a word, and walks off, leaving me next to another heavily tattooed guy.

This guy hasn't had as much work done as Fox. He's sitting in boxers too, showing a colorful array of tattoos running up his arms and covering his chest and shoulders, but that's it. Normally, that would seem like a lot, but next to Fox's it seems almost reserved. They are beautiful though; I notice as I try to check them out without him seeing. I spot an Alice in Wonderland one, but Alice is a zombie, which looks amazing and reminds me of how I feel this morning.

"Here." I jump, finding Jack in front of me with a steaming cup of coffee. I take it with shaky hands and thank him quietly.

"You gonna make me a coffee as well, Jackie boy? Or do I have to blow you to get one?" a new voice asks. I look up as a sandy-haired man strolls out of one of the rooms looking like he's about to head to work in his suit. Who the heck gets dressed up to go to the clinic?

"Fuck off, John. I'm not your bitch boy, make it yourself." Jack stomps off to his room. The guy called John is quiet for a moment, but I notice the clench of his teeth and the tightening of his jaw. He is not a happy bunny. I guess in his regular life he's used to people doing what he asks. I remember what Jack told me last night about who everyone is and my brain falters when I realize John is the tax-evading rapist. To be fair, he does give off this vibe. Not a rapist vibe, there's no such thing, but I don't doubt for a second he could reel people in with his wit and charm if he wanted to. Add that to his all-American-boy-next-door looks and I can see many a girl accepting a drink from him that she would later regret. But if you look at him closely, past the fake smile and the expensive suit, his eyes are completely void of anything. Empty and cold, that's the feeling I get from him. I don't think I'll have any problem remembering to keep my identity hidden from him, that's for sure. My body literally goes on high alert just being in the same room.

"You." I ignore him when he barks at me, keeping my head down and sipping my drink. A kick to my legs has my coffee sloshing over the side of my cup and over my fingers. I wipe my hand on my jeans, feeling my fingers throb from the heat, but I refuse to show this asshole the reaction he wants. I lift my head slowly and stare at him with indifference. As much as I don't want to piss him off, I know I can't afford to let him walk all over me.

"You can be my bitch boy. I take it black with two sugars." I keep my eyes on his cold ones and lift my coffee to my lips as if he never spoke at all.

"Are you fucking deaf?"

"Oh, I bet, like me, he wishes he were fucking deaf. Just once I'd like to wake up in the morning without having to listen to you bitch and moan all the time," the guy next to me says.

"I wasn't talking to you, AJ, so keep out of it."

"Jesus. I just want to drink my fucking coffee in peace before I have to go and let those fuckers jack me up with whatever shit they've concocted," AJ mutters.

John moves to kick me again but freezes when Fox walks in.

"Knock it off, John. Either make your own coffee or go without. You aren't at your fucking country club now."

Fox is now dressed in black jeans and a black T-shirt much like he was yesterday when he knocked me to my knees. His black hair, still wet from his shower, curls slightly at the ends, making him seem less severe than usual. More boyish. He sits down next to me on the sofa and snags my coffee from my hands before leaning back and sipping it.

I close my eyes in defeat. Normally I would protest, but the coffee I've already consumed is lying heavy in my stomach. There is a good chance I'll be seeing that again later. I watch the glare John throws my way before he storms out.

"The bus will be here in ten minutes," Jack tells us as he walks back into the room with a cute brown-haired guy behind him. He stares at Fox. The cute guy appears younger than the rest of us, well, except for me, seeing as I been mistaken for a teenage boy. Like me, he looks like he's having a rough morning. He has a sprinkling of freckles over his nose and cheeks, but at the moment, they provide the only color on his otherwise pale-as-snow skin. His gray eyes are dull and filled with pain and, judging from how sunken in they are and the dark circles underneath them, I would say he had a rough night too.

"Cam, can you manage?" Jack asks me quietly. Despite everything I have learned since I've been here, I think Jack is actually a good guy, but there's not a chance I can let him help me without exposing my secrets. I nod my head, telling him I'm fine.

"Right, well, let's hustle. Oh, before I forget. Guys, this is Cam. Cam, you've met Fox. The guy on the other side of you is AJ and behind me is Dylan." My instinct is to wave but that doesn't seem very manly, so I just tip my head in greeting.

I shuffle forward and try to stand but my legs buckle underneath me. AJ catches me before I hit the floor.

"Seriously, dude, what is your malfunction?" AJ asks in a pissed off tone.

"That would be the fucking cancer that's eating me from the inside out," I snap out, embarrassed.

I glance up at Jack and ignore the look of pity he throws my way.

"Let's just get the fuck out of here. I'll shower when I get back," I tell them, needing to get out of here and away from them.

"Sure, if you make it back, Nemo," Fox sneers.

"Oh, fuck you, Fox." I am so done with all this bullshit.

He winks at me, the fucking psychopath. "Maybe we should see how you feel later first. Fucking a corpse is not my idea of fun."

"Here, I've got you." Jack pulls me up and takes my

weight as Fox did earlier. He helps me to the elevator and then out and onto the bus that is already waiting for us. We sit tight, waiting for the others to climb aboard before the doors shut, sealing us in and sealing our fate. It all begins now.

Dylan sits down in the seat that faces mine and takes me in.

"Rough night?" he probes.

"Hello, Pot. I'm Kettle."

He laughs but it quickly turns into a wheeze that rattles in his chest. "Touché."

"Hey, I'm Levi." I look up as a dark-haired god-like man sits next to Dylan, rendering me momentarily mute.

"Yeah. The space cadet here is Cam. Don't take his silence personally, he had a rough night and a run in with John this morning," Jack explains from beside me when it becomes apparent that I can't talk.

"John's a dickhead just ignore him. Hopefully, he'll be the first of us to keel over and die." Levi laughs

"Don't bank on it," I manage to get out.

"I can hear you fuckers, you know?" John calls from a few seats in front of us but we all ignore him.

"That guy over there." I look where Levi is pointing to the seat across the aisle from ours. The blond guy is tall, built, and sexy as fuck. He is one of the oldest of us; I would put him at thirty easily.

"That's Nate. He's the last of the guys sharing our apartment. He doesn't speak much either. Everyone else is from the other three floors. So, what did you do to end up getting stuck with us? I don't remember you from Talson's."

"That's what I would like to know," I mutter under my breath.

"What was that?"

"Just lucky, I guess." I sigh.

It takes us five minutes to get to the clinic. It seems ridiculous to send a bus for such a short distance but then I remember I can barely put one foot in front of the other and realize they might be on to something.

I manage to find a burst of strength from somewhere and walk myself into the clinic without falling flat on my face. The sickly yellow waiting room is full, so I make my way to the nearest wall and slide down it before my legs give out. Jack and Dylan follow suit on either side of me. Fox and AJ stand near the exit talking while quiet guy, shit, what's his name again? Nathan or Nate is leaning against the wall on the opposite side of the room, taking everything in. I can't see Levi or John, but I don't bother looking for them as I am too busy checking out the people that went in for testing before us. They must be waiting for the bus to collect them and take them home but what concerns me is their movements, or lack thereof. Row after row of people sit with their backs straight, hands in their laps, and their eyes closed. It's creepy as fuck, in a robotic kind of way. I hear the bus pull up and watch, stunned, as they all turn as one to the window. When the bus comes to a stop, they all stand and line up single file and head outside to board the bus. Fox and AJ look over at us with a confused expression on their faces.

"What the fuck was that all about?" Jack asks. I turn to face him as he stares wide-eyed at the bus pulling away.

"So, it wasn't just me then?"

"What, that noticed the sheeple people leaving?"

I snort out a laugh. "Sheeple people?"

"You know sheep, followers. I mean, tell me they didn't look like a bunch of fucking robots to you?"

Before I can agree with him, a woman and two men walk into the waiting room carrying clip boards.

"Line up, please, in your designated groups. Your group is who you share an apartment with." Jack helps me up and we make our way over to where she indicates, then follow her down the corridor into another, smaller waiting room. This one is snot green, making me wonder if their decorator was either color-blind or on drugs.

"Your name will be called when we're ready for you. Please sit and wait. We won't be long." This time we all sit in chairs as the room is empty except for the eight of us. I think about the people who were in here before and the way in which they came out and get a very bad feeling about all this. Given my colossal shitstorm of the last twenty-four hours, that's saying something. I know I signed up for this but nowhere in the contract did it mention turning us into fucking mindless droids. Logically, I can see the sense in it. There's no need to police a town if you can control their minds. It's something I was wondering about. Desperate people do stupid things, often not giving a fuck about the consequences because what could be done to them that's worse than dying? But given my circumstances, I can't afford to lose myself like that.

"Dylan Gibbs? Make your way to treatment room one, please," a voice crackles over the intercom. I watch as he stands and makes his way to the treatment room before disappearing inside.

"Levi Adams, treatment room four, please." My palms are sweaty, and my heart begins to race as I wait for my name to be called.

"Valentine Fox. Can you make your way to treatment room three, please?" He looks at me briefly and scowls before standing and strutting his way over like he doesn't have a care in the world. One by one, their names are called until I'm the last one left. The door opens to treatment room one and an orderly of some kind walks out holding up a barely conscious Dylan. He sits him in the chair at the end of the row I'm sitting in, lifts Dylan's hands, and folds them into his lap. The orderly doesn't acknowledge my existence before he walks to one of the other rooms, but I can't take my eyes off of Dylan.

"Dylan?" He doesn't answer me. I'm not sure he can even hear me at this point.

"Dylan, are you okay?" No response, not even an eye twitch, nothing.

"Cameron Miller to treatment room one, please." I stand up slowly, feeling like I'm making my way to the gallows. I guess in many ways, I am. I walk sluggishly, my body protesting every step I make. I'm about to pass Dylan when his hand shoots out and grabs my arm so hard that I let out a startled pain-filled cry. I yank my arm, trying to pull away from him, but he's too strong. At this point, I'm beginning to think the lights are on but nobody's home.

"Dylan. Let me go."

He forces his head up to make eye contact each movement looks like it's taking every ounce of strength he has.

"Pill," he whispers.

"What? I don't understand." My arm is going numb where he grips me. My fingers are starting to tingle from the lack of circulation. Any minute now I expect my arm to snap in two.

"Pill. Don't take it." He chokes out the last word before blood starts pouring from his nose. He finally lets go of my arm, but before I can say or do anything else, he drops to the floor at my feet. I watch in horror for a second as his body flails and convulses in front of me before springing into action. I run to the treatment room waiting for me and push the door open, slamming it against the wall.

"Help, quick." A man and woman, both wearing white coats, spin around in shock when the door crashes open. But they react to my words and my panic-stricken face and race out to the waiting room.

"Stay here," the male doctor orders me and slams the door in my face. I don't know how long I stand there frozen in shock, staring at the door, but when it opens again the woman steps through, covered in blood.

"How is he?"

"What did he say to you?" she questions.

"I'm sorry, what?"

"We saw him say something to you on the camera feed. What did he say to you?"

What were they checking the cameras for? Do they think I had something to do with it or is it something else? Paranoia wars inside me as I debate what to say. If I lie and they already know what he said to me, I could be in serious trouble.

"Ill. He grabbed my arm and said he felt ill. Then the next thing you know, he's on the floor and bleeding everywhere. Is he going to be okay?" She seems relieved with my answer. Best to keep the lie as close to the truth as I can get it.

"I'm sorry but I can't discuss another patient's condition with you. Now if you'll undress and hop up onto the bed for me, please."

"Yeah, about that. I have a major problem I need your help with. I have been housed with a group of guys. Not just any guys but convicted criminals."

"I'm sorry you're unhappy with your accommodations but once you've been assigned somewhere it can't be changed."

"Even though I'm a fucking girl?" I growl out, my mood going from upset to flat out pissed off.

"Excuse me?"

"I. AM. A. FUCKING. GIRL." She looks shocked at my outburst for a second before a mask drops back into place.

"As I said, all housing situations are final. It won't matter after tonight, anyway. Here, take this." She hands me a plastic cup filled with water and a small white tablet. She takes off her blood-soaked coat and throws it into the bin before walking over to the sink and washing her hands. I look down at the tablet and remember Dylan's words.

"Don't take the pill," I mumble to myself before slipping it into the back pocket of my jeans. I drink the water down and place the empty cup on the counter next to me.

"All right, undress, please, and climb up onto the bed." I can't argue with her. I don't know how long these tablets take to kick in, so I need to fake compliance for now, but a little bit of me dies inside thinking about taking my clothes off and revealing what's underneath. I do as she asks but leave my underwear on. She doesn't say anything, and I have to hold back my sigh of relief so I don't give myself away. She grasps my elbow and helps me up onto the bed before combing over every inch of my uncovered body with a fine-tooth comb, recording every mark, scratch, and blemish she finds.

"This looks painful," she comments to herself as she gently runs her fingers over the hostile red fingerprint marks on my arm caused by Dylan's grip. I don't say anything; I just count silently in my head willing this shit to be over with. She walks to one of the drawers beneath the counter and returns with a syringe filled with fuck knows what. All I know is its vivid color makes it look like lava and when she stabs it into the crook of my inner arm and pushes the plunger, it also feels like lava burning through my veins. I bite my lip to stop myself from screaming out, my teeth cutting through my skin. When the darkness threatens to suck me under, I bite down harder until I can taste blood. I refuse to leave myself vulnerable, half naked, and unconscious around anyone in this place. Finally, when I don't think I can hold on any longer, the pain begins to recede and my heart rate slowly starts to return to normal.

"That's all for today, Cameron. You can go ahead and get dressed now."

I sit up and slide off the bed, expecting my legs to buckle underneath me but, if anything, they seem stronger than before. Must be all the adrenaline pumping through my system. Whatever the reason, I'm grateful. I hurry to get dressed, taking comfort from the added layers of protection, and wait quietly while she calls for a porter.

The door opens a couple of minutes later, revealing the same guy that escorted Dylan out before. He doesn't speak to me. He takes my arm—thankfully my uninjured one—and walks me out to the waiting room. He sits me in the chair I was in before and places my hands in my lap before leaving, all without a word. I can see Jack out of the corner of my eye sitting like one of the robot wanna-bes from earlier and realize I might be the only person left that is all there mentally. I look down at the floor where Dylan had fallen, finding it sparkling clean, without a speck of blood, as if the earlier incident was nothing more than a hallucination. But I know better. The pill in my back pocket tells me all I need to know.

"Your bus will be arriving shortly. Please make your way back to the main waiting area for its arrival. Once it's here, you are free to leave and head home to sleep." The intercom goes off, leaving the waiting room in silence again. Was that some kind of subliminal message or am I just reading into this shit too much? How long will the effects of these tablets last? As bad as it sounds, I could really use a shower. So if these pills are going to zombify the guys for a while, I'm going to take full advantage.

# THREE

The bus drops us off outside our building. I spot the camera mounted on the edge of the brickwork as it turns to watch us, so I mimic the guys' robotic movements until we are in the living area and out of sight. There are no cameras in our apartment. I'm assuming it's like this for everyone but I can't figure out why. Surely the tablets will wear off at some point and when they do, people are going to be pissed. Isn't the privacy of our own home the place we would make escape plans if we had any? Unless, of course, they do have cameras up here but they are super tiny and hidden from our sight. I freeze, making Jack bump into the back of me. He stops, turns, and walks around me without speaking. Everyone files off to their own rooms, leaving me frozen on the spot. Are there cameras hidden here, watching our every action and reaction? I shake my head and sigh. If there are, I'm already busted. There is no point crying about it now. I can't put the genie back in the bottle and there is no way I'm going to be able to pretend to be a part of the robot squad indefinitely. I turn the handle to my room and find Fox on top of his bed, fully clothed, with his eyes closed. I would bet one hundred dollars the other guys are all doing the exact same thing. I don't waste any more time worrying about it. I grab my bag from under my bed and hurry to the adjoining bathroom that Fox and I are sharing. I lock the door with the world's flimsiest lock and set a new speed record for showering before climbing back out and toweling off. I guess having no hair comes in handy when time is of the essence. Before the chemo and radiation treatments, my hair was long, dark and thick, skimming my waistline, taking forever to wash and dry. I used to complain about it all the time, never really appreciating what I had until it was gone. Isn't that always the way?

I rummage through my bag, thankful I'm a tomboy through and through, and select a pair of baggy black jeans, black T-shirt, and a blue hoodie. I have no need for a bra but I do need underwear. These are my only concession for being a girl. I like pretty lacy underwear in a variety of colors. Colors I won't wear on the outside, as it makes it harder for me to blend into the crowd.

I slip on a pair of pink, lace bikini briefs and step into the jeans. I'm pulling the T-shirt over my head when my eyes catch on my reflection in the mirror. After Jack's comments this morning, I was expecting the worst, but I have to say I don't think I look that bad. My normally pale skin has a flush of color to it, my eyes, although weary, have some life inside them and the purple circles underneath don't look as dark today. I pick up the hoodie to slip it on and notice the arm Dylan had grabbed earlier. The angry red and purple marks have completely disappeared. I twist my arm around to see the other side, but it's blemish free. How strange. I guess he didn't squeeze me as hard as I thought after all. Sliding the hoodie over my head, I locate my toothbrush and toothpaste, and brush my teeth while I think about all that has happened in the last twenty-four hours. I wonder if Dylan is all right and, if he is okay, where is he being kept? I need to find a way to thank him for warning me.

Wondering how he even figured it out to begin with, I pack up everything and go over to the bedroom, sliding my backpack under my bed before walking slowly over to Fox. He is in the exact same position he was when I went for a shower. He looks like he's sleeping but there is nothing natural about it. He's a fraction too still, a touch too stiff, and he isn't making that cute little snoring noise he made last night. I lean over him just watching the rise and fall of his chest. It's comforting in a fucked-up kind of way.

All these guys are a potential danger to me but the thought of being trapped here in this place alone while everyone around me turns into some kind of puppet terrifies me more than anything else at the moment. His fingers twitch on his left hand a little. I look up at his face and find his eyes open and staring at me. I let out a little shriek and find myself flat on my back with a very heavy Fox on top of me. He stares at me, looking dazed and confused for a moment before his eyes glaze over again and he rolls off me. I'm about to make my escape when an arm snags me around the waist and pulls me back against him.

How in the fuck I manage to find myself in the classic spooning position, I don't know, but when he throws his leg and arm over me and holds me tight, I know I'm not going anywhere. Fuck. In another time and place and with another person I'm sure this would feel like heaven, but as it stands now, I'm trying to get my head around the fact that I'm wrapped up in the arms of a former gangbanger who thinks I'm a guy.

I have to fight back an irrational giggle. There is a rapist across the hall that would be a danger to me if he knew I was a girl, and I'm in bed with a criminal that wants me as a guy. Well, both are going to be sorely disappointed. I'll have to wait for him to settle down again. I'll just lie here until he loosens his hold on me and then I'll slip away. The sad thing is, this could be the last time anyone holds me so I might as well enjoy it.

Something tugs on my ear. I try to swat it away but I can't move my arms. I blink my eyes open and become simultaneously aware of two things. One is that the thing tugging on my ear is a set of teeth and the other is a hard dick stabbing me in the ass. I try to throw myself out of the bed, but he must anticipate my actions because he grips me tighter.

"Want to tell me why you're in my bed, Nemo?" He talks seductively into my ear, making my whole body shiver. When he grinds into me, I know damn well he noticed it too.

"Let me go, Fox." I try to keep my voice firm, but it cracks at the end.

"Now why would I want to do that? Besides, you still haven't answered me. Why are you in my bed?"

"You were sleeping earlier; I was checking that you were still breathing, but then you yanked me down onto the bed with you and pinned me down."

He's quiet behind me, dropping his head to rest against my shoulder blades.

He holds me still but not as tightly as before. It's almost like he needs the comfort, the connection I often so desperately crave, but that's ridiculous. This is Fox we're talking about.

"What happened earlier, Nemo? I remember going into the treatment room and that's about it until I felt you pressed up against me.

"I don't remember either," I lie. "I was the last to get called. Dylan came out just before I went in. He was bleeding from his nose and started having some kind of fit on the floor. They wouldn't tell me how he was when I asked. I can't remember anything after that."

"We always knew that not everyone was going to make it, Nemo," he tells me callously. "You better get used to that shit." He rolls over and sits up on the edge of the bed. He turns back to look at me, his face softening fractionally before he stands up. "Come on, let's get some lunch. I'm fucking starving."

I'm pretty hungry too, I realize, which is unusual for me. My appetite has been nonexistent for ages. It'll be nice to make the most of it.

AJ is standing in the kitchen with his back to us, making scrambled eggs, when we walk in. He's wearing low slung sweatpants and nothing else, showcasing the pretty colors inked into his skin. He looks at us over his shoulder but doesn't speak. Turning back to the eggs, he slides some onto a plate next to a slice of buttered toast. He hands the plate out to me as I approach before doing the same for Fox.

"Thanks." I'll admit, I'm a little surprised. That was kind of sweet of him.

I find a seat at the table and watch as Fox sits at the other end, acting as if the whole bedroom situation never happened, and that suits me just fine. I have enough going on without adding a boy to the mix.

The smell of the food rouses everyone else and one by one they end up at the table as AJ cooks eggs for us like it's an everyday occurrence.

"Anyone seen Dylan?" Levi asks.

"He got sick at the clinic," I answer between mouthfuls.

"You can remember what happened at the clinic?" AJ asks me sharply, sitting down beside me with his own plate of food. "Because I remember getting up this morning and everything before walking into that treatment room. I remember taking the meds they gave me and closing my eyes, then nothing for the next three hours," he says, checking the time on his watch.

"No. He came out of the treatment room before I went in. He...umm... His nose started bleeding and then he was on the floor having a fit or something. I have no idea what happened after that."

I push the eggs around my plate, my appetite vanishing in an instant as I try to commit to memory the face of the boy who may have saved my life. Well, for now at least.

"Well, Levi can move in with Jack then and I can get the room to myself," AJ comments offhandedly. I want to yell at him for being insensitive but he's only stating facts. It means very little that we haven't had confirmation of Dylan's death, deep down, we already know.

"What are we doing this afternoon, then?" AJ manages to ask around a mouthful of eggs. "I'm not spending my last days cooped up in this shit hole with you assholes."

They want to hang out together? No, thanks. I think I'll just stay here and chill out.

"I'm just going to stay here and watch TV. I'm not hanging out with you faggots," John says, glaring at me.

Okay, change of plans then.

"I'm in. There isn't a great deal to see from what I noticed last night, but I'm curious to see how some of the others got on at the clinic and whether they can remember anything." I notice them studying me and fight the urge to squirm.

"What's to know? Worried they might have knocked you out and had their way with you?" John taunts.

"Why? You jealous?" I fire back. Fuck it. I know I shouldn't rile him up, but this guy gets on every single one of my nerves. He stands up, forcing his chair back with a screech.

"What the fuck did you say?" This is a bad idea, Cameron, do not engage. I repeat, do not engage.

"I'm sorry. Do you need me to dumb it down for you?" For fuck's sake. Why do I never listen to myself?

"Either sit down or fuck off, John. Jesus, do you have to pull this crap every time I eat something? I swear you talk so much shit, I can smell it on your breath," AJ snaps at him, slamming his fork down onto the table beside his plate.

"Fuck you, AJ." John storms off to his room, taking the tension with him.

"Ignore him. He's just trying to get a rise out of you." Jack tells me something I've already figured out.

"I wouldn't mind getting a rise out of you." Fox wiggles his eyebrows at me. Jack looks down at his plate with a frown as I flip off Fox and head back to the bedroom to splash some water on my face and brush my teeth before heading out. I'm slipping my Converse on when Fox strolls in and starts undressing. I focus on tying my laces, trying in earnest to ignore the disregarded clothes piling up on the floor around his feet.

"Tell the guys I'll be out in a minute." I look up instinctively when he speaks and find myself staring at Fox's naked body, yet a-fucking-gain. A hard-in-all-the-right-places kind of body wrapped up in a thousand pictures. I want to study each and every one of them as I have a feeling they all mean something to him. I tear my eyes away, deliberately avoiding his groin area and head for the door.

"No worries."

Levi and Jack are already waiting when I walk in. They both glance up but dismiss me with a look when they realize I'm alone. I get the impression Fox is their leader of sorts.

I spot an earbud in Levi's ear and feel a pang of jealousy. I miss music more than I thought I would.

"Hey, I thought we weren't allowed to bring in any electronic devices. Something to do with them interfering with the medical equipment and testing."

"Yeah, and? Are you going to snitch on me, Nemo?"

Great, the name is catching. "It's Cam, and no, of course not." I sigh and plonk myself down on the sofa next to him. "I just miss music, that's all."

He slips out the bud and slides it into his pocket before turning to face me. "What else do you miss?"

I can't tell if he is genuinely interested or trying to distract me. "Now, that's a loaded question, Levi." I lean my head back and close my eyes and think about the things I miss the most. "I miss having the freedom to come and go as I please. I miss the ocean and music and my big comfy bed. But most of all, I miss Charlie."

"The drug?" AJ perks up from the sofa opposite like I suddenly just became so much more interesting.

I frown at him but then remember that *Charlie* is a slang word for cocaine. I shake my head. I'm beginning to feel like Dorothy when she realized she wasn't in Kansas anymore.

"Charlie, the boy," I tell him, feeling the pang in my chest that his name always invokes.

"You have some dude back home? What's he think about you being here?" AJ seems genuinely curious now. His intense eyes bore into me, waiting for an answer.

"He's my kid brother. He turns six in a couple of months."

"This has gotta be rough on him. What about your parents?"

I think of Charlie's tears when I left. He had wrapped his little arms and legs around me, hoping he could make me stay. I wish with every fiber of my being that I could have. I shut down that train of thought. Bursting into tears now is not an option.

"My dad died when I was a kid. My mom lost her marbles. She spiraled out of control. Having a small kid to look after didn't do anything to help pull her out of the darkness, if anything, I made it harder for her. Anyway, long story short, she developed a drinking problem and I ended up getting bounced around the foster system. Sometimes I would end up back home, but inevitably she would fuck up and I would be gone again. Eventually, she got clean. She met someone at an AA meeting, and they hit it off. They got married and a year later Charlie came along. He gets the mother I hoped for and his dad, Tony, adores him. So, although this sucks, he'll be okay. My relationship with my mother is more one of friendly acquaintances than anything else. It's been fractured too many times over the years to be anything more. I miss her, and Tony too, I'm not saying I don't, but Charlie is my person."

"And he's the reason you're here now so he gets something from your death." Jack guesses correctly, having come in halfway through the conversation.

"Schooling is expensive. I don't want him to have to struggle to make ends meet or sacrifice his dreams just so he can eat."

"That's kind of cool, Cam."

I smile at Jack, but it's hard to miss the sadness in it. No amount of money changes the fact that Charlie would rather have his big sister than a check.

"You bitches ready?" Fox strolls out of our room in his standard outfit of black ripped jeans, a black T-shirt, and black combat boots.

"Fuck you, Fox. We were waiting for your pampered ass." AJ stands, grabbing a black leather jacket off the back of the sofa and shrugs it on over his own black jeans and white wife beater. Jack and Levi are dressed similar to me in jeans and hoodies. Jack is in head-to-toe black like Fox, making Levi stand out among us in his bright red hoodie.

Heading towards the door, I suddenly remember we are still a man down.

"Where's Nate?"

"Behind you."

I swing around, thankful as fuck I managed to hold back

the girlish scream that threatened to bubble free from my lips.

"Have you been here the whole time?" I ask, looking up in shock at Nate.

He just nods before walking around me and down the stairs.

Levi laughs at the expression on my face. "You get used to it. The guy's a ninja. He was leaning against the far wall when you came in."

I just nod and mentally remind myself to be super vigilant from now on.

It's quiet when we make our way outside but I guess that's to be expected. In a town this size, we maybe fill a quarter of it, if that. The closest buildings to ours are empty so we head toward where the bus dropped us off yesterday, keeping our eyes peeled for other people.

"I have to say, Cam, you look a hell of a lot better now than you did this morning. Truth be told, I wasn't sure if you were going to make it back." Jack walks beside me, talking quietly.

"Surprisingly, I feel better than I have in a while. I don't know if it's because I didn't take my usual cocktail of drugs last night or what. They do have a tendency to make me feel like shit."

"I guess." I look up at him. His skeptical tone makes me wonder what he's getting at.

"There are a couple of guys over there," AJ calls back to us over his shoulder. I turn to where he's pointing and see two men standing outside one of the buildings, arguing. They stop when they see us and watch us warily as we approach them.

"Can I help you?" the tallest one says, keeping himself at a safe distance.

"You had treatment yet?" Levi asks him. He stands just in front of AJ and Fox with his hands in his pockets, trying to make himself seem non-threatening. With this motley crew, that's an impossibility.

"Yeah. We were the first group in. They collected us about an hour after we got here yesterday. What of it?"

"Just wondering what you remember after you went into the treatment room."

The guys scan us, deciding whether they want to answer, but I have a feeling it isn't just us they don't trust.

"Nothing. I don't remember anything after entering that room until I woke up in bed hours later," the shorter of the two guys answers. He has a bald head just like mine.

"How did you feel when you woke up?" I ask him curiously.

Everyone turns to face me, surprised when I speak up.

"Like shit. How do you think we felt?"

I ignore the tall guy and focus on the bald guy. He looks at me closely, taking in my frail frame and hairless head. His features soften as if he feels some camaraderie with me. Guess you need to actually have your body eat itself from the inside out to recognize in others the strength it takes to not just lie down and give up.

"Better than I did when I arrived there. Not healthy or anything, but for the first time in ages I managed to eat and keep it down."

I nod, letting him know it was the same for me. The guys look at me and I know they're thinking about me sitting and eating with them earlier.

"Either way, we're better than the others." The hostility seems to be leaking out of the tall guy as his shoulders drop and he looks down, defeated.

"What does that mean?" Fox asks him.

"When we woke up, it was to find that only Ben and I made it back." Baldy, or I'm guessing Ben, nods in agreement.

"What the fuck? How many of you arrived at the clinic to start with?" Fox questions him but I'm still reeling in surprise.

My mind flashes to Dylan. Did they all have the same reaction he did?

"We started out as a group of thirty-two. Now it's just Ben and me."

# FOUR

His answer snaps me back to attention.

"Thirty-two? Holy fucking shit," AJ curses. We all stare at each other in shock.

"What about you guys?"

I glance around our little group, suddenly realizing that not one of us thought to check the guys from the floors below us. I see the exact moment Fox realizes this too because his eyes widen before looking at me in question. I shake my head, spin on my heel, and run back to our apartment. I can hear the guys' footfalls behind me a second or so before they speed past. By the time I get there, the guys are already inside, making their way floor to floor, checking to see who made it back. I bend over and grasp my knees, trying to catch my breath and not throw up in the process.

"Come on, Nemo, stop fucking around," Fox shouts from

our apartment window, not caring in the slightest that I can barely breathe, let alone walk.

A hand on my back startles me and has me spinning around, losing my footing in the process. The same hand stops me from face planting on the steps. I look up and find Nate gripping my arm tightly. He waits until I find my balance then lets go.

"Thanks," I tell him.

He nods and indicates for me to head inside. I do as he wants and take my time as I painstakingly make my way upstairs. Nate keeps pace with me the whole way up before opening the door and nudging me inside.

"I don't see what the fucking problem is. We all knew we were going to die, so why are you all acting like a bunch of fucking bitches?" I hear John complaining as Nate and I make our way toward them.

"You took your fucking time," Fox growls. I don't know if he's talking to me or Nate, but I'm not in the mood for his bullshit. I step to walk past him and into my room, but he blocks my path.

"Don't you want to know how many of us are left?" Part of me does but part of me knows it will only serve as a reminder that I might be next.

I don't answer. I just glare at him and wait for him to speak again. It shouldn't take him too long. The asshole clearly likes the sound of his own voice.

"Fifteen people made it back—that's including us," he tells me, waiting for my reaction.

"Out of how many?" I ask him.

"Thirty-three." The room is silent. Even John has shut up as he absorbs Fox's words.

So that's it then. Less than half of us made it back. The reality of that means tomorrow will probably be our last day, if not for all of us, then for most. I glance out at their faces, the group of misfits, criminals and, in John's case at least, psychopaths, and feel the strangest urge to laugh. So this is how I'll spend my last night here. My rumbling stomach has me turning toward the kitchen and grinning. Fuck it. Fuck it all. No point crying over something I can't change. I shove away from a surprised Fox and make my way back downstairs, ignoring the shouts from behind me. Eventually, I hear footsteps and look over my shoulder to find them all following me. Nosy bastards.

"Looks like the newbie has finally snapped." I hear John mocking, but I shut him out. He has no fucking clue.

"Cam?" I turn to find Jack walking beside me with a look of confusion on his face.

"Where are we going?"

"I'm going shopping. I don't really care where the hell you guys are going. But if tonight's going to be my last night here, I want something more than eggs now that I finally have an appetite."

His confused expression clears before a burst of laughter erupts from him.

"We thought you were gonna try and break out or something."

"Trust me, if I didn't need this money for Charlie, I'd be gone like a shot. So it's not playing out in here like I thought it would? It doesn't change anything, really. I'm still dying. What does it even matter anymore? I just want some nice food, a movie, and a good night's sleep and if that's how I spend my last night on earth, that's fine by me." A pained look briefly crosses Jack's face before he masks it again. Shit. Just because I have accepted my mortality doesn't mean he has.

"Sorry, Jack, that was insensitive of me."

"Nah, it's all right. You aren't telling me anything I don't already know." I turn in the direction of the shops I saw yesterday on my travels and head toward them. Taking in the deserted buildings around me, I wonder idly if people lived here before us or if this place was custom-designed just for the participants of the Phoenix Project, offering us a taste of normality perhaps, to balance out the fact that the reaper is checking us all off his list.

When the shop finally comes into view, I head toward it, ignoring the grumbling voices behind me.

"Shopping? He wants to go shopping?" I hear John scoff in disgust. I spin around to face the group, clenching my hands at my sides, and stomp over to them.

"Is there any chance you could just die already so I don't have to listen to you fucking moaning every two seconds?" I yell at John, whose face is turning a comical shade of red.

"What'd you say to me, faggot?" He steps forward but is snagged back by Levi.

"Leave it, man," he tells him.

"Fuck you, Levi, fuck you all. Ever since cancer boy turned up, you've turned into a bunch of fucking pussies. So what? So you can all get a quick fuck in before you kick it? Just fucking take it if that's what you want, there are enough of you. What the fuck is going to happen? Nothing, that's what. Nobody cares if you fuck the little faggot up the ass. We're all going to be dead soon. Rules were made to be broken and they don't mean jackshit in a place like this anyway."

We stand there in stunned silence for a moment. Did he really just tell everyone to get on and rape me already?

The rage boiling inside me is all-consuming. I don't stop to consider my actions, I react purely on instinct. I'm skinny, scrawny, and weak thanks to the cancer, but it wasn't always this way. Before my body decided to turn on itself, I was a fighter. The foster system is not a safe place for young girls so when I was old enough, I started going to boxing and martial arts classes put on for free at the local youth center. I knew how to defend myself and, most importantly, I knew how to fight back. He's too tall for me to land a punch to his smug looking face in any way that will hurt, so I grip his shirt and pull him toward me as I lift my knee and drive it as hard as I can into his rancid dick.

He makes a pained squeak before dropping to the floor and cupping himself. I swing my leg back to kick him but find myself pinned within Fox's arms and being pulled away.

"That's enough," he tells me quietly. All the fight drains out of me as I realize I've just made myself a bigger target.

"You need to stay out of his way. He'll kill you for that," he warns me, looking angry. I shrug out of his hold, pissed off with all of them, and head inside, calling out over my shoulder.

"He's gonna have to get in line. Seems like everything is trying to kill me lately."

I grab a basket and make my way up and down the deserted food aisles, throwing things in that I haven't been able to keep down in years. Steak, baking potatoes, and sour cream. I grab the ingredients to bake chocolate chip cookies and head to the wine section which, unfortunately, is empty. No drinking allowed. I guess I can see the logic in that. I grab a two-liter bottle of Coke instead and head to the checkout. They are all self-serve and instead of paying at the end, you just swipe your apartment key card. The guys are wandering around now, loading themselves up with junk food, making me smirk. Not so stupid after all, huh?

I leave them to it, not even bothering to tell them I'm going. I need some peace and quiet, which is impossible with them around.

The empty apartment is a soothing balm to my frayed nerves. I pop my food in the fridge and assemble the ingredients to bake cookies. I make enough to feed an army, which is handy as I'm just getting the first batch of cookies out of the oven when the door opens and the guys start pouring in.

"Mmm... Something smells good. I didn't know you could bake," AJ comments, snagging a cookie from the counter.

"We know nothing about each other, AJ, so why is that so surprising?"

"Not many guys make cookies, is all." He shrugs before snagging another. Shit. I never even gave that a thought.

"So, I like baking cookies, sue me. You made eggs for everyone earlier."

"Not the same thing, Nemo." I sigh because he's right.

"Oh, cookies." Jack swipes two before Levi takes one and flops down on the sofa.

"Help yourselves, guys," I mutter, stepping back when John walks up to the counter and swipes all the cookies off the tray and onto the floor before stomping on them. I stand there watching him, refusing to show him any kind of reaction, even when inside I want to carve his heart out with a spoon.

Happy with himself, he heads into his room, slamming his door behind him and making it rattle in its frame.

Levi leans down from the sofa and swipes a cookie off the floor that escaped the stomping and shoves the whole thing into his mouth. I watch him with my mouth open as he chews and swallows. He must feel my eyes on him as he looks up to find me staring.

"What? Five second rule." I shake my head and pull the next batch out of the oven as the timer beeps.

“Where are the others?” I ask, grabbing a few cookies for myself, knowing if I don’t, there will be none left.

“Fuck knows where Fox is, but Nate’s behind you.” I spin around and come face to chest with Nate.

“Goddamn it, Nate,” I shout, making the others laugh.

“Sorry,” he mumbles, eyeing the cookies in my hand. I sigh and hand them to him before turning back and grabbing some more. I leave them to it and sit down on the end of the sofa opposite Levi and switch on the massive TV. Flicking through the channels reveals the only thing available to watch are movies.

“We don’t have regular TV channels?” I ask Levi

“Nope. Guess they don’t want us watching the news and shit. Probably worried we’ll start missing home and make a run for it.”

“Yeah, sure,” I reply, not believing that crock of shit for a second. It’s just another power play to cut us off from the rest of the world if you ask me.

I pull up the list of movies and pop on *The Water Boy*. If anyone can get me laughing tonight, it will be Adam Sandler. Everyone finds their own spots to watch from until Fox strolls in five minutes later. He takes us in without a word and heads over to me, plonking himself down beside me and effectively pinning me into the corner of the sofa despite there being plenty of space on his other side. I open my mouth to ask him to move when he snags the remaining cookie out of my hand and shoves the whole thing in his mouth before turning back to watch the movie. I snap my mouth closed again with an audible click. What's the damn point?

I must have dozed off at some point because the next thing I know, I am opening my eyes to a blue screen and Fox softly snoring in my ear. I look over the room and see AJ asleep and sprawled out on the sofa to the left of me but everyone else must have gone to bed. I carefully try to stand up but Fox chooses that moment to turn and rest his head on my shoulder, making me freeze. You have got to be fucking kidding me!

What is it with this guy? I think about moving again but decide against it. I know it's wrong and fucked-up on so many levels, but I miss human contact. I miss being held. So instead of slinking away to my own bed, I stay exactly where I am, basking in the warmth of the gangbanger who likes to snuggle. When did my life become so weird?

"Aww, how sweet. Guess Fox was impressed with his cock sucking skills." The mocking tone seeps through my sleep fog and into my brain.

"He's better than you, that's for fucking sure," Fox grumbles as he pulls himself away from me.

John fumes. "Eat shit, Fox. I ain't into any of that gay shit."

"I think you protest too much, John. I think you're a jealous fuck who would love nothing more than to wrap your lips around my cock. I might have even considered it for the two seconds of peace and fucking quiet it would bring me, but the truth is, the idea of you anywhere near my dick makes me limper than when I fucked your mom."

"You fucking asshole." I hear scuffling and open my eyes to find John being held back by AJ.

"Aww, did I hit a nerve there, Johnny boy? Have some unresolved mommy issues, do we? Is that why you seek girls that look just like her, so you can hatefuck them like the sick fucktard you are?"

John seethes. "I'll kill you."

"I can't wait for you to try," Fox replies calmly before standing and stretching.

"Okay fuckers, time to get ready. The bus will be here in twenty minutes." He looks down at his watch. "Time for a morning wank, you know, just in case it's my last. Come on, Nemo, you can help." He grips my wrist and yanks me to my feet, before dragging me into our bedroom.

"Fuck off, Fox, I'm not going anywhere near your dick," I tell him as he closes the door and spins me, pinning me to the other side of it with my wrists above my head.

"Stay away from John today. If you find yourself alone in the same room as him, leave. He has a hard-on for you and I just pissed him off even more. Hopefully, karma will be on our side and the fucker will die today, then we won't have to deal with his shit anymore." He shoves off me before he starts stripping, heading for the bathroom and leaving a trail of clothing behind him. Why do I constantly find myself around a naked Fox?

"You coming? My dick's so big, I could use the extra hand." I flip him off and head to my bed, ignoring his laugh as he closes the bathroom door behind him. Dragging my bag out from under my bed I slip my hand inside the little zip pocket and pull out the photo I take everywhere with me. It's of me and Charlie back before my hair fell out. Our heads are pressed together, my dark curls and his lighter ones spread out around us, our arms are wrapped tightly around each other as we laugh about something stupid that only the two of us would have found funny. I rub my finger down his cheek in the photo and take a deep breath. If this is it, my last day breathing, then at least I can go out knowing that Charlie will be set for life. That little boy right there is worth everything that might happen from here on out. Although this might not have played out the way I thought it would, it's still the right choice, the only choice.

The shower turns off, letting me know that Fox is done so I shove the photo back into my bag and grab my toothbrush. I ignore Fox when he strolls out in nothing but a towel, a billow of steam following him, and head inside to brush my teeth. There will be time for a shower later when everyone else is zombified. Or I'll be dead and won't ever have to shower again. Either way, a shower is out while Fox is around. I don't trust that he won't just burst in while I'm in there.

Everyone is ready when we head back out, John standing as far away from us as possible, which suits me just fine. Yesterday the bus had been filled to capacity, but today we don't even fill half of it. The empty seats leave behind a poignant reminder of what happened, and of what's to come.

"You okay?" I look up and find AJ sitting beside me. I shrug. Are any of us really okay?

"I guess. You?" He looks out the window beside me, thinking about his answer.

"Everything is a little different than I thought it would be." I look at his face, taking in the words of a man who is generally pretty evasive, and agree.

"On the plus side, I think we all wear fucked-up pretty well. We could all be rocking in a corner somewhere, but we're not. For the most part, I think we've all accepted that this is just how our stories are meant to play out. Not everyone gets a happy ending," I tell him.

"Ain't that the truth," he agrees. "The fucked-up thing is that a project this size costs billions. Billions that would be better spent on prevention and cures." He sighs. "But what do I know?"

We pull up to the clinic as I contemplate AJ's words. It sounds good in a perfect world but that isn't how it works out in real life. Tell the government you want more money for cancer treatments and they give you the runaround, crying poverty. Yet when it comes to something like this, testing biological agents that can potentially be turned into weapons, that same government is willing to throw dollar bills like they're in a strip club.

We head in through the double doors, quietly taking in everything around us. The seats that were filled yesterday hold fifteen people today, each of them in the same blank stare pose from the day before. Despite the fact that there is plenty of space, the guys and I head back to the same place we occupied yesterday, and we wait.

For the next few weeks, it's all we do. We get up, eat, visit the clinic, go home, and repeat the monotonous cycle as we fall into a bizarre routine, waiting for the next person to die.

# FIVE

"What are you making?" a voice asks quietly from behind me. I spin around in a knee-jerk reaction and end up flinging pancake batter all over the wall of chest I find myself up against.

"Fucking hell!" I gasp out in shock. The body takes a large step back, revealing an awkward looking Nate staring down at me.

"Sorry." He bends a little, almost like he's trying to make himself look less imposing, but for a guy whose six-foot-four frame dwarfs my five-seven, the only way that would work would be if he was on his knees. A flush works its way over my cheeks at the thought of Nate on his knees before me, wearing a little less than the gray, soft-looking T-shirt and navy blue sleep pants.

I wave off his apology. It's not his fault I'm jumpy. The

problem with that, of course, is that I wave him off using the hand that's still holding the wooden spoon and end up splattering even more batter over him.

"Erm... oops?" I offer and jump in surprise when he laughs out loud. It's a great sound and I pledge to make him laugh at every opportunity.

"Well, I was attempting to make pancakes but at this rate you'll end up wearing more of the batter than I actually get in the pan," I tell him, making him smile. Gah, the dimple gods have been working overtime with these guys. Jesus.

"Can I help?" he asks in that soft tone of his that's so at odds with his large body. I shrug, trying to play it cool, but being up close and personal with any of these guys is a challenge in itself.

"Sure. Do you like cooking?" I question as I pour some batter into the pan.

"I like the idea of it but I suck at the execution. I'm pretty sure I could burn water." I offer him a smile of my own.

"I can teach you if you want. Nothing fancy, but enough that you don't have to live on takeaway food for the rest of your life." My smile slides off my face at the slip of my tongue. What life? It's easy to forget while we're here caught in limbo that we'll all be gone soon. Who the fuck wants to spend what little time they have left learning to freaking cook?

"Shit, I'm sorry, Nate, I wasn't thinking. Of course, you don't want to learn to cook, I didn't—" He places his huge hand over mine, making me snap my mouth shut. I look down at his hand, thinking it feels strangely intimate. The expression on Nate's face tells me he surprised himself with that move. He pulls his hand away and tucks it into his pocket. I wonder if it's because he feels weird now or if it's to stop himself from doing it again?

He coughs before speaking, the easiness between us suddenly feeling a little awkward.

"I really do want to learn how to cook. Thank you, Cam, I appreciate it," he says, and I believe him. I nod and turn back to the pan, ready to flip the pancake over.

"I taught my little brother to make pancakes. I'm pretty sure a smart guy like you will pick it up in no time."

"Yeah, you say that now..."

I shrug my shoulders. "It's just pancake batter. If you fuck it up, I'll just make another batch, it's not a problem." I watch him take a deep breath and note that some of the tension in his shoulders has slipped away.

"Money was tight when I was a kid. Wasting food because I couldn't grasp the basics of cooking wasn't an option, so I never learned. When I got older, I always found it a little intimidating." He gives me a self-deprecating smile as I take the pancake out and hand him the ladle to pour some more mixture into the pan.

"You can add four dollops around the pan this time. I just like to cook a single one to start with to make sure everything is right."

He nods and I watch in fascination as he pours out mixture for each pancake. His focus is absolute like he's defusing a bomb instead of making breakfast, the tip of his tongue poking out the side of his mouth as he concentrates. Who knew big old Nathan Adler could be so stinking cute?

"How's that?" I snap out of my thoughts and stare back down at the pan. They are a little uneven and more blobish than circular, but that won't affect the taste any.

"Looking good, Adler. Now, wait for the little air bubbles to start popping over the surface, then flip those bad boys over." He follows my instructions to a tee and when he slides the misshapen golden-brown pancakes onto a plate, I smile big at how proud he looks.

I pick one up and take a bite. Closing my eyes, I exaggerate my moan a little before I think better of it and eat it in four mouthfuls.

"So good, Nate. Congrats." I open my eyes and find Nate's eyes on my mouth as my tongue licks away the stray crumbs from my lips. When he sees me looking, he turns away and starts pouring another four rounds of batter into the pan. We work together in tandem, him cooking the pancakes as I talk him through the ingredients.

I don't miss the look of confusion that keeps crossing his face. I thought it was over the cooking at first, but now I realize it's over me. My moaning, him looking at my lips, I think he's kind of drawn to me but confused about it. He's not the only one feeling confused here. I feel like I'm being pulled in so many directions, I'm not sure which way is up anymore. There is a connection between us, a tangible thread of possibility that links us together but with so many obstacles in our way, I can't ever really see it becoming anything more. He doesn't know I'm a girl for one, even if his subconscious seems to have figured out there is more to me than I'm letting on.

I'm going to need to be careful around this one. Not because I think he could hurt me, but because if I'm not careful, I could hurt him. Concealing who I am was only ever meant to keep me safe, but standing here right now, it just feels like exactly what it is, a huge freaking lie.

The guys stumble out for food, the smell enticing them away from their beds as usual. We eat in companionable silence. Even John, for once, manages to keep his mouth shut as we contemplate facing another day.

"I need a hobby." I sigh, looking out the window as the rain that had been threatening to fall for the last hour finally makes itself known.

"I'm down for something, anything, actually. I'm bored as fuck. This waiting around to die shit is exhausting," Levi moans.

"What you got in mind?" Nate asks from the seat beside me.

"I have no idea, but for once I agree with Levi. I'm so fucking bored."

"You could always practice your dick sucking skills," John sneers; his silence never does last long.

"I've told you before, John, you're just not my type. I like my men, well, a little more manly, no offense." I smile sweetly at him. There is no playing nice with John. It doesn't matter how many times I get up with the intention of ignoring him, he always seems to know just which buttons to press.

He doesn't answer, just tosses his plate into the sink before walking off back to his room.

"Well, I vote for Xbox," AJ states from down the table, making me look up. Fox is staring at me in a way that makes me squeeze my thighs together. I think back to the comments I made to John and realize I managed to inadvertently turn Fox on in the process. Fuck me and my big mouth.

"I'm game if you are. I'm surprised you guys haven't had it set up already."

"Honestly, most of the time we're either zapped out or watching a movie," AJ admits.

"Good point. Jack, it's your turn to clean up." I turn to face him and catch the look he throws Fox. Oh boy. Jack has a big ole crush on Fox and Fox is as oblivious as they come.

"Sure, no worries," Jack answers with a smile. The rest of us head into the sitting area. I sit and wait while AJ sets everything up and Fox and Levi argue over what to play. Naturally, Fox wins.

"Okay, Cam, *Call of Duty* is a first person shooter game. Need me to run you through everything?" he questions.

"Nah, I'll pick it up quickly enough. I'll watch you guys play first to get the hang of it." I let them duke it out about who's up first and whatever else they feel the need to squabble over. I sit for the next hour, watching them banter back and forth between themselves, making me realize we've become a makeshift family of sorts.

"Okay, Cam, you're up." Fox tosses me the controller and sits down beside me. He tells me which buttons are which and then I'm up. I tune everyone out and get myself into the zone, running around the digital jungle firing at the enemy. It isn't until Fox jabs me in the shoulder that I look up and realize everyone is staring at me with their mouths open.

"Nemo, have you played this before?" he asks with a smile playing on his lips.

I shrug casually. "I've spent months on and off confined to a hospital bed. There is only so much daytime TV you can watch before you start to lose your mind."

"Damn, Nemo, talk about hustle." Levi whistles. I realize, looking at the screen, I pretty much annihilated everyone else, except for Jack who isn't too far behind.

"I beat you fair and square and I'm about to do it again." I laugh at him as a look of determination crosses his face. These guys are so competitive, it's hilarious.

We head out to the clinic after that game. When we come home, I let the boys sleep it off as I wander around the apartment aimlessly. What was once a comfort is now my least favorite time of day. The silence seems to stretch on forever when the guys are sleeping, their life-size personalities on hold as their bodies fight off the effects of their drug-induced slumber.

We all made it back today, another day we were never guaranteed, and when the boys wake up, everything will go back to being loud and boisterous while we ignore the elephant in the room.

SITTING up here on the roof of the building, staring down at the vast deserted place, I try to wrap my head around the fact that I've reached the two month mark. Every morning I wake up is another day I'm surprised to see.

When I came here, the doctors told me I wouldn't survive the month, and yet here I am. But it's more than that. Instead of getting sicker, I actually feel better than I can ever remember feeling. Even when I was in remission the first time around, I never felt as good as this.

I haven't said anything to anyone because I don't want to rub salt in their wounds. Although saying that, the guys don't really seem to be declining either. John is the only one who looks sicker than when he arrived. But hey, at least now his outside matches his inside.

I have no idea what to expect now as all my plans and expectations revolved around me dying. Being stuck in limbo while you wait to die stops you from really living at all.

Now, after sixty-one days, our town's starting population of 6,472 has dwindled to only fifteen. Seven of those survivors live in this apartment. That seems like a crazy coincidence. I don't know if I should be questioning those odds or buying a lottery ticket.

Something fucked-up is going on, that much is clear, and

yet I'm still as helpless now as I was when I got here. Maybe in a twisted fate kind of way, I'm even more helpless. When I arrived, I knew with certainty I was going to die. Game over, end of story. But now I'm questioning if this is really the end of my story or merely the end of a chapter. I can't help but feel like I might live. Out in the real world, that would be fantastic news but here I was never meant to leave in anything other than a body bag. I might not have all the answers but I know the Phoenix Project simply can't afford for me to become a loose end.

"What's got you thinking so hard up here?" Levi sits beside me, his feet dangling over the edge of the wall next to mine.

"Just wondering what's coming next." He doesn't say anything as I study the side of his handsome face. They've all grown on me since I've been here, with the exception of John. Each of them doesn't quite live up to the stereotype I had placed upon them.

"We're probably better off not knowing. Sometimes I think it's a blessing we can't remember anything afterwards."

I don't answer so I don't have to lie to him.

"Come on, Jack wants to watch one of those shitty horror movies you both seem to like so much." I can't help but snort at that. Despite trying to play it cool, Levi has a slight aversion to clowns. I'm not sure if anyone else has picked up on it. Not everyone is as hypersensitive to the people around them as I am. He does a good job of hiding it if you don't count how rigid he suddenly becomes.

"Hm... I quite fancy the movie *IT* tonight. What do you think?" He turns to scowl at me, catching himself at the last minute and wiping his expression clean.

"Didn't you watch that shit last week? Watch *Saw* or something; everyone likes that." I pretend to think about it for a while.

"Hmm... maybe, oh, wait, I noticed they have the original version of *IT* on there too. That's like four hours long if I remember correctly. We can watch that instead of the remake for a change." His footsteps stumble for a second, making me laugh.

"You asshole," he grumbles. "Do the others know?"

"I don't think so. I'm pretty sure if they had figured it out, you would have woken up with a clown in your bed already. You know what the guys are like." He grimaces at that.

"Don't worry, your secret's safe with me." We head back down to the apartment where everyone else is gathered around yelling at some pre-recorded boxing match that's playing. I look around and realize John, Fox, and Nate are missing.

"Where are the others?" I ask AJ, who is on the sofa closest to me, before heading to the fridge and grabbing a can of Coke.

"Fox is getting changed. John's been throwing up again so he's in bed and Nate is—" I cut him off.

"If you say Nate is behind me, I will throw this can at your head." His grin is infectious, making one of my own appear.

"Actually, Nate has gone out to get popcorn." Okay, that's an acceptable answer.

I plonk myself down on the sofa next to him and sigh.

"Why the long face, Nemo?" Levi asks, leaning against the counter.

I shrug my shoulders, not really wanting to get into it but knowing these guys are like a dog with a bone. If I don't give something up, they won't stop pestering me.

"I don't know. I guess I'm feeling like the walls are closing in. It's been two months. Guys, I never expected to make it a week. The numbness of the whole situation is wearing off. Now I really just want some answers. Answers that you and I know I won't get." I pop the can open and take a big mouthful before I give anything else away.

"Yeah, I feel that. I'm not one for lying around doing nothing either. I never considered when I came here, that one of the ways they might kill me off would be with boredom."

The door to my room opens, revealing Fox, slightly damp from the shower and wearing nothing more than a pair of black basketball shorts. I look away quickly, ignoring the way my heart speeds up whenever he's near me, and because this is Fox—the guy who literally has no boundaries—he is always freaking near me.

"What's everyone doing?" he asks, drawing my attention despite everything I just thought, with the timbre of his voice.

"Going to a club. I thought we could do a little dancing,

maybe—" My voice cuts out when Fox lobs the wet towel he was previously using to dry his hair in my face.

"Fucker," he grumbles but even I can hear the amusement in his voice.

"We were about to watch a movie. Cam, it's your turn to pick. What are we going for?" Jack asks from the end of the sofa on my left, the remote poised ready in his hand as he attempts to inconspicuously check out Fox's chest.

I watch Levi freeze by the counter with his own can held against his lips.

"I don't know about you guys, but I'm in the mood for something spooky. I was going to suggest *Saw*." I don't miss the way Levi's shoulders soften in relief before I throw him under a bus, metaphorically speaking of course.

"But then Levi mentioned how he hadn't seen the original *IT* movie and wanted to see what all the fuss was about, so why don't we go for that one instead?" I tell everyone but I don't take my eyes off Levi who is scowling at me. My lips twitch in response as I try to fight my smile, but it's no good. Seeing the disgruntled look on his face makes me laugh. I stand up to go over and tell him I'm just joking when a strange noise makes me pause. I tilt my head, trying to get a better read on what it is and where it's coming from, but my head starts to pound.

"What is it? What's wrong?" Jack asks, staring at me, which makes everyone else look at me in curiosity too.

"Can you hear that?" I ask the room at large, the noise

sounding almost like a dog whistle that's gradually getting louder.

"Hear what?" Levi asks, his eyes dropping to my nose. He curses, reaching over the counter for the roll of paper towels.

"Cam, you're bleeding." He tosses the roll to me but I make no move to catch it. I watch distantly, my mind sludgy and my limbs leaded as the paper towels bounce off my chest and hit the floor.

"Fuck!" Levi yells before running toward me.

"Fox, Cam's eyes are bleeding, what's happening?" I don't know what anyone's answer is as I suddenly lose what little control I had and fall helplessly to the floor when my legs crumble beneath me.

"Move! Fuck! Nemo?" I feel a hard slap to my face and look up to see Fox's worried eyes looking back down at me.

"You're really pretty," I tell him, my words slurring over each other before my body snaps rigidly, then starts convulsing on the floor.

I can't hear anything beyond the blood rushing through my body. I can't feel anything except blinding pain in the back of my head before everything blissfully stops and then I feel nothing at all.

# SIX

When I come around, I'm surprised to find myself in my room and not at the clinic. I groan as I try to peel my eyes open, wincing as the light makes my head throb. I realize there is an arm around my waist when it tightens around me, making me tense until I recognize the smell of the man beside me, Fox. When I feel his rough fingers trailing across the skin of my stomach, I freeze as ice floods my veins.

I'm naked, my body bare for all to see, displaying the secrets that haunt me. Tears run down the side of my face in tiny rivers, part in fear, part in embarrassment.

"You've got some explaining to do, Nemo." Fox's voice rumbles over me, making my already sensitive skin tingle.

I can't hold back the tiny sob that escapes, making Fox lift his head and look at my face. When he sees my tears, he curses and tucks me into his chest, wrapping his strong arms around me as I fall apart. He doesn't speak while I cry, he just runs his fingers up and down my spine in a surprisingly sweet gesture.

When I'm all cried out, he pulls back and lays me flat on the bed before leaning down over me, his eyes roving over my face.

"Talk to me," he implores.

"What do you want me to say?" My voice croaks.

"How did you end up here with us lot when you are clearly not a guy?"

"Well, you know what they say about assumptions, right? They figured that because my name is Cameron James Miller, I was a guy. I didn't realize they had fucked up until the day we moved in here."

"Jesus. Why didn't you say something?" he bites out.

"I told the housing coordinator and she told me all decisions were final before telling me the safest option for me would be to pretend I was a boy to avoid any unfortunate behavior." My voice drips with sarcasm.

"Fucking bitch. What about someone from the clinic? They could have moved you."

"Yeah, that's what I thought too. But again, apparently, all decisions are final." He looks livid but it doesn't seem to be at me, so I relax slightly.

I watch him watching me and swallow at the intensity in his eyes.

"I knew there was something different about you. I

thought you were just softer than the rest of us who had spent most of our lives in and out of a jail cell. Fuck, I should have figured it out." He sounds pissed at himself now, which almost makes me smile. It's only the uncertainty of the situation that's holding me back.

"How could you have known? I have no hair, no boobs, and no curves. Short of seeing me naked—which I was never going to let happen—you had no way to tell." He dips his head and lifts himself up a little, looking down at my chest. I instinctively move to cover myself, but he grips my wrists and pushes them above my head. He holds them in place with one hand and uses the other to drag a finger down my face and neck, over my collarbone, and down to the scars that show the trauma my body went through. A fresh round of tears spill over my cheeks, but Fox doesn't notice. He seems completely enchanted by my biggest shame. He traces the scarring softly with the pads of his fingers, making me gasp in surprise.

"That hurt?" He looks up as he waits for my answer.

"N-no… the area is just a little sensitive."

"Good." He doesn't say anything else before dipping his head and tracing each of the scars with the tip of his tongue.

I'm openly weeping now. I don't even try to hide it as all the emotions I've been holding at bay rush to the surface and pour out of me in a twisted mess of pain and confusion.

What I don't feel, though, is scared, at least not of Fox. He isn't hurting me or taunting me, each flit of his tongue and press of his lips against my skin is giving me back a little piece of my identity.

"Fox," I say his name softly, making him look up at me.

"These scars make you more beautiful than you can ever know. You stand here every day and take part in this shit show we call life even though the odds are stacked against you. What you see as flaws, Nemo, I see as warrior wounds."

I try to respond, but words fail me. I feel like any second now, I'm going to wake up and this will all have been a dream. I've been praying to wake up from this nightmare for months, but right now the thought of waking up and not finding Fox beside me leaves me feeling sick.

"I-I Fox?" He lifts his head and stares into my eyes. There is no look of disgust or repulsion like I saw reflected back at me from my ex. All I see is desire and something else, something unfamiliar and darker.

"Who else knows?" I ask biting my lip with worry, making Fox's eyes focus there.

"What? That you're a girl? Everyone except John—and he doesn't need to know. The guys will keep your secret, don't worry."

"Are they mad at me?"

"Mad? No. Surprised as fuck, but not mad." He sweeps his hand over my brow and frowns. "How are you feeling?"

I take a minute before answering to see if any pain registers now that the haze of sleep has worn off, but all I feel is achy.

"Just tired more than anything. I feel like I've run a marathon. What happened?"

"That's what I'd like to know. One minute you were fine and the next you were bleeding from your eyes. I swear to god, Nemo, if you scare me like that again, I'll blister your ass." I squirm beneath him as an unexpected rush of warmth races through my veins.

Fox doesn't miss a thing, his eyes flashing with hunger. Before he can speak, there's a knock at the door and AJ pokes his head inside. He takes in Fox pressed over me with my hands still pinned above my head before looking down at my flushed face.

"Hey, how are you feeling?" AJ asks like it's perfectly normal to be in this position.

"I'm okay, just tired," I whisper, feeling embarrassed and confused. He nods, then focuses on Fox.

"If I come over and steal a hug, are you going to disembowel me in my sleep?" he asks him.

"Probably," Fox answers him, making no move to get off me.

"Fox. Come on, I didn't just scare you, I scared everyone." He still doesn't move but his grip on my hands loosens enough for me to be able to slip one free. I reach up and cup his jaw, his dark scruff tickling my palm.

"I'm okay, Fox, I swear." He scowls at me before finally relenting. He leans over me and scoops up his black T-shirt from the floor. Blocking me from AJ's view, Fox slips the T-shirt over my head and helps me maneuver my arms through. Rolling us, he angles our bodies so I'm now facing AJ and Fox is pressed against my back with his hand on my hip.

AJ just rolls his eyes at him, not bothered by Fox's antics at all. He walks over to the bed and lifts the blanket before climbing in and tucking my face against his chest and slipping an arm around my back, making Fox grumble and me laugh. The bed is tiny, way too small for the three of us. One false move and both Fox and AJ will end up on the floor, but nobody complains. They just press themselves as close to me as they can get and guard me as I drift back to sleep.

When I wake up, I see the sun streaming through the windows alerting me to the fact that it's morning. Both guys are still wrapped around me, making me smile that they stayed with me all night. I don't want to move, I want to stay in this moment for just a little longer but unfortunately, my bladder has other ideas. There is no way for me to get out of bed without disturbing at least one of the guys. Looking up, I see AJ staring down at me with a soft, sleepy expression on his face.

"Hey," he rumbles gently..

"Hey. I really need to pee," I tell him, without beating around the bush. But let's be honest, it's better than peeing on him. He smiles at me before surprising me by dropping a kiss to my forehead. He climbs out of bed and holds out his hand to help me up. I gently extract myself from Fox's hold and slip my hand into AJ's, letting him help me up since my legs still feel a little wobbly. When I turn to head toward the bathroom, I stop short and gasp. Lying on the floor, buried under quilts and blankets, I see Jack and Levi fast asleep. I glance over at my bed and there's Nate, snuggled under my covers.

"They wanted to be near you. They were worried. We were all worried." I turn my head toward AJ and give him a wobbly smile. The way he's looking at me lets me know that everything is different now.

"I'm sorry I scared you all." He steps up to me and wraps me in his arms, breathing me in before answering.

"Just don't do it again. I thought I'd gotten used to losing people, but the truth is, Cam, I don't think I'll ever be ready to lose you." I swallow down the lump in my throat and lift up onto my tiptoes, placing a soft kiss against his jaw. Cat's out of the bag now, so I doubt I'll get punched for it.

"The day we were born, we were all given an expiration date. Some of us just have a shorter shelf life than others."

He squeezes me a little tighter, frowning. "Don't talk like that, Cam, I don't like it."

"To have hope in a place like this is a very dangerous thing. None of us are walking out of here alive, AJ, but that doesn't mean I don't plan on squeezing every drop of life out of this existence until my heart stops beating and the darkness finally comes for me." He looks like he's going to argue with me, but I place my fingers over his mouth and shake my head. His words won't change our fate. The stones of our destiny have already been cast.

I leave AJ to ponder my words and step around the guys, padding softly across the room so I don't disturb them.

I take care of business and decide to brush my teeth and jump in the shower while I'm in here. It feels weird, knowing I don't have to hide anymore—at least from the guys in my room, anyway.

I check out my face while I brush my teeth, surprised to see some color in my cheeks and, dare I say, a healthy-looking glow. I guess the strain of having to hide who I am has been taking more of a toll than I realized. There is some dried blood under my nose and a streak down the side of my neck, which I'm guessing came from my ear. My eyes are a little bloodshot too, but overall it could have been worse. I woke up, that's always a bonus.

I turn on the shower and wait for the small room to steam up a little before stripping off Fox's T-shirt and climbing in. The hot water feels good against my sticky skin, soothing away the remaining aches from yesterday's episode.

When the shower door is yanked open, I squeal and try to cover myself. Fox doesn't give a shit though, he just steps into the shower with me, closing the frosted glass door behind him, enclosing his large sculpted body with mine in a shower cubicle clearly designed for one.

"Fox," I whisper when his hands land on my hips. The water rains down over him as he spins us around so his back is keeping the water from me.

"Let me help, Nemo." He grabs the shower gel and squeezes a blob into his hands before lathering them together. Without waiting for permission, he runs them over my body, washing away the remnants of the blood and sweat from yesterday.

"What's going on? Why are you all acting so weird? I'm the same Cam I was yesterday, it's just today you know I'm lacking in the penis area." He smirks at that before sobering.

"Everything's changed, Nemo. You might not have noticed, but each and every one of us has grown attached to you. I think most of us thought it was a protective thing. Being inside, it's hard to forget the smaller newbies crying when they missed home or, worse, were made someone's unwilling bitch. None of us wanted to get attached, it's hard enough keeping our friendships with each other in check without factoring in someone like you, and yet here you are."

He spins me into the water, rinsing the soap from my body before turning me back out again.

I watch him as he soaps himself up, dragging his hands over his chest and thick, corded arms, down his intricately tattooed chest to his rock-hard cock. I gasp when I see it, snapping my eyes to his when he growls and presses me against the wall, his dick hot and hard against my stomach.

"If you keep looking at me like that, I'm going to do things, Nemo, that I just don't think you're ready for."

I stare up into his dark eyes, his body rigid—in more ways than one—as he tries to hold back.

"I thought you were into g-guys," I splutter out.

"The only thing I'm into is you, Nemo. You might have no hair, boobs, or cock for that matter, but you have heart. You have strength, humor, and determination in spades. My soul is so dark, it's pitch black, but you're all sunshine and rainbows and, fuck me, I'm drawn to it like a moth to a flame. What do you say? Want to play in the shadows with me until the reaper comes a-calling?"

I dip my head and lean against his chest, knowing if I fall for this guy or any of them, I stand to die more than once. A part of me will fade away a little every single time one of them dies. The alternative, though, is to stop living and that is something I promised myself I wouldn't do until the end.

"Okay, Valentine. Let's see where this thing goes," I mumble into his chest, expecting him to push me up against the wall harder and thrust into me now that he has finally been given the green light. Instead, I feel the tension leave his body as he reaches over to shut the water off.

He climbs out before me and holds a towel open, wrapping me up tight before wrapping another one around his waist.

"Well, that was anticlimactic," I grumble to myself as my arousal starts to cool.

Fox laughs before leaning down and nipping me on the shoulder.

"Oh, the things I'm going to do to you, Nemo, are going to blow your mind." I roll my eyes at him and huff as I shove him back a little.

"First of all, that's big talk from someone who just left me high and dry when I gave him an access-all-areas pass. Second of all, I'll have you know, I have a vivid imagination and a large collection of porn, well, I used to at least. I might not have had access to a lot of cock but these fingers are expert level talented. Too bad I won't be showing you just what I can do with them." I pull the door open and stomp out to the bedroom and right into a wall of compact muscle hard enough to make my eyes water when my poor nose smacks into one of his pecs.

"Ouch." I look up, blinking back tears, and scowl at the tower of muscle.

"Nathan Adler, I swear to god I'm going to put a bell around your neck," I snap, but when he lifts me clean off my feet and wraps me up tight in a bear hug I forget I was mad at him and his concrete chest.

"Thanks, Nate. With the way you're holding her, I've got one hell of a view from down here." I hear Levi from somewhere on the floor, making me blush. I squirm to get down but Nate just walks us over to my bed and sits with me in his lap.

"You okay?" he asks me softly, his voice always so at odds with his gruff exterior.

"Surprisingly, yeah," I tell him.

"What happened out there, Cam? One minute you were fine and the next it was like someone had cut your strings. It was freaky as fuck," Jack asks.

I look over and see him and Levi now sitting with their backs to Fox's bed, while Fox himself pulls on a pair of sweatpants from the floor. AJ is sitting on the windowsill, giving me the once over but it doesn't make me feel uncomfortable. It makes me feel cherished and cared for.

"I heard something. Like a high-pitched whistle that just kept getting louder and louder, making the pressure build in my head until it all became too much. You guys really didn't hear anything?"

They look around at each other but all end up shaking their heads.

"Great," I grumble. Maybe I'm finally going crazy.

"Nope," Nate grunts out, making me turn to look up at him. "You didn't imagine it any more than we imagined the blood pouring from you. I don't know why you were the only one affected, but I hope to fuck this was an isolated incident because I think you just aged me ten years."

The room is silent for a moment before Levi breaks in. "Holy fuck! I don't think I've ever heard Nate use so many words on purpose before." Jack reaches over and shoves him. Levi doesn't move. He's nearly twice the size of Jack, after all, but he shuts his mouth.

Everyone is quiet for a while before Jack speaks up.

"So, a girl, huh?" he questions.

"Apparently so," I answer him, not sure how he feels about the fact that I lied to him.

"When were you going to tell us?" he asks and this time there is no hiding the hurt in his voice. After everything, all the lies I've told, I decide to give him the unwavering truth.

"I wasn't ever going to tell you, Jack. I wasn't going to tell any of you."

He swallows but looks away. I notice Levi frowning at me like he isn't any happier with this news either.

"I get that you don't like it but, honestly, it kept me safe," I tell them.

"We would never hurt you!" Jack snaps at me.

"And I would have known this how, Jack? Stop acting so butt hurt about things and think for a second. Put yourself in my shoes and think back to my first day." I can see him looking back, trying to make himself understand the decision I made, until finally, he sighs. He might not like it, but he gets it.

"Care to explain to the rest of us?" Levi asks, frustrated.

"I found out I was being housed here when you did. It took me less than thirty seconds to realize I was the only girl in the group. The bitch guide told me I should pretend I was a guy as the side effects of the drugs were unpredictable. They could cause aggression and... other side effects." I leave that hanging for a second and look over to see a tic spasm in Fox's jaw.

Jack groans out loud and dips his head, making me smile.

"What?" Levi asks him.

"Then I decided to give her the scoop on who we were, where we were from, and what we were in for," he admits, and I realize he never told them. They all look at me in shock before understanding dawns. They have actively tried to avoid talking about their pasts. I'm not sure they knew I was aware of their crimes.

"Shit, you must have been terrified." AJ drags a hand through his hair.

I lift my hand and wave him off.

"I figured out early on you were more than the label you were branded with, so don't think I've been living in abject terror for the last two months because I haven't."

"Then why didn't you say anything?" Jack asks.

"Because John Davis might like punching little boys, but he likes touching little girls more." Nate goes solid beneath me.

"Did he touch you?" he hisses through gritted teeth. I rub my hand in a soothing manner up and down the arm that's banded around me.

"Never. He thinks I'm a guy, remember? More than that, though, he thinks Fox has some kind of claim on me. He might act the fool, but he isn't stupid. He knows better than to break one of Fox's toys."

Fox stalks toward me like a lethal predator, ripping me from Nate and hauling me up into his arms. I wrap my legs around his waist as he pushes me against the wall and slams his lips down on mine.

Now, I'm not a virgin. My first time wasn't special or sacred or even with someone I loved. The truth is, I just didn't want to die without ever experiencing that kind of intimacy with someone. It wasn't earth shattering or life changing. It was just a nice experience with a nice guy who let me have control of my body which constantly failed me.

This kiss, however, is anything but nice. It's forceful and dominating and consumes me, making me forget we have an audience. When he finally rips his lips away from mine, he's breathing heavily and the proof of his arousal presses against my core.

"You are not a fucking toy," he tells me. All I can do is nod.

"I think I just came," I hear muttered from somewhere, making me snort and bury my head against Fox's shoulder as my face flames with embarrassment.

"So, what happens now?" Nate asks, making me train my gaze on him over Fox's shoulder. He's looking at me, but the words are for Fox.

He doesn't answer for a second. His eyes bore into mine and flash with something that's too fleeting for me to read.

"We carry on as we always have and what will be will be. As far as John is concerned, it would be better if he still thinks of Nemo as a guy." As much as I've loved being myself around these guys, I know Fox is right. Baiting a tiger with a juicy steak—or in my case, at least, a snack—is just asking for trouble.

# SEVEN

I lie on my bed, listening to the guys puttering around in the kitchen, knowing we have to head out to the clinic soon but I'm reluctant to move. I listen to the shower and think of Fox soaping himself, running his hands up and down his delectable body.

I should be getting dressed but lying here in another of Fox's T-shirts and surrounded by his scent, I'm struggling to rein in my body's reactions to finally being allowed to be a woman again. It's like my cork has been popped and all the urges and desires I had to keep simmering below the surface are erupting out of me in a wave of want and need.

Taking advantage of my moment of peace, I slide my fingers beneath my underwear, not surprised at all to find my clit already swollen and needy. I dip my fingers inside myself and draw some of the gathering moisture over my fingertips before swirling them over my clit once more. I circle around it, again and again, applying a little more pressure as everything inside me starts to tighten. My breath comes out in little puffs and in an attempt to be quiet, I bite my lip when I feel a groan trying to escape. I slide my hand down farther and fuck myself with two fingers, imaging it's Fox's cock thrusting its way inside me. I move faster and faster, dragging myself closer to the edge before finally flicking my clit hard twice. It's more than I can take as my toes curl and I whimper in relief as my orgasm crashes over me.

I'm so lost in my own world I never hear the shower shut off or the bathroom door open. When I open my eyes, it's to find Fox's heated glare burning into mine. He presses his hand over my mouth before I shriek. Both of us breathe heavily, our faces inches apart and separated only by his hand.

When he knows I'll be quiet enough to avoid having the guys come running in here, he pulls his hand away only to replace it briefly with his lips. I mewl when he pulls away, but watch wide-eyed as he grabs the wrist of the hand I was just touching myself with and raises it to his face. He inhales deeply, making me blush, but he doesn't notice it as his eyes drift closed, a groan of his own escaping.

"Oh, fuck." My greedy pussy spasms as Fox sucks the two fingers I just fucked myself with, twirling his tongue around them until he has licked my essence clean.

"Fucking delicious, Nemo. I'm going to lock myself out there with the guys while you get yourself showered and dressed for the clinic. I don't trust myself with you right now." His voice is rough and filled with need. I squirm on the bed in protest, wanting him to stay, fuck the clinic and the consequences, but I know he's right. I sigh in frustration, making him chuckle.

"Don't worry, Nemo. When we get back, I'm going to sample your enticing nectar straight from the source," he tells me with a wink before he pulls himself away and leaves me a squirming mess for the second time in twenty-four hours.

One thing's for sure, if the Phoenix Project doesn't kill me, Valentine Fox will.

TODAY'S clinic experience starts off a little differently than usual. We are gathered together in a large room at the back of the building waiting for someone to come out and speak with us. This is new, that's for sure. When a tall, somewhat familiar looking, thin man with cold eyes walks into the room wearing a navy three-piece suit and stares us down, I have to fight back my snort. When I see Fox's lips twitch, I realize I wasn't as quiet as I had hoped. Not that you could blame me. If this guy thinks he's intimidating, he's clearly never met my guys. I see he figures that out pretty quickly when he pays attention. He starts fiddling with his tie before swallowing hard.

"Gentlemen. My name is Mr. Davis. I'm here as a

representative of the Phoenix Project. I'm introducing myself because some of you may see me around. My role here is merely as a consultant. I shall be looking around the facility, seeing if and where improvements can be made and, of course, I'll be checking how you are getting on as you transition to the next stage of treatment. We are incredibly happy with how you have responded so far." *Translation—you haven't died yet like the others.* I wonder if they're actually happy with that or if we've become a nuisance.

"What the hell is the next stage of treatment?" I ask Jack, figuring if we were told about it, Jack would remember.

"I'm not sure, but it looks like we'll soon be finding out," he comments, looking uneasy.

"You will still come here each morning for your medications and monitoring. If you have any questions, or you notice any changes in your body that seem... odd, please don't hesitate to approach me."

I raise my hand and wait for him to nod in my direction.

"Define odd, sir?" The guy unbuttons then rebuttons his jacket before answering.

"As you know, the serum is still in its testing phase. This means we simply don't know all the possible side effects at the moment. How it affects one won't necessarily be how it affects all. Any feedback you can give us, no matter how insignificant, could prove to be useful information that will help with your continued treatment." When nobody responds, he bids us goodbye and walks out, his posture so stiff he looks like someone has shoved a poker up his ass.

"Gotta love vague answers," I whisper, making Fox look down at me from his spot to my left.

"What do you think that was really all about?" AJ asks from the other side of me. "We never had anyone talk to us at the beginning of our treatments, so why now?"

"Maybe because they didn't want to acknowledge that most of the people they would be talking to wouldn't be around long enough to ask questions. Who knows? There is something a little off with that guy though..." I trail off with a sigh. "In all honesty, I'm not sure we can trust anyone but each other."

"Fucking know-it-all. Everything is going great you paranoid fuck. All this place needs is some pussy, then it would be like heaven. Why the fuck do you want to mess up a good thing?" John spews his venom.

"I have neither the patience nor the crayons to explain this situation to you, John, so why don't you go back to ignoring me, for both our sakes," I tell him with a big wide smile that's as fake as me being a boy.

"Fucking prick," he blasts before our names are called over the intercom. When each of us is given a room to report to, we make our way down the corridor, splitting off into the one we are usually assigned to. I open the door and see my usual doctor typing something on her laptop.

"Good morning, Cam. You know the drill, clothes off, and take your medication please."

She doesn't look up and I don't answer her. I take the pill and slip it into my pocket before drinking the water from the little plastic cup next to it. Next, I take off my clothes, sans panties, and climb up gracelessly onto the bed. I still hate every second of being exposed this way, but after Fox's words yesterday, I feel a little stronger today. Stronger and more determined.

Something tripped in my brain last night. When the darkness came, I thought my time had come. When I woke, I swore I would stop preparing myself to die and start fighting to live. I don't want to die here anymore, so I need a damn good plan to get out of here. It occurs to me as I lie here, I should have told the guys not to take the pill, but I wasn't thinking clearly. I feel guilty until the doc walks over and plunges the needle into my skin. Then I remember that at least they don't have to feel this. I grit my teeth as liquid fire races through my veins and steals my breath from me.

I take myself away to my happy place, to Charlie and me lying under the stars on his trampoline trying through fits of laughter to find the constellations. His smile, his happiness, everything that makes him, him, is what pulled me through the darkness time and time again. Doing this for money when I had no other options seemed smart at the time, but now I know if there is a chance I'll survive, I'll fight for it. I'm smart enough to know if Charlie had a choice, he would choose me over money every single time. In a society that judges based on your income and tax bracket, too many people fail to see that the richest people are always the ones who love and are loved right back.

My thoughts are interrupted by the voice of a second person entering the room.

"Dr. Conners, report your findings," I hear an unfamiliar male voice ask.

"Yes, sir," my doctor answers anxiously. "Patient has shown baseline responses to stimuli. Superficial abrasions and contusions heal rapidly. Status at the moment is a class one, but that could change as the serum is administered. Out of all the test subjects, this one seems to be the most stable, showing almost no negative side effects."

What the actual fuck are they talking about?

"Excellent. I would like you to administer a second dose of the serum, doctor, and observe the patient closely. Keep them here for monitoring for the next twenty-four hours if necessary."

"But, sir, that much serum is likely to be lethal, and at this stage..."

"Might I remind you, Dr. Conners, you are not running the show here. I have been given orders to have all remaining class ones double dosed. If they aren't showing any additional changes afterward, they will be removed from the program."

"But, sir," she tries again.

"Do it, that's a direct order," he barks at her.

"No, I'm sorry, sir but—" He surprises me by cutting her off with a curse. I fight back the bile rising in my throat, trying to figure out what to do. Fuck. What can I do?

"Leave. I will do it myself." I hear angry footsteps move

away from me and the door open and close as I try to come up with a plan to get out of this without giving myself away. It turns out I can't do anything. Before I can give in to the rising panic, another needle presses into my arm, streaking white hot lightning across my skin. It's impossible not to cry out. My back arches off the bed, every muscle in my body pulled tight, every bone threatening to snap under the tension.

I scream. I can't help it. My organs are boiling from the inside out, liquefying everything into molten lava. I thrash on the bed, trying to escape the pain, but nothing helps. Eventually, I feel the darkness creep over me as my movements still and my heartbeat starts to falter.

"What a waste!" he proclaims, his voice grating over my skin. I hear the door open and angry voices before it slams closed again. My vision fades out now as my heart skips a beat, its pattern irregular and too damn slow.

"Not on my fucking watch! I'm not losing you today, Cameron, so hold on." I hear the panic in my doctor's voice seconds before I feel her cold hands on my chest.

"Initiating phase two." Her words echo from far away, making no sense to me. Nothing makes sense anymore. My brain finally shuts down as my heart beats once, twice, and then stops altogether.

PEELING MY EYES OPEN, I blink as the bright light blinds me. I take a deep breath and wait until I can focus again. My mouth is dry and my throat feels like it's been rubbed down with sandpaper.

I turn my head, realizing belatedly that I'm still in the treatment room. Someone has covered me with a white sheet, which slips down as I sit up and gingerly swing my legs over the side of the bed. I don't know where the doc or the asshole who tried to kill me are, but I'll happily take this reprieve while I take stock of my body. My muscles are sore and aching like I'm coming down with the flu. Apart from that, I feel okay. Better than I thought I would. I look down as I stand, feeling cold as I'm still only in panties, and frown when I don't see something that should be there but isn't.

*My scars.*

I lose my balance, knocking the little table over and sending the small plastic water cup tumbling to the ground.

I look down again and whimper when the view remains the same. I stumble over to the sink. What I see in the mirror above it takes my breath away. With a trembling hand, I reach out and touch my reflection. How is this even possible? My mind drifts back to the double dose of those fucking meds I could hear them arguing over before the blinding pain and then the bliss of nothingness.

I keep expecting the mirror to twist and warp my image like those reflections you see in a funhouse, only this time it would reveal my true reflection. My smooth head, my sparse eyebrows, and my nonexistent eyelashes that frame my dark jaded eyes. Instead, what looks back at me is perhaps the cruelest form of punishment. An image of what I would have looked like if my body hadn't been consumed by cancer and riddled with chemicals. Dark sculpted eyebrows and lashes so full, they look almost fake, make my usually androgynous face look pretty and delicate. Rich brown hair, the color of the darkest chocolate, reaches my shoulders, looking softer and shinier than it ever had in any memory I could conjure up. My eyes are the exact same shade of brown as my hair, an odd anomaly that used to catch people's attention before I lost my hair and they stopped being able to look me in the eye at all. Only now, as I feel my emotions start to spiral, I see what almost looks like an echo of fire in them. Bright, burning embers melt through my chocolate orbs. I focus my gaze lower, my vision starting to blur as the tears threatening to drown me begin to fall. I trace a finger over my chest, imagining the curve of where my breast would be, watching in the mirror as my fingers move over my pale, flawless skin. My scars are gone, my smooth skin is unbroken, my touch now feeling both foreign and familiar. I can't stop touching myself, wondering if this is all some kind of fucked-up hallucination. The scars I always hated that marred my skin like a barcode with an expiration date have been completely erased and I find myself feeling unexpectedly angry. Fox was right, I earned those scars. They reminded me every day that I had kept on fighting even when the odds were stacked against me. And now someone has wiped them away, erased them like they meant nothing at all. Like I didn't bleed, cry, and scream over them after making the agonizing choice I had been forced to make.

I think of Fox's lips trailing over the sensitive scar tissue, burning through my layers of self-loathing, and sink to the floor with a sob. Wrapping my arms around myself and burying my head against my knees, I cry so hard my head throbs from my inability to suck in enough air.

I thought I had come to terms with all I had lost. I had made a kind of peace with it, knowing Charlie was going to be taken care of for the rest of his life. This horrid life stealing disease had somehow given me the means to provide the single best thing in my life with a future. A future I just wouldn't be a part of. And that was fine until I started to get better and truly looked at what I had already lost.

Losing my hair, my breasts, and then, finally, the ability to have children left me feeling stripped bare and exposed for the whole world to see. I felt less than a woman. Unworthy, defective, and flawed. It took coming here to die to finally see my own worth and realize I wanted to live.

The smell of smoke catches my attention, making my head shoot up and look around. Nothing appears to be out of place until I catch a glimpse of my hand and notice the smell is coming from me. I turn my left hand over in front of me and see the skin is so red it looks like it's been submerged in boiling water, except there's no blistering. After using my hands to examine my chest, I know for sure it hadn't looked like that a few moments ago.

I pick up the discarded plastic cup that I had knocked over as I scrambled from the bed and watch in fascination as it melts into my palm, the previously white plastic running freely through my fingers like sticky white slime. But how is that possible, and more to the point, how isn't it hurting me?

I focus my gaze on the ceiling but I don't see any cameras. They don't have them in the treatment rooms, not because it's unethical, but because there would be a record of the nefarious shit they do to us.

The door opens, making my head whip around. The doctor looks at the bed and frowns before scanning the room and finding me curled up in a ball under the sink.

"Cameron," she calls softly like she's placating a wounded animal. At this point, she's not wrong. I don't answer, I just watch her warily as she approaches, crouching down on the floor in front of me.

"It's okay," she tells me, offering me her hand. I stare at it like she has the plague.

She blows out a breath and sits down with a sigh. I take her in and realize this might be the first time I've seen her looking anything less than perfectly made up.

"I don't understand what's going on," I whisper, afraid if I speak too loudly the spell will be broken, that my healed body will go back to being broken.

She studies me a beat before standing up and hurrying over to the door and locking it.

"Okay, I don't have much time. Come over here." I stand, wrapping my arm around myself and walk toward her, sitting in the chair she indicates.

"I will tell you what I know, which honestly is not much. I need you to trust me though," she pleads and sits beside me.

I don't speak, hoping she might be able to give me some of the answers I've been searching for.

She takes a deep breath, making me brace myself, and starts talking.

"I took this job to make a difference. We had the potential to make real headway toward the eradication of dementia and Alzheimer's if caught quickly enough. The trouble was, the serum needed a lot of tweaking. The success rate was stuck at around ten percent and the possible side effects were harrowing, with multiple cases ending in death." She stops talking for a second as she collects my clothes and hands them to me. I blush, slipping them on. As soon as she started speaking, I forgot all about my nakedness, my thirst for knowledge overruling everything else.

"So that's why we're all here? Why not just tell us that? That's more noble a cause then being used as a test subject for chemical warfare."

She looks at me with sharp eyes.

"Noble maybe, but people wouldn't understand why they couldn't just up and leave if they changed their minds. People needed to think they would be exposed to something that could be harmful to others. You wouldn't want to put your family at risk now, would you?" I shake my head, realizing how effective a tool that particular lie had been.

"Exactly, and that's what they were counting on."

"Well I hate to say it, doc, but I don't think your serum is working as well as you guys had hoped. Whatever the reasons behind it, it doesn't change the fact that out of the thousands of us who arrived here, only a dozen or so are left. Those are not good odds."

"Actually, it is working. It's just not being used for what it was intended for and the results have been... extreme."

I stare into her troubled eyes and swallow.

"What do you mean?"

"Some of the patients have started showing signs that they are adapting, mutating, if you like, in other areas." I think of my hands melting that cup earlier and feel my pulse quicken.

"So now instead of side effects being bleeding from the eyes, it's laser vision?" I half joke.

"Maybe not lasers but you're not far off the mark. I'm talking accelerated speed, increased strength, and amplified agility. Only, these aren't side effects, this is what the Phoenix Project was always about. Tell me, Cameron, can you imagine how priceless it would be to have a soldier, or an army of soldiers for that matter, who are stronger and faster than every other army out there? Soldiers who could self-heal?" I look down at my body and suck in a sharp breath and shudder at the implication behind her words. Self-heal. My scars. Fuck.

"What happens to the ones who show potential for these changes?" I ask, even though I have a feeling I already know the answer.

"They are moved off site to an undisclosed secondary location. They will become the ultimate weapon until their bodies give out."

"And if they don't want that?"

"They aren't given a choice, Cameron."

"Fuck! I guess a part of them must be grateful they aren't dying anymore." But the doc's shaking her head before I even finish speaking.

"No, Cam, they're still dying. Ironically enough, whatever was killing them, hasn't healed at all. In some cases, the disease has stopped spreading, but as I'm sure you know, everyone was already at the terminal stage before they got here."

She turns to the cupboard behind her and pulls out a set of hair clippers, making me jump off the stool and step back until I bump up against the wall.

"No, please don't," I plead, my voice breaking. Surely she wouldn't be this cruel.

She looks like she's fighting back tears herself as she plugs them in.

"You, Cam are the key to everything. I checked your scans after I stabilized you earlier, before destroying them and replacing them with doctored versions of the ones you arrived with."

She walks over and takes my hand, pulling me to sit on the stool by the desk.

Surprising me, she cups my chin with her hands, forcing me to look at her.

"You're cancer-free, Cameron. Not in remission either. It's like you never had it to begin with."

I'm glad I'm sitting or I would have fallen on my ass. I

don't try to mask my tears. I let them roll down my cheeks, feeling them cover her shaking hands still holding my jaw...

"You are their success story, Cameron. The serum opened up your ability to self-heal completely. We knew it would heal bumps and bruises from the start but to kill cancer... that's huge. I have so much more to tell you but we just don't have the time today. I need you to listen to me very carefully, okay?" I nod and inhale deeply to clear my head. When she steps back to pick up the clippers, I cringe away.

"You have to keep hiding. Act sick and weak, Cam, your life depends on it. Tell nobody what I've told you. Do you understand? It's imperative that you stick with the facade of being sick or I fear the next set of tests run on you will be far more horrific than either of us are prepared for."

Leaning down again, she presses her forehead against mine.

"I swear to you, it will grow back. Close your eyes and don't watch." I close my eyes, jolting when I feel the blades against my head. I fight back a wave of nausea as I feel my hair drop to the floor around me. It's just hair, I know it is, but it doesn't stop me from nearly biting through my lip from the injustice of having something I so desperately missed returned to me only to have it cruelly stripped away again.

"There, all done. Do you have access to a pair of these in your apartment?" I nod. I guess being housed with guys finally came in handy for something.

"You need to keep this to yourself, Cameron. Keep coming here as usual and I will try to find out everything I can to help us get the fuck out of here." I look down at her as she sweeps up my fallen hair.

"Why are you helping me?" I ask quietly. I remember how dismissive she was when I first came here. When I told her I was a girl.

"I wanted to help save the world, Cam, not destroy it. I'm sorry I was a bitch to you at the start, but I just couldn't afford to get attached to anyone knowing you were all going to die." She takes a moment to collect herself before looking at me. Beneath her professional mask, I glimpse the pain she has been hiding. I don't know how she hid it because seeing it now makes my heart ache for her.

"I lost my husband six years ago after a brief battle with bowel cancer. The only thing that kept me going was that I was eight months pregnant. What I didn't know, and what my husband didn't know, was that we both carried the Tay-Sachs gene. Abigail started showing symptoms when she was six months old. That's when I found out. She died when she was two and a half and there wasn't a single thing I could do to stop it. What the hell was the point in being a doctor if I couldn't save the people I loved?

"That's when the Phoenix Project approached me. They promised radical treatments and testing to prevent a huge number of incurable diseases. I needed to believe in something and I wanted it to be true so badly, I ignored every red flag that smacked me in the face.

"I know now that they played me. They sought me out because I was vulnerable, riddled with guilt and grief and so fucking angry at the world." She stands and reaches for my hand, giving it a slight squeeze before walking over to dispose of my hair.

"My intentions were pure, Cameron. I refuse to dishonor my husband's and daughter's memories by doing something I know is wrong."

"So we're going to run?" I ask.

She turns to look at me before nodding. "But first we need a plan."

# EIGHT

For the first time since arriving, I walk the five-minute journey back to the apartment instead of taking the bus. There is nobody around, the ghost town hiding my secrets as well as its own. I think about the doctor's words and how they have yet again pulled the proverbial rug out from beneath me.

I make an effort not to think about my hair or missing scars or the fact that I might very well be the only person left here who isn't sick, but it's impossible to think about anything else. How ironic is it that being healthy again paints a target on my back that will likely kill me faster than the cancer ever could have?

I hurry up the steps to my apartment, knowing I've been out of it a few hours more than I usually would have been, which means I need to hurry so as not to raise suspicions. As much as I want to tell the guys what's going on, I know I can't. These guys won't take this lying down. They'll storm the castle, so to speak. As mighty as they are, they won't stand a chance against the Phoenix Corporation and a squad of super soldiers.

I open the door to the apartment and find it eerily quiet, just like always after clinic visits. I peek into each of the rooms and find everyone accounted for, so I quickly tiptoe into the room I share with Fox and grab my bag before closing myself in the bathroom.

I take a deep breath and brace my hands against the sink, preparing myself before I look in the mirror. One day I'll be able to look at my reflection and feel something more than sadness and regret.

I lift my head and stare into my eyes. I blink once, then twice before blowing out a stream of air.

"Fuck," I grumble. Concealing this is going to be impossible. My head, smooth fifteen minutes ago, now has soft fuzz upon it. My eyebrows and eyelashes, which had just started to grow back after I stopped chemo, are significantly fuller. When I strip out of my clothes, I find a sprinkling of pubic hair which I swear I will never take for granted again. I fight back a wave of hysterical laughter. I know if I let it out, it will turn into great heaving sobs. Girls my age used to talk about shaping, shaving, and lasering off their pubic hair but I've never been so happy to have some grow back.

Hiding all this isn't going to be an option, plus lying to

these guys makes me feel shitty but I really want to be able to hide this shit from John a little longer.

I finish up and get dressed in jeans and a shapeless flannel shirt before digging around in the bottom of my bag for a beanie. I pull it on, using it a little like camouflage so I don't shock the shit out of them when they wake up.

I wrestle back the surge of panic at just the thought of explaining it to them. I mean, how can you explain something you don't understand yourself?

'Hey guys, the booby scars are gone, oh and my hair has grown back too in all the right places.' A wild thought has me choking and running back to the bathroom and whipping the hat off to stare in the mirror. Am I going to end up like some kind of fucked-up version of Rapunzel? Will it just keep growing at an accelerated speed? Shit, that has me looking down at my crotch with a grimace. Fuck no, I don't want to be tucking my pubic hair into my damn socks. I need to go back to the clinic, I need answers, I need—

"Nemo? You in here?" I yank the beanie back into place a second before Fox strolls into the bathroom. I watch with detached fascination as he lifts the toilet seat and whips his cock out for a piss before I turn away. This guy gives zero fucks about propriety.

"You're quiet," he observes, nudging me away from the sink with his hip so he can wash his hands.

I try to find the words to tell him what's going on but it's like the English language has been erased from my brain. I open my mouth and close it again with a frown.

“Earth to Nemo?” I look up and find him watching me with those dark, hypnotic eyes of his.

“I need to talk to you guys,” I manage to whisper, my tone implying I’d rather gargle with glass.

“What’s going on?” He crowds me against the wall, running the pad of his calloused thumb over my cheek. I know the second his brain registers my eyebrows and lashes as he freezes solid against me.

“Nemo.” He breathes out before he takes my lips in a blistering kiss. I start to lose myself in him, but he pulls back, making me grumble in protest.

“Is that what’s got you acting all weird? It must be a shock but the shit they’re pumping into us must have stimulated your hair follicles.”

I reach up and pull off the hat and show him my head.

He barks out a laugh before rubbing his hands over my now fuzzy head.

“Cute. Makes me want to stroke you. You get hair in other places too?” he asks, wiggling his eyebrows, making me laugh.

“A little, for now at least. I might end up with a seventies afro and I don’t mean on my head,” I tell him.

“Is it really freaking you out that much, Nemo?” My lack of enthusiasm finally becomes apparent to him.

“It’s not that, Fox, it’s… fuck!” I shove him back a little and grip the edge of the sink as I glare at the reflection in the mirror.

“I have so much more to tell you guys, but I’d rather only

do it once." I stare at his reflection behind me and see him frown.

"I'll go gather the others." I watch him leave and try to summon the strength for the barrage of questions that are bound to be thrown my way. Questions I'll more than likely not have the answer to. I don't know how long I stand there contemplating my words before Fox comes back and drags me to the common area. All the guys, minus John, are gathered around on the sofas—apart from Nate who is leaning against the kitchen counter drinking coffee. I let go of Fox's hand and walk straight to Nate who picks up a cup from behind him and hands it to me. I stand next to him and lean my head against his arm, taking in the guys who are still in the process of waking up properly.

"Okay, fuckers, wake up and pay attention. Nemo has something to say." Fox throws himself on the sofa next to Jack who rubs his eyes and slides his glasses back on.

"Fucking hell. Tell me there's more coffee," AJ grumbles, standing and striding toward us. He presses a kiss to my forehead before walking over to the coffee maker and pouring himself a cup.

Fox leans over and clips a softly snoring Levi on the back of his head, making him jump.

"Fuck you, Fox. I'm awake," he yells, flipping Fox off.

"Well, aren't you just a little ball of sunshine this morning?" Fox snarks at him.

"I might have risen but I refuse to shine," Levi tells him with an imaginary flick of his hair.

I can't help but snort at his antics. He turns to me and winks before smiling hugely.

"Hey, Nemo's got a little fuzz growing. What's next, a beard?" I frown at his words, hoping like fuck that doesn't happen.

"That's not funny, asshole," I grumble, taking a sip of my coffee and placing the cup behind me on the counter.

"Where's John?" I ask, not really wanting him to hear any of this.

"He didn't make it back," Nate says from beside me. Huh, it's been a while since we lost someone.

"Finally, something positive," I mutter, making the guys laugh.

"So bloodthirsty, Nemo." Fox laughs.

"It's not that, I just refuse to be a hypocrite and sit here pretending to be sad for him. He was a dick with a capital D who would have loved nothing more than to inflict a little pain on me and that's without him knowing I'm a girl," I remind them.

They nod in agreement. John might have come with these guys from prison, but they were far from friends.

"So I have something to tell you and not all of it is good. Save your questions to the end and I'll answer them if I can, okay? You know those blackouts you have, from when you arrive at the clinic to when you wake up back here in bed?" They all nod, clearly used to it now, even if they don't like it.

"Yeah, well, I don't black out. I never have," I tell them and wait for them to absorb what I'm saying.

"Are you serious?" Jack asks with wide eyes. "You have some kind of immunity?"

"Not quite. Do you remember that first morning when we lost Dylan? Well, everything that I said happened to him was true, I just left out the part where he told me not to take the pill. I had no idea what he was talking about until I went into the treatment room and they gave me that small white tablet. I slid it into my pocket and played along. When I came out, you were all acting like mindless robots. It didn't take me long to figure out that the pill is what makes us complacent and malleable.

"Why the fuck didn't you tell us sooner?" barks Fox.

"I was the only girl, dropped into an apartment full of ex-cons, one of whose favorite hobby was rape," I snap back at him, remembering my stark terror in the early days.

"I used the time to shower, knowing you wouldn't walk in on me and discover my secret. It was the only time it was safe for me to be me. I'm not saying it was the right decision, but I didn't know you all back then and I was terrified out of my ever-loving mind. Truthfully, guys, I doubt I would make a different decision even if I could go back and change it."

"So, wait, if you're not taking the medication then how are you, well, not dead?" Jack asks bluntly, leaving me confused.

"I am being medicated, I'm just not taking the sedative."

"Sedative? Explain," Fox orders me quietly.

"The small white tablet they give you. It makes you open

to suggestion and leaves you with around a four-hour gap in your memory."

"Cam, that's what we signed up for, to be tested on. If they find out you're not taking them, they'll get pissed or worse, you'll relapse again." Jack tries to reason with me and, again, I'm confused by their reactions. The sedative isn't the reason we're here, it's the serum they give afterwards.

"Oh my fucking god!" I gasp out as I finally understand what I missed before.

"What?" AJ asks.

"You don't remember anything after taking the tablet, do you?" I wait for them to confirm. When they do, the pieces click together.

"The tablets are not what's being tested on us. That's just to make their job easier. It's the serum they inject into us that they're interested in." Everyone is quietly staring at me, gauging the truth in my words.

"You're saying they're knocking us out and pumping shit into our veins while we're unconscious?" Fox asks, his voice low and filled with anger that hopefully isn't aimed at me. I nod and watch as he lifts his arm and inspects it before looking at me in question. "There are no needle marks," he points out.

"I'm getting to that part." I fidget on the spot, trying to think of the right words to say but I can't find any. Fuck it. "I passed out after this new round of treatment… When I woke up, I had hair." I take a deep breath, watching their confused faces. They clearly think I'm losing my mind.

"I had hair that reached below my shoulders," I tell them.

"What the fuck, Nemo? You're not making any goddamn sense right now." I groan with frustration at Levi's words.

"I know, okay! It all seems so fantastical, even to me. I've actually lived it and I still can't wrap my head around it, so how the fuck am I expected to get you guys to believe me?" I scrub my hand over my face and move to sit on the coffee table. I watch as Nate and AJ walk over and find spots on the sofas with the others.

"I woke up with a full head of hair and freaked the fuck out. The doctor found me and told me a few things, but there wasn't a lot of time to get it all and she swore me to secrecy, shaving my head in the process."

"And that doesn't seem shady as fuck to you? Come on, Nemo, you can't be that naïve!" Levi snaps, making me glare at him.

"Everything about this place is shady as fuck, Levi, so why don't you keep your judgments to yourself? The doctor was recruited after she lost her husband and kid. She was told they were looking for a cure for a variety of diseases using drugs that wouldn't make it through FDA approval due to the side effects. That's why all of us terminal guests were invited to stay," I tell him, a patronizing lisp to my words.

"She found out that everything she was sold was a lie, just like what we were told."

"Oh, yeah, and what did she tell you that's so important, Cam?" he mocks, making me want to punch him.

"The serum they're giving us heals." They are all quietly staring at me, wanting more.

"Well, I hate to state the obvious, but if that were true then people wouldn't keep fucking dying," AJ points out.

"I'm not sick anymore. I can self-heal relatively quickly, if the hair growth is anything to go by. I'm willing to bet you guys can too, which explains why you don't have any needle marks." They look at me like I've lost my mind.

"Oh, come on, none of you are deteriorating. People are dying because of the side effects, not because of their illness. The doc says the illnesses themselves seem to freeze at the stage they're at. Never progressing any further, at least with the serum being administered."

"If what you're saying is true, why do you seem so pissed off? The serum saved you," Nate answers.

"We came here to die, Nate, not to get better. They aren't going to let us leave, not now that they have what they want."

"Nemo, I'm trying not to be a dick here but you're talking in fucking riddles." Fox stands and starts pacing behind the sofa.

"Some of the side effects are extreme. They...They're making super soldiers, Fox. People who are abnormally strong and fast, who can also heal. If you wanted to start a war, tell me, how much would you spend to acquire soldiers like that?"

Nobody answers but there's something about the way they're looking at me that makes the hairs on the back of my arms stand up on end.

"How sure are you about this?" Fox asks, his voice sharp as a blade.

"It's secondhand information. I haven't been to the other camp and seen them with my own eyes but—" Nate cuts me off before I can finish.

"Camp? What camp?" he barks. I can see what I'm saying is beginning to sink in and they don't seem any happier with this than I was to hear about it.

"It's where the people who have shown 'potential' have been relocated to."

"So why haven't they taken you, if you're so convinced you can heal?" Levi asks, with that damn mocking tone. I tamper down my anger at his attitude, knowing everything I'm saying sounds like something out of a b-rate sci-fi movie.

"Seems that healing isn't limited to me. It's something I'm betting at least some of you can do but that by itself is not enough. They want to force other mutations." I stomp around the counter and yank one of the drawers open, grabbing a small sharp knife and, before anyone can say anything else, I slice it across my palm.

"Motherfucker, that hurt more than I thought it would," I grit out as Nate growls, stalking toward me. He pulls a clean kitchen towel from one of the other drawers and wraps it tightly around my hand.

"You are fucking crazy, Cam." He presses against my palm as the makeshift bandage quickly turns red.

"Honestly, Nate, I'm kind of at the point where I wish I was."

"Show us then, Cam. If you really are superwoman, let's see your magically healed cut," Levi calls out, making me glare at him. I pull away from Nate and unwrap my hand despite his protest and show him my palm. The cut is still open and deep but the bleeding has slowed so I'm not leaving a trail everywhere.

"I don't know what the drugs are doing to you, Cam, but your hand is definitely still cut open. I think maybe you should lie down for a little while," Jack tells me in what I'm sure he thinks is a soothing voice, but it comes across just a touch too patronizing for my liking.

"Wow, you really are an ass," I tell him, making him frown.

"I almost wish I hadn't told you guys. Jesus, all right, fine, believe what you want, you're going to anyway but just be fucking careful. If you get marked down as a potential, you'll be gone."

"What's your plan then, Cam? If what you're saying is true, there has to be an end game. If you don't die but don't show signs as a potential, then what? You can't stay here forever," AJ states.

"That's just it, AJ. In here it's black and white, die or become a soldier that they control with orders, drugs, and blackmail. There is no in-between for someone like me. Eventually, they'll have exhausted every avenue, pushed every drug upon me in hopes of forcing a change. And if that doesn't work, they'll kill me themselves, purely because they can't afford to let me live."

"Cam, I'm not trying to be an asshole here, but you have to understand how far-fetched this all sounds," AJ points out, and it's the truth. It sounds utterly ridiculous. Hell, if the roles were reversed, I'm sure I would be thinking he had lost his mind.

"It's gone," Fox speaks quietly, the first words he has spoken while everyone around him has voiced their opinions.

"What's gone?" Nate asks. Fox nods to my hand. I lift it to look and sure enough, the skin is smooth. If it wasn't for the dried blood coating my fingers, you would never have known it was cut to begin with.

"Holy fuck!" Levi blurts out. Fox stands up and stalks toward me, lifting my hand before gently running his finger over where the incision was.

Reaching over, he lifts the knife from the counter where I tossed it. I flinch for a second, thinking he's going to cut me again, but instead he draws the knife across his own palm.

"Well, that's sanitary," Jack mumbles, making me snort.

"You can't catch cancer, Jack," I tell him, rolling my eyes.

"Not what I was thinking, Cam. Do you know how many diseases are passed on through the blood?" he asks me sternly.

"A lot, I'm sure, but we were tested for everything under the sun before coming here and I don't believe a single one of you would willingly put me in danger, so quit your bitching," I snap, my chest rising and falling rapidly.

As Jack and I argue, the others watch with various

degrees of curiosity as Fox bleeds before standing and following suit with slices across each of their palms. Jack stands with a disgruntled sigh.

"This feels a lot like some kind of fucked-up initiation," he comments, making me laugh.

"I wouldn't know. That's more Fox's area than mine. What's the saying, Fox, blood in, blood out?" His lips twitch in response but he doesn't take his eyes away from his hand.

"What's that saying, a watched hand never heals?" AJ asks, watching Fox with a cocked eyebrow.

"I think that's a watched pot never boils," Jack mutters, AJ's sarcasm having gone right over his head.

I look around at the guys who are all staring at their bloody hands, feeling conflicted. Part of me hopes none of them heal, that they can still hold on to the last pieces of their humanity, the other part desperately hopes I'm not in this alone. I know I haven't told them everything, but I just don't think they can take anymore. Plus, what am I supposed to say? *Hey, guys have you seen that move* The Fantastic Four *with the guy who's a human torch? Yeah, well, I'm the sequel.* I shake my head. In fairness, I might not be able to do anything more than get hot hands but still, that is some seriously fucked-up shit.

As the time ticks by and nobody starts to heal, I begin to worry I might be the only freak. Judging from the looks I'm getting thrown at me I'm not alone in these thoughts.

Fox looks up at me and frowns, reaching up a hand and

wiping my top lip. When he pulls back I notice his hand is smeared with blood.

"Eww, Fox." I swipe my sleeve across my face.

"It's not mine, Nemo." He tells me quietly.

I reach up and realize my nose is bleeding. That's when I notice it, humming softly in the background, just underneath the rumble of the guys talking among themselves. The whistling noise from the day before. With wide eyes, I slap my hands over my ears to muffle the sound. Fox pulls me against his chest and places his large hands over mine, making another barrier against the sound. I keep my head pressed against his chest even though I know I'm bleeding all over him. We stand there for a while before I calm down enough to realize I'm still standing and not convulsing all over the floor like last time. I pull away as Fox hushes the others enough for me to strain my ears. Nothing but silence reaches me, thank god, making me blow out a big breath in relief.

"I'm okay. It stopped, thank god." He nods, then his eyes open wide when he glances down at his hand and sees that it's completely healed. Whipping around to face the others I find them all with similar reactions. Nate and AJ's hands have healed over completely like mine and Fox's. Levi's is still showing a faint pink line and Jack's looks like it has only just started to knit back together.

"Well, fuck. Looks like we might be superheroes after all. Please tell me we're going to get some other really cool powers," Jack jokes. I look away and force out a chuckle before swallowing hard. I open my mouth to tell them about what happened with my hands at the clinic but decide against it. I need more time to get my head around it myself before I start blurting that shit out. Plus, looking at Levi's face and seeing the wonder on it, I'm worried he might end up throwing himself out the window just to see if he can fly. Nah, it will keep until tomorrow. Let's just deal with one thing at a time.

We stress and overanalyze stuff until I think I might lose the will to live. That's the thing about this place, we have too much time on our hands to pick apart every little detail. Once we've exhausted everything, the boredom sets in again. It's a vicious cycle. There are only so many movies or Xbox games to play before the guys come up with stupid shitty ideas to occupy themselves with. This is exactly the reason I find myself standing here staring at them incredulously as they announce their intentions to hold a hot dog eating contest. And that's my cue to leave. I have no idea why eating twelve hot dogs seems like such an awesome feat, but it seems boys as a whole are just plain weird. At least it will keep them busy for a little while. I leave them to it and head up to the roof for a while, snagging a blanket off the sofa on my way.

The winter brings early evenings but I don't mind it one little bit. I shake out the blanket and spread it flat on the ground before lying down on it and drawing the edges around me to keep out the chill. I close my eyes for a while and drift off, listening to the faint peals of laughter coming from below. When I do open my eyes again, it's to a darker, clear sky littered with dozens of stars. I burrow down a little farther into the blanket and watch the stars twinkle, thinking about Charlie, wondering if he's watching them back home, thinking of me.

A body stands above me, blocking my view of the stars.

"I thought I might find you up here," Levi tells me, looking down at me with a smile. "What are you doing?" he asks, before surprising me by lying down next to me.

"I'm stargazing," I tell him, focusing back on the night sky. The door creaks open again a second before AJ appears above us. He doesn't ask what we're doing, he just lies down on the other side of me.

"What's that one called?" he asks, lifting his hand and pointing to one of the constellations.

"The big digger," I answer with a smile as Levi laughs beside me.

"I think you mean the Big Dipper." AJ nudges me, making me snort.

"Nope. I meant the big digger. Charlie and I were useless at picking out the constellations and when we did finally manage to find them, we could never remember their proper names. So Charlie decided to rename them to things we would easily remember. Therefore we have the Big Digger," I point to a cluster of stars to the left of us, "the Intergalactic Cupcake and," I look around until I spot it and point, "Rex the Astro-dino." They chuckle beside me, easing my melancholic mood a little.

We lie quietly for a while, just enjoying the peace and each other's company before AJ speaks.

"Want to talk about it?" I should have known they would pick up on my mood. It's incredibly difficult to live in such close quarters with people and keep shit to yourself.

"I'm okay, just missing home, I guess. I keep wondering what Charlie is up to and if he's okay..." I trail off with a frown.

"What? Say whatever you want, Cam, we won't judge you for it," Levi urges me, before reaching down and linking his fingers through mine. I stare at him in surprise but I don't pull away. I guess them knowing I'm a girl means they are going to be more touchy-feely toward me. As someone that seems to crave human touch so much lately, they'll get no arguments from me. I cough to clear the strange lump in my throat and answer his question.

"I've lived in so many different places over the years, always moving from one home to the next, but Charlie was my anchor. I guess being here and not being able to see him or talk to him has left me feeling adrift." I feel AJ take my other hand in his and give it a squeeze.

"I have you guys, I know I do, but sometimes I can be surrounded by you all and still feel awfully alone. It's silly," I tell them quietly.

"It's not silly," Levi says softly. "Back when I first got sent down, I thought the loneliness would eat me alive. I would lie in my cell, surrounded by two hundred other inmates and feel like I was the only person on the planet. It wasn't until AJ got sent down too that I started to make connections again. Sure, Fox looked out for me, but he was distant and jaded, just like I was. AJ, however, is a goof." I laugh at that. He's not really but he has his moments.

"Hey, I resent that. I am the epitome of maturity," AJ declares, making both Levi and me laugh.

"The point is, he was a tenacious fuck who wouldn't shut up, so in the end I was forced to respond," Levi adds.

"Okay, that part is mostly true," AJ concedes. "But it was only because I knew you. Better the devil you know and all that." I look up at AJ when he says that but he's still gazing at the stars.

"You guys knew each other before you went to prison?" I question.

"We grew up in the same neighborhood," Levi answers me. "I was actually friends with his brother, Chase, so I had seen him around but he's two years younger than me, so we never really ran with the same crowd," he continues.

"Not until you both had to start wearing orange every day," I point out.

"Exactly," AJ says.

"So when your brother came to visit you, AJ, he could visit Levi too. That's kind of handy, one bird, two stones."

"Chase died six months after I got sent down, in a drive-by shooting," AJ tells me.

"Shit, I'm sorry." I squeeze his hand tighter, then remember he was also Levi's friend. I squeeze his hand tighter too.

"It's okay, really. We were never close and he was on a downward spiral since the day he left my mother's womb. Not that I have any room to talk, but I like to think I learned from my mistakes instead of repeating them over and over like he did. He survived longer than most. In our neighborhood, the only way you got out was either in a police car or a hearse."

"That makes my heart hurt for you guys. I'm sorry life dealt you both a shitty hand, but in the end, I guess I'm a little thankful too." Even though I can't see them I can imagine matching frowns upon their faces.

"If you had chosen different paths, your road wouldn't have led you here. It wouldn't have led you to me."

They don't say anything to that but they move closer, each of my hands still wrapped up in one of theirs as they lie next to me in silence. No words are needed, their grip on me conveying just enough to remind me that no matter what, I'm not alone.

I'M ODDLY NERVOUS TODAY, sitting on the bed at the clinic now that the doc and I have given up the pretense. Knowing the others are going through their treatments without the little white pill to numb them makes me nervous too, even though it's out of my hands now.

"Okay, so here's what I was able to dig up," the doc says, handing me a cup of water.

"The other facility is actually a training camp. The soldiers are being trained whether they want to or not. Refusal to train means they withhold the drugs. Knowing they will deteriorate rapidly without them, it forces their hand."

"Wait, so if I stop taking the serum my cancer will come back?" I ask, my voice cracking.

"Not for you, no. I told you that you were different, remember? Your cancer is gone, the others, well their ailments are just frozen, if you like. The drugs act as a pause button. Without them, everything will start to play out again in real time." I close my eyes in despair thinking about the guys. They are tied to this place and they don't even know it. How the fuck am I supposed to tell them this?

"I haven't been able to find out the second camp's location yet but I'll keep looking. With the small number of people we have left here, it's not going to be long before they shut us down. From what I can tell, this location was only ever meant to be temporary. So we need to get out of here before then. Do you understand, Cam? There will be no second chances." I nod, knowing she's right but how can I leave the guys behind? I might be able to get help for them, but at what cost? If I returned, and that's assuming I could find this place again, there would be no guarantee what I would find. The guys might get moved to the secondary location or worse, if deemed unworthy, they might be disposed of completely.

"Why haven't they shut us down already? There are less

than fifteen of us left. Surely keeping us here must be costing them a small fortune?"

"Oh, it is, but they weren't quite ready to give up looking for their proverbial unicorn. The one who surpasses everyone's expectations." She looks at me with pity, making my stomach flip.

"You are everything they dreamed of and more, Cam, which is why we can't ever let them know. If they get their hands on you, you will spend the rest of your life in a cage, pulled out only to be poked, prodded, dissected, and tested in ways you don't want to know about."

"Fuck! What makes me so special? So, I can heal, the others can too right?" She raises her hand to get me to quiet down.

"Cam, you are completely healthy, one hundred percent. You don't need the drugs to heal and, from this point forward, I'm willing to bet my life you'll never get sick again. The nanos will keep your body in tip-top shape, preventing illness, and if you get injured, assuming you don't suffer a fatal wound, you will heal every single time. The nanobots adapt, they become a part of your very core. In time, you'll heal quicker and quicker until it's done faster than you can blink. Unless someone cuts off your head, you won't die, Cam." I gape at her. That is a lot of information, way too much to process but—

"Nanobots?" What the fucking fuck?

"Nanobots are tiny synthetic transducers capable of taking the raw unharnessed energy generated by the human body and turning it into mechanical power with the sole purpose to repair. Virtually undetectable, nanoparticles are so small they measure in at around 0.1 micrometers. They move around the body harmlessly until they're needed.

"After you were double dosed with the serum, you reacted badly. Your heart stopped for two and a half minutes, so I made the call to inject you with the nanos, which is technically stage two testing here at Phoenix, and usually reserved only for patients in containment at the other location. We only keep a limited supply here on site, I'm just thankful I had access to them.

"The nanos are meant to stabilize the body, making repairs inside you, all while you are completely unaware of them. Given that not all human bodies are created equally, some nanos perform better than others depending on their host. At a basic level—a class one—the nanos would be able to stitch the skin back together from superficial wounds and heal almost all bumps and contusions. The other end of the scale is a class four. A class four has nanos that react in a slightly differently way. The nanos here self-replicate, leaving the host in the one hundred percent health range. We are talking superhero status, which even we thought was something out of a comic book, until now. In most cases, the serum works with the nanos in tandem until the body can be weaned off the serum altogether.

"When I tested you and found out you were cancer-free, I also noticed some anomalies in your blood exams that had been associated with the chemotherapy on your first round of testing. It wasn't until I used electron microscopy that I realized you had pre-existing nanos all over your cells." She tells me all this, looking like she expects me to say something. But I have no idea what I could possibly say.

"What I meant to say is that I detected nanos in your system that have been there for years, Cameron. Nanos that absolutely shouldn't have been there. I'm going to dig around in your file tonight to see if I can find out anything else. Either way, the level of nanos you now have will keep repairing your body with or without the serum."

"I have a thousand questions and yet I don't know what to say right now, doc." She nods in understanding. Well, at least someone understands because I'm utterly clueless and freaking the fuck out.

"So nobody else has had the nanos apart from me yet? But why? If they had the nanos all along and they are as powerful as you say, why use the serum at all?"

"The serum is the first step. The nanos wouldn't work without it. The serum works at a molecular level. It interacts with specific regions on your genetic code and causes mutations to your DNA. It also manages to hold the disease at a standstill while this process is happening. So while it won't completely cure, it will beat back the effects of various diseases, prolonging life expectancy. The problem with the serum is the side effects. The nanobots are safer because they just act at a cellular level. It maintains the health of everyone who receives them, but without the serum, there wouldn't be super soldiers. Sure, they would just be stronger, fitter, and faster but there wouldn't be any mutations and that's why the Phoenix Project won't allow the nanos to be administered until after the serum has changed people into 2.0 versions of themselves."

"But if the soldiers make it to stage two and start receiving the nanos, won't that mean they won't need the serum anymore either? They could leave and be free of the Phoenix Project once and for all." If that's true then there is still hope for my guys. I just need to find out how to get my hands on the nanos.

"That's the beauty of it, Cam, they will never know. They will just assume the serum is keeping them alive. They will never know about the nanobots. There is no chance for them to revolt if they aren't privy to all of the information."

I let that sink into my brain, my heart bleeding for all the people caught up in the Phoenix Project's web of lies and deceit. I feel a need begin to rise inside me, an ember start to glow and burn deep within at the injustice of it all. So many people's lives toyed with.

"See if you can find out the location of the second site," I tell her, my voice quiet but threaded with steely determination.

"Cam, you need to get out of here and never look back. You can't mess with these guys. I want to help, I do, but we just aren't strong enough. Besides, you have no idea what kind of people you'll be dealing with. The Phoenix Corp will send their soldiers after you. These are people who have been irrevocably changed by the serum, they're not who they used to be."

"None of us are who we used to be, doc, I understand that more than anyone, trust me." I hold her eyes, willing her to flinch. I never told her about what I could do, what I did to that cup and yet she doesn't seem to be surprised at my hinting about me having an extra ability. "You already know." It's a statement, not a question, and explains why she seems to be keeping her cool here.

"When you were still unconscious, your body temperature soared to the point that I couldn't touch you. I tried to take your temperature and you melted the thermometer. It was the double dose of serum that forced the change. So yeah, Cam, I already know and like I said you are the perfect weapon for this corporation. It's why we need to get you out of here. If your secret is discovered, it doesn't just put you at risk but everyone else left here. They will wipe out this town, having no need for it anymore, and wipe out everyone left in it."

"Shit! Fine, but first I have some questions. My hair grew back, but what about other things?" I look down at my chest and back at her.

She looks at me sadly and shakes her head.

"No, Cam, I'm sorry. Your body will heal, even stimulating dying cells and reviving hair follicles for instance, but it can't regenerate what isn't there.

"Repair, not regenerate. Got it." I nod. I suspected as much.

"I'm sorry, Cam, I wish there was more I could do."

"It's fine, doc, you've saved my life. That's more than enough."

"It will never be enough," she tells me vehemently, grabbing my hand and squeezing it tightly for a moment before letting go. "I'll find out everything I can for you, Cameron, but we need to go and it needs to be in the next couple of days. While I'm digging for information, can you scope out the area? Discreetly, of course, but we need to find the best course of action for getting out safely."

"I can do that, doc." I stand and walk to the door, tugging my beanie back in place. "Thank you. This is random, but please tell me I'm not going to end up like Rapunzel or with pubic dreadlocks?" She looks at me with confusion for a beat before bursting out laughing. The sound is so foreign coming from her I can't help but stare in wonder.

"Oh, god. No, Cam. I'm sorry, I should have said something. No, the nanos work with your own neurons. Your hair will reach whatever length your brain pictures and stop. Perhaps, on that note, you should try not to picture yourself as Rapunzel." She smiles at me, making me smile back. Her face turns solemn after a moment, the seriousness of our situation washing back over us.

"Stay safe, Cameron."

"You too, doc."

# NINE

After leaving doc's room, I go out and wait like a good robot for the rest of the guys to appear. One by one they make their way to the plastic seats, never making eye contact and assuming the hands on lap pose. We wait in silence for the bus to arrive, shuffling out in a perfectly straight line when it does, wordlessly climbing aboard and taking our seats. The driver looking back at us in his rear-view mirror ensures that we continue with our act until we are safely behind the closed doors of our apartment. As soon as Nate, the last of us, walks through and closes us inside, Jack spins around next to me and engulfs me in a hug that's just a touch too tight for comfort.

"Holy motherfucking shit! I can't believe that all this time we've been losing hours of our lives for nothing. I mean, sure, it's not the most pleasant of experiences, but being sedated is hardly necessary." I roll my eyes and chuckle. Only these guys would describe fire burning through their veins as an unpleasant experience. I hug him back, glad they all made it in one piece.

"Stop hogging her, asshat." Fox yanks me none too gently from Jack and kisses me hard. When Fox finally pulls away, I'm left gasping for breath.

"Nothing like the taste of you to remind me I'm still alive." He tucks my head under his chin and turns us slightly so we can both see all the guys.

"So what normally happens now?" Jack asks, perched on the arm of one of the sofas.

"You guys would sleep for a few hours and I would shower and just relax until you woke up." They all look at me like my answer is slightly anticlimactic, but what were they expecting exactly?

"Did you guys notice there were only ten of us on the bus home?" I don't know if they were paying attention to their surroundings or just concentrating on their reactions.

"Yeah, we noticed," Nate responds quietly. Nobody says anything for a while, making me wonder if they are as worried about losing me as I am about losing them. I want to tell them not to worry, about me at least, but I just can't. Plus, how the fuck do I say anything without it seeming like I'm rubbing salt in their wounds?

"Let's get something to eat and then chill out for a bit. I don't know about the rest of you, but I feel like shit. Plus, I'm thinking we won't be getting a lot of downtime in the future."

With a slap on my ass, Fox nudges me toward the kitchen area.

"Feed me, wench," he calls to me before throwing himself down on the sofa.

"You can suck my metaphorical dick, Fox." I flip him off and stomp to the kitchen. I ignore everyone laughing and grab a bowl, filling it with cornflakes and ice cold milk before yanking open the drawer and snagging a spoon.

"I'll suck anything you want me to," he taunts back.

"You should be so lucky. Pick another fortunate victim instead. Jack, I'm tagging you in." As soon as the words leave my mouth, I want to suck them straight back in again when I catch the look that passes over Jack's face.

"Fuck. Jack, I'm sorry." He raises his hand, making me shut my mouth.

"It's all good, Cam, don't sweat it. I'm going up for some air, be back in a minute." He disappears out the door, leaving me feeling like an utter bitch.

"Dammit." I walk around the counter and pass the bowl of cornflakes to Fox.

"What? What did I miss?" Fox appears completely oblivious, but I can see the other guys know exactly what's going on.

"I just put my giant foot in my mouth, that's all," I mumble, taking a step back but I'm halted when he wraps his free hand around my wrist.

"What's going on?" he asks, this time more insistently.

"If you haven't figured it out then it's not my place to say anything." I pull my wrist free and head out the door, taking the stairs up to the roof. I find Jack sitting at the edge of the building with his feet dangling over the edge, his mind a million miles away.

"Penny for your thoughts?" I ask him softly before sitting down beside him.

"Ha, not sure if they are even worth a penny these days."

"I'm sorry, Jack. I opened my big mouth before I even thought about the words spilling out."

"It's not your fault, Cam. We both know I overreacted. I guess he's figured it out now, huh?" I nudge him gently with my shoulder before snorting.

"That boy is so freaking smart and yet so freaking dumb at the same time. I've left him down there scratching his head in confusion. It's a good job he's so pretty to look at." Jack barks out a laugh at that, the tension dissipating.

"How long have you been in love with him?" I ask softly. I knew he had a crush on him, you'd have to be a blind man or apparently Fox, to miss all the covert looks he threw Fox's way but I didn't realize how deep those feelings ran until the stark look of longing crossed his face downstairs at my words.

"Pretty much from day one. Fox is, well, Fox, he's..." He drifts off, looking for the right words to describe the enigmatic Valentine.

"Easy to love," I answer for him. "Fox is surprisingly easy to love." I slip my fingers through Jack's and grip them tightly.

"I'm sorry, Jack. If I hadn't come along and—"

"No, Cam. If you hadn't come along nothing would have changed. He hasn't seen me as anything more than a friend for the last two years. You've done nothing wrong. Fuck, none of us have done anything wrong. The fact is, sometimes you love people who just won't love you back."

"He does love you, Jack, he loves all you guys." Despite the cocky air he radiates.

"I know. He loves me in the same way I love you and I'm good with that. I mean, would I like to see the mighty Valentine Fox on his knees sucking my dick? Sure, who wouldn't? But I'll get over it. Woah, easy there." Jack pulls me back and wraps an arm around my shaking shoulders to stop me from tumbling off the roof as I laugh so hard my stomach cramps.

"Jesus, Jack, warn a girl next time. So, are you gay or do you do a little muff diving too?" Now it's Jack's turn to laugh. The look of horror on his face is answer enough and sets me off laughing again.

"Ah, no. The only charms I succumb to are that of the one-eyed snake, so you are out of luck, lady," he manages to spit out through his laughter.

"Hey, for a time you thought I was a guy. I was a handsome fellow too, thank you very much!" I joke with fake indignation.

"You looked like a toothpick with a cue ball balanced precariously on top. So, not my type."

"You bitch!" I roar.

"Oh, please, don't even bother, it seems we both have the same taste in men. Tall."

"Tattooed," I add.

"Muscular," Jack adds wistfully.

"Unhinged." I smile at him.

"And definitely psychotic," Jack agrees.

"So, we're okay? I'll try to make sure Fox tones it down between us while you're around."

"No, Cam, don't do that. When you care about someone, you want them to be happy even if it's with someone other than you. And you do make him happy, Cam, make no mistake about it. Try to remember that the next time he pisses you off."

I nod, knowing he's right.

"Love you," I tell him, laying my head on his shoulder.

"Back at ya, Nemo. Now let's head back down before those assholes eat all the food again."

The guys are arguing over the boobs of a buxom blonde actress on the television when we walk in.

"I'm telling you, they're real," Levi protests to AJ, who is shaking his head. Fox looks over to me, taking in Jack's and my hands linked together and dips his head in silent question. *Everything okay?*

I send him a small smile and a nod before heading toward him, dragging Jack behind me.

"Come on, Nemo, help me out here, real or fake?" Levi asks as Fox pulls me down on his lap. Jack groans and sits beside us.

"Seriously, Levi? Have some fucking tact," Jack bites out.

"Huh? What?" I watch as Levi's eyes dip to my chest for a second before they widen a fraction and a pink flush steals across his cheeks.

"Shit, sorry, Nemo, I didn't think." I shrug my shoulders. Truth be told, I didn't either. For the first time in a long time, I feel comfortable in my own skin.

"I'm with AJ on this one, they're fake. She's past the perky stage by about twenty years," I say studying her.

"Fake," Jack agrees. I look over and smile, jumping when I see Nate sitting on the other side of him.

"Goddamn it, Nate!"

"What?" he asks, looking around in confusion before glancing at the TV. "Fake," he comments before refocusing on me.

I sigh and give up. Leaning back against Fox, I glare at Nate

"I'm starting to think you don't so much walk as you glide," I tell him. His lips twitch but he doesn't confirm or deny it. Hmm, I wonder if he has developed a gliding power? I dismiss that thought as soon as it arrives. The boy was probably born a ninja, popping out of his poor mama wearing black fatigues and carrying a samurai sword.

I turn back to the TV and watch as the blonde runs up the stairs in a white shirt held together with one button, hurrying to avoid both a serial killer and a nip slip.

"I never thought about getting implants. It all seemed so bloody pointless but who knows, maybe if I don't die anytime soon, I too could be the proud owner of boobs the size of my head."

Fox nips the side of my neck, making me squirm in his lap. I feel everyone else's eyes on me but I refuse to be embarrassed.

"I'm not going to claim to be a boob expert here, Cam, but I'm pretty sure with titties that big you'd topple over." Jack snorts.

"I volunteer to walk in front of you and offer them—I mean, you—all the support you might need," AJ offers.

I grind down on Fox's hardening dick and grin evilly when he groans.

"What about you, Fox? Think I should get implants?" I ask him, feeling myself starting to react to his thickness beneath me.

"I think you are goddamn perfect the way you are." He nibbles up my neck, biting down on my lobe before surprising me and covering my flat chest with his large hands.

"It's your body. That means you get to call the shots. Unless, of course, we're in the bedroom. Then this body is all mine." Fox has this unique ability to make me feel like a goddess without even trying. He has never kept his attraction of me a secret, even when he thought I was a guy. He just genuinely likes me for who I am inside. For my soul beneath the layers of scars and imperfections. To him, this is just the skin I'm in. And I'll be damned if it doesn't make me lose another piece of my heart to him. I turn in his lap and lick my lips, feeling bold and nervous at the same time. I press my lips against the shell of his ear and whisper, feeling him shudder from my words and my breath against his skin.

"I really, really want to feel you inside me, Valentine." He growls, not for a second masking his desire, before standing with me in his arms and tossing me over his shoulder. He slaps my ass to the sounds of hooting and hollering from the others before closing us within the confines of our room. Slowly, he slides me down the front of his body, the evidence of his arousal thick and hard between us.

"You want this?" he asks, crowding me against the back of the door.

I nod, my mouth suddenly dry.

"Words, Nemo. Do you want this?" he asks again, his voice caressing my skin, making me shiver.

"Yes, Fox. I want you. No, I need you." His lips are on mine before I can take my next breath, devouring me, reminding me who is the dominant one in this relationship. When he pulls away, it's my turn to groan.

"Patience, Nemo. When we are in here, you do as I tell you okay?" I nod, a rush of wetness seeping into my panties.

"Words, Nemo," he barks.

"Yes, Fox." I lick my lips. "Do... do I need a safe word?" I ask a little nervously. I want this and I am aroused beyond belief, but I am way out in the deep end of the pool and have only swum in the shallows.

"I'll never hurt you, you never have to question that. I might push your boundaries but never beyond what I think you can handle. Until you know that and feel comfortable, your safe word will be Phoenix." I laugh softly. Yeah, that will definitely feel like a bucket of iced water being thrown over us.

"Now, strip." He steps back and folds his massive arms across his chest.

I hesitate, my fear and insecurity eating at me.

"I'm waiting, Nemo." I take a deep breath and pull my hoodie up over my head and toss it on the floor by my feet. I unfasten the button on my jeans and slide them down my legs, dropping them partway down and letting gravity take over before I kick them away. That leaves three things. My black tank top hiding my blemish free skin, my hot pink panties that seem to have Fox mesmerized, and the beanie I've left on. The boys haven't commented on it, probably figuring I was a little self-conscious, but it's not that. Now that I know I have some control over the nanos just by my sending them a mental image, I've been picturing the length of my hair since leaving the clinic. A quick trip to the bathroom earlier had me fighting back happy tears at the girl who stared back at me. And right now that girl wants to get laid. I pull the beanie from my head and shake out my long luscious locks before tossing it back, relishing in the feeling of it cascading around my shoulders.

"Holy mother fucking god," Fox croaks out. He doesn't move and neither do I for a second while his eyes scorch their path across my skin. I slowly grab the hem of my top and pull it over my head, closing my eyes at Fox's sharp breath.

His hands are on me before I can open them again, his restraint finally snapping. He grabs a handful of my hair and yanks it back, hard, making me groan and shamelessly grind myself against his thigh.

"Nemo," he whispers against the column of my neck. "You are so fucking beautiful." He lets go of my hair and trails his hands down to the smooth skin of my chest, gazing at me in wonder.

"Is it weird that I miss them?" I ask him quietly. "I spent so long resenting them, then you made me look at them differently, as something to be proud of and it changed everything. I'm angry that the marks that made me shed so many tears are now gone. It's stupid, I know." He grips my chin and stares into my eyes.

"It's not fucking stupid at all. Those were yours, you earned them. But, Nemo, just because you don't have scars on your skin doesn't mean you don't still have scars in your heart." He holds his hand over my heart to emphasize his words. "'And though she be but little, she is fierce.'"

Be still my beating heart as I place it in the palm of the Shakespeare quoting gangbanger I'm falling for.

A devil's smirk takes over his face a second before he picks me up and tosses me onto his bed, making me bounce. I let out a shriek that Fox silences again with his lips.

"By the time I'm finished with you, you'll have a whole

collection of pretty little marks across this delectable body of yours." He dips his head and bites my shoulder.

"With my teeth." He rakes his fingers down my ribs, making me arch up with a gasp. "And with my fingers. Oh, the things I want to do to you, Nemo." He slides down the bed until he's eye level with my pink lace-covered pussy. Before I protest or beg, I'm not sure which, he pushes my legs open and licks me through the lacy material.

"Oh, shit," I wheeze. Fox sucks and nibbles, bites and blows against my heated core until I'm two seconds away from beating him on the head or begging him to fuck me.

"Hands on the headboard, Nemo. If you let go, I'll stop. Got it?" I nod frantically, doing his bidding. I'm pretty sure I'm at the stage where I would happily sell my soul just for some relief. He hooks his fingers into the flimsy material covering my sex and drags it down my legs before standing up with my panties in his hand. He bites the scrap of fabric, holding it between his teeth as he snags his T-shirt and pulls it off over his head in that one-handed way that only guys seem to be able to do. My body writhes of its own accord as I take in the canvas of Fox's skin. I whimper with need as he opens his fly and slides his jeans down his legs. His hard cock stands loud and proud, having escaped the confines of his boxer shorts, which are now on the floor beside his jeans. I rove my eyes over his body, watching his cock jump at my perusal of him, my brain still trying to process that this god-like man wants me.

He climbs onto the bed on his knees between my legs,

taking my panties from his mouth and looping them over his cock like some kind of tangible token of lust between us. The look in his eye as he strokes himself is almost enough to bring me to orgasm on its own. He looks every inch the conquering warrior, which I guess makes me the spoils of war.

"Fuck me, Fox," I plead. He ignores my words, using one hand to spread my legs wide once more. The other he uses to continue stroking himself as he stares at the most intimate part of me.

"I want to come all over this pretty little pussy." I feel myself drip at his words. "I want to mark you as mine."

"Do it, please, Fox."

He nudges his cock head at my entrance, my pink panties still hooked over his length, before looking into my eyes.

"Tell me you're mine. Body, heart, soul. Be mine," he orders.

"I'm yours, Fox," I cry out as he slams his full length inside me in one smooth move. I'm so wet that my slick walls welcome him inside, but his sheer size leaves me gasping for breath. Breath which Fox refuses to let me catch as he thrusts into me again and again so forcefully that the only thing stopping me from sliding across the bed is the death grip I have on the headboard.

"Fuck, I knew you'd feel like heaven," he moans, impressing me with his ability to still talk, whereas I'm reduced to a drooling fool over here.

I lift my hips, meeting him thrust for thrust, chasing the rush I know is on the horizon.

"We should do this all day for the rest of our days. I think I'll die happy with your cock inside me," I pant.

"I think the guys would appreciate the show." My pussy spasms at his words, of the thought of their eyes on me as Fox fucks me into oblivion.

"I think you like that idea, Nemo. You want the guys to see me fuck you hard and deep. What if they did more than watch? What if AJ flicked your swollen needy clit while Levi fucked your mouth with his tongue? Or what about Nate, maybe you could take us both at the same time. Would you like that, both of us filling up every inch of you? You'd never feel empty again."

"Oh, god." My head thrashes from side to side at his words as I soak his cock with my arousal.

"Come for me, Nemo, come all over my cock." His words detonate the bomb inside me, making every nerve ending flare white hot for a moment before Fox roars my name, pulling himself free of my body and shooting his cum all over my throbbing sex.

We both stay quiet for a moment; the only sounds are our rapid breathing as we try to catch our breaths. I watch Fox watching me, or more specifically, I watch him staring at his seed coating my skin and flush. He dips a finger into it and swirls it over my inner thigh, a look of satisfaction on his face that seems almost primal.

"I like seeing my cum on you, Nemo. It lets the other

predators know you're already taken." I roll my eyes and chuckle.

"You're the big bad wolf, baby. I think everyone knows that, you don't have to worry. Besides, you're the only one who sees me like that. You see past the outside of me, not many others do."

"Bullshit! Well, except for the wolf bit, that much is true. But that crap about others not wanting you? You're insane if you think that. What you see is clearly very different from what the rest of us see."

I don't try to stop the huge smile that spreads across my face. The big bad wolf is nothing but a poet at heart.

"I can see you don't believe me," he mutters, climbing from the bed and snagging my sheet from my bed. My eyes widen a fraction when he rips the sheet straight down the middle.

"What the fuck, Fox?" He doesn't answer, he just walks over to me and, before I can guess his intentions, he uses the sheet to bind my right ankle to the right-hand corner bedpost.

"What are you doing? Fox, dammit!" I wiggle but I'm no match for Fox, who restrains my other ankle to the other side of the footboard leaving me open and exposed.

"I'm going to prove to you just how goddamn sexy you are." He picks up my panties, which somehow ended up at the end of the bed and, with a quick yank, he tears the material until he's left with one long pink strip of fabric.

Taking both of my wrists in one hand, he fastens them to

the headboard before standing back and admiring his handy work.

"So fucking beautiful," he mumbles to himself and, with his dick hard yet again, I'm left with no choice but to believe him. Walking to the side of the bed he bends so that his forehead is against mine.

"I will never hurt you, not you, Cam, not ever." I swallow hard at my name on his lips. It sounds foreign coming from him.

"I need you to trust me. For the next five minutes, I need you to put your faith in me. Please, Nemo." It's the please that does me in, the whispered plea has me unable to tell him no.

"I trust you, Fox."

"Good girl." I watch as he stands back up, naked as the day he was born and, in a classic no fucks given move, he opens the door to our room and calls for the guys.

# TEN

I squeeze my eyes shut but I feel my body trembling as the adrenaline pumps its way through me. I said I would trust him but I'm not ready for this. My safe word is on the tip of my tongue when I hear a groan followed by Levi's voice.

"Holy fucking shit."

"You are such a lucky fuck." I hear AJ's voice filled with something... Is that lust? I feel a hand on my cheek and slowly open my eyes, bracing myself for their reaction.

Nate's navy blue eyes blaze down at me as he searches for something. Whatever it is he's looking for, he must find it because he places a soft kiss against my lips before pulling back.

"You good?" I have a feeling if I said no, Nate would rip me from this bed and punch Fox in the face. I mean, Fox would kill him, but I suspect Nate would do it for me anyway. I look from him to AJ and Levi who are standing at the foot of the bed staring at Fox's cum dripping from my pussy.

"Fox." I don't know what I'm asking for, but he does. He walks over to me and leans down so he can whisper in my ear even though he's still loud enough for Nate, who is on the opposite side of me, to hear him.

"Make no mistake about it, Nemo, they want you. All three of them are wishing you were painted in their cum instead of mine." I whimper at his words, feeling another rush of wetness seep from within me.

"Damn, Fox. Whatever you said to her is turning her on like fuck. She is so wet I can see her glistening from here," Levi tells him.

"She's thinking about you three coming on her. She likes the idea a lot even though the naughty girl knows she's mine." My body squirms in reaction to his words but I don't refute them.

"Fox..." AJ implores. Fox looks into my eyes at AJ's plea and never breaks my gaze as he replies.

"You're allowed to come, boys. But no touching, not yet at least. You have to earn that." He waits for me to say something. To freak out and tell them to stop but I can't. I'm literally just a bundle of sensation.

Quietly now, and for my ears only he asks, "You remember your safe word?" I nod in response.

"Words, Nemo, it's important. What is your safe word?"

"Phoenix." My voice croaks loudly in the sudden quiet of the room.

"You heard her, guys, she wants this. Let's show Nemo just what kind of effect she has on us," Fox instructs them, moving aside again so his lips are against my ear but I have a clear shot of Levi and AJ. I watch them in anticipation as they pull their erect cocks from their jeans, stoking themselves, their eyes never leaving my exposed pussy.

"Look at them, Nemo, they can't take their eyes away from you." I can't tear my eyes away as they fist their cocks and start sliding their hands up and down their lengths.

"They want to cover you in their cum. They can't help themselves, there is a need instilled within them to mark you, to please you. Tell them, though, who you belong to Nemo. Tell them."

"You, Fox, I belong to you," I gasp as cum shoots across my chest, surprising me. I turn to face Nate, who I had forgotten about while I watched the others. He stares at me with a heaving chest before tucking himself back inside his pants. He looks at me with zero apology in his eyes but a smile tips up the corner of his lips as a faint pink hue colors his cheeks.

"I had to sit out there listening to you guys going at it like bunnies. It was like listening to live porn. I'm surprised I managed to make it through the door before blowing my load."

Fox chuckles softly from beside me just as Levi groans and comes, shooting over my belly.

"Fuck!" I gasp at the sensation, looking up at AJ who is now watching my face. His movements speed up, his breathing getting faster. I lick my lips, which seems to be his undoing.

"Motherfucker." He comes over my pussy, covering Fox's offering, and I just know somehow, before the day is over Fox will feel the need to take me again to prove a point.

"Do you believe me now, Nemo?" Fox's voice breaks through everyone's heavy breathing. He moves his hand down to my clit, rubbing his and AJ's cum into my skin. He soaks his fingers before pushing them inside me. Fuck! I'm vibrating with need when he slides his fingers out and swirls them around my clit, over and over, picking up speed before pinching it hard. I scream as I come, adding my own juices to the mix.

"You are sexy, gorgeous, beautiful, and all the other things you refuse to see when you look in the mirror. The next time you need reminding of this, I might just let them fuck some sense into you," Fox tells me, stroking me lightly as I ride out the last of my high.

"Pretty sure I went straight for a moment there too," Jack announces from the doorway where he is leaning against the frame, nonchalantly eating a bowl of cereal.

"Then I realized it was probably all the dick stroking that was getting me going, so false alarm." He crunches down on his cereal as the others start to laugh around us. Nate disappears and reappears a moment later with two large towels. While Levi, AJ, and Fox free me from my bindings,

Nate uses one of the towels to wipe my stomach, before gently wiping between my legs. As soon as I'm free, I sit up and let Nate wrap the other towel around me. He covers my sweat slicked body as a naked Fox climbs on the bed behind me, pulling me back into his arms.

"You okay?" I nod and snuggle back into him. For once he lets my lack of words go without reprimand.

"Good. Okay, I hate to shit on what has so far been a pretty spectacular afternoon but we need to figure out what's going on around here. Nemo, I want you to take a shower, then I want you to pack up all your shit. Make sure you collect everything you don't want left behind. We need to be ready for anything. I can't shake the feeling we're on borrowed time somehow." He mutters the last part almost to himself.

"Nate, I want you to scope out the rest of this town. If anyone can get in and out undetected, it's you. I want a list of possible exit points. I also want to see if there are any bodies around out there unaccounted for." Nate nods at him.

"AJ and Levi, I want a cohesive list of shit we'll need if we need to make a run for it." Fox looks down at me with a wink. "Don't forget we have a woman in our crew now so make sure you add any essentials she might need."

Damn, this is not a conversation I wanted to have just yet.

"Ah, no, it's fine. I don't get periods. The damage from the chemo fucked up my uterus and the radiation therapy destroyed all my eggs. I'm infertile," I tell them, waiting for the pity. As if sensing my pain, Fox carries on talking, even as he holds me a little tighter, giving me time to collect myself. It's not news but the word infertile always sucks the air from my lungs. I never knew I wanted to be a mother until the option was taken away from me. I take a deep fortifying breath and blow it out. I won't cry, I've already cried a million tears over what could have been and it didn't change a thing.

"Jack, can you get into the files here and find out anything we might need to know?" That catches my attention. Shit, the only way Jack will be able to get his hands on a computer is if he breaks into the clinic. I'm not sure that's a good idea.

"Fox..." I warn him but Jack cuts me off.

"Sure, if you can get me in, Fox, it's no problem." I close my mouth. It's not my call to decide what they can and can't do and truthfully, any decisions we make now come with possible consequences. I look around at these guys working together like a well-oiled machine and feel a pang of sympathy for them. In another life, if they had all made different choices, they could have been a formidable team.

After a kiss from each of them everyone goes their separate ways, leaving me alone in the quiet apartment. It gives me a nice reprieve to take in everything that my brain has been desperately trying to compartmentalize.

I stand under the hot shower spray marveling at that I have to wash my hair, something I will never take for granted again. As I step out and dry off, it dawns on me that none of the guys even mentioned the head of locks when they walked into the room. I flush with color when I realize my head was the last thing they were focusing on. I pull on some clean underwear, a dark pair of baggy jeans, and a white long-sleeved button up shirt that is far more fitted than anything I've been wearing since I got here. I stare at the face in the mirror and, for the first time, I see the potential in me. My face is flushed and my usually dull eyes sparkle with mirth. I look healthy. Happy.

I'm not sure I've processed everything that just happened with the guys or what it all even means but I want to explore all there is to offer.

I step out to the room and snag my bag off the bed. Rummaging around, I find the picture of Charlie and me. Looking down at it, I smile. "I'm coming, Charlie," I whisper, placing a kiss against his cheek before tucking it back into the bag.

"Well, well, well. If it isn't the little bitch who wants to be a boy." I freeze, hearing John's voice from behind me. What the fuck is he doing here? We thought he was dead. I turn to look at him and realize I'm not far off. If he wasn't standing here speaking I would have mistaken him for a corpse.

"It's not an issue for me, though. I have no problem fucking bitches up the ass until they bleed out. That what you want, little girl? Just this once I'll let you decide where you want it, the first time at least." His smile is sinister and every bit as evil as the villains from the horror movies we all gather to watch and scream at. And now here I am stuck in my own version, all alone with the psycho in the way of the door. With us being on the top floor, the window is out and the lock on the door is laughable, even Charlie could break it down.

I square my shoulders and raise my fists like my old sensei showed me and try to calm my racing heart.

"You look like death warmed over, John. Maybe you should go lie down before you fall down. Me kicking your ass won't do anything for your ego."

He stalks forward, not bothered by my words at all, unbuckling his belt as he approaches, making bile rush up the back of my throat.

"I want my turn with the whore. You fuck all the others and think to deny me. ME!" he shouts, spittle flying from his mouth. His entitled attitude wipes out any other kind of logic, if there was ever any there to begin with.

I feign a move to the left and then run to the right, knowing that getting away is always the best option wherever possible. He catches my arm and pulls me hard, making me fly backward across the room. My body crashes against the wall before crumpling to the ground as the air rushes out of my lungs.

He's on me before my winded body can catch its next breath, straddling my waist and pinning my hands above my head.

He's strong. Too strong. It's unnatural—shit! He's like me. Something has changed in him too. He holds my hands in place with one of his and uses the other to rip open my shirt, the buttons pinging off and scattering across the floor from the force. I squirm under him, but it's like being pinned in place by a truck.

I scream as loud as I can, praying someone will hear me.

"Shut the fuck up!" He slaps me hard before squeezing my face and shoving his tongue in my mouth.

He lets go of my hands so he can reach down and unbutton my jeans. I pound my fists against his head and face but it's like he can't feel them at all. I bite down on his tongue until I can taste blood and he pulls back with a roar. He punches me in the face once, splitting my lip, twice, making my jaw shatter like kindling, three times, making something in my eye pop as my vision starts to fade in and out. I can feel him grab my wrist, bending it backward hard until it snaps. My body starts to shut down as the pain becomes too much. Everything now seems to be happening to someone else as I float somewhere above myself.

Another snap and the other wrist is broken too, stopping my ability to hit him. The tears fall, feeling icy cold against my skin, surprising me that I can feel anything at all beyond the pain. He shoves his hand down my pants, making me pray for oblivion until something tickles the back of my consciousness. Smoke. My whole body is heating up, that's why my tears feel so cold. John's so focused on his end goal he hasn't noticed. When his fingers slide beneath my underwear and he starts trying to find my entrance, I use the last of my strength to lift my arms and wrap them both around his neck and hold on tight.

"Fucking knew you wanted me. You like it rough, huh?

Open your legs, whore." He pushes my legs apart and I let him so he can settle between them. Then, before he can slide his finger inside me, I wrap my legs around him too, locking them behind his back at my ankles.

"What the fuck? Get off me," he yells when he finally realizes something isn't quite right. He struggles but I hold on like my life depends on it because, at this point, it does. If I let go of him now, I'll be dead. I clear my mind and repeat one word over and over. *Burn*. Focusing all my pain, rage, and hopelessness into my grip, I hold on. I ignore his angry bellows which quickly become terrified screams as his body catches fire in my arms. I hold on as he fights and even as his struggles start to diminish. I hold on until there's nothing to hold except ash. Only then do I let go and let the peace of death pull me under.

THE POUNDING in my head has me rolling over with a groan. Nausea forces its way up my throat, but I swallow it down, straining to open my eyes against the light of the room. I lift my head gingerly, wondering why the fuck I'm hungover with no memory of getting wasted in the first place, when everything falls back into place, making my body start to shake. I gaze around and realize I'm tucked up in my own bed. Drawing back the quilt, I see I'm in one of Fox's large T-shirts and a pair of boxers. The question is, how? When? I don't have the answers but I need to find out, so I sit up gently, surprised to find the pain is mostly limited to my head.

That reminds me, I look down and see that my arms are fine. I turn them slowly, rotating them softly, checking their dexterity and finally conclude they are healed completely, thank fuck. Having no idea what time it is or how much time I've lost, I slip out from the blankets and walk to the door with soundless steps. The door is open a crack so I can make out the voices talking quietly to each other as I approach. I'm ready to push it open when some of their words catch me off guard, making me freeze.

"HER FILE IS FAKE, Fox or, at least, the information being fed to it is. There is some mention of her healing abilities but it's labeled as class one superficial healing. Looking over other files, that puts her at the bottom of the spectrum, which we both know isn't the case. Class one is for healing capabilities that repair abrasions, contusions, and shallow cuts. Class two is for abilities that heal wounds and tissue damage without leaving scarring. My hand is still scarred from when I sliced it, I would say that makes me a class one, but not Cam. I don't know what the fuck happened while we were gone but her wrists were definitely broken and from the bruising on her face, I would say her jaw was too. You've just checked on her and seen for yourself that she is completely healed. That puts her in class three, the second highest category. Class four is classified so it will take me longer to crack. Regardless, though, there is no way she could have known any of this without these kinds of extensive injuries. We need to keep this quiet for now. At least until we find out what the fuck happened here."

"Can you use the laptop we swiped to check the camera feed?" Fox asks him, his voice sharp and simmering with rage.

"I've already checked, the feed conveniently shut off five minutes after we left. It's still off. I've made a copy of some of the older footage and looped it to repeat. As soon as the feed goes back up I'll upload the footage so it looks like real time. That will buy us a little anonymity. It will make moving about easier." Fox must nod as I don't hear his answer. The next voice I hear is Nate's.

"What's the plan now, Fox? We can't keep playing dumb here. Cam is going to get hurt and I don't mean physically. She's been through enough. We need to either come clean or cut her loose, but I'm not comfortable lying to her anymore." His deep voice has quieted to barely above a whisper.

"Fuck! You think I don't know that? Tell me how, Nate." He sounds frustrated, making my heart beat faster. Nothing fazes the unflappable Fox and that alone has every single red flag in my subconscious popping up, leaving me feeling a huge amount of fear and trepidation.

It's enough to stop me from pushing the door open and demanding they explain. I stay and take a quiet deep breath and prepare myself to absorb the blows that are bound to come from his words, from the secrets they've kept from me.

On one hand, it feels hypocritical to be pissed about them hiding shit from me. I mean how can I be mad when I'm guilty of the same damn thing? The flip side of it all, though, is making me realize how little I actually know these guys beyond their touches and smiles. These guys were convicted and incarcerated for committing serious crimes and yet I opened my arms and legs and let them in.

Into my body and into my heart. It's too soon to throw around the word love but, then, in a life or death situation, can it ever really be too soon when every day is potentially your last? I do love them, maybe not all in the same way, but if I die tomorrow, I want to at least be able to admit that to myself even if I'm not able to admit it to them just yet. So, the question remains, what is it they are hiding and is it something that is going to leave me emotionally bleeding out on the floor?

"How do I tell my girl that none of us are sick? That we all stood here with our thumbs up our asses as everyone around us died? How do I tell her we sold our souls for our freedom?" Fox continues, unaware of my presence.

A gasp escapes me at his words, making me stumble back. I hear a curse and feet moving rapidly toward me, but I back up into the room, holding my hands out to ward them off as I press myself up against the window. My heart races out of control, leaving me feeling caged in and panicky. They all pour in with varying expressions of guilt and worry.

"You were never sick? Why? Why would you lie about that?" I ask in a whisper, my words coated with pain.

"We had to. It was part of our agreement. We had to, for all intents and purposes, appear to be just like everyone else. They wanted to see how their serum would work on a healthy body. No one in their right mind was going to agree to that. No one but a group of prisoners who had nothing left to lose," Fox tells me, his eyes never leaving mine as he edges closer to me.

"But Dylan and John..." I trail off. They were sick, I could see that with my own eyes which just rubs in how stupid I've been.

"It's why none of you ever talk about your illnesses because there isn't anything to talk about. And to think I didn't bring it up because I didn't want to upset anyone. I'm such a fool." I shake my head, disappointed in myself.

"Hey, don't do that. This is on us, not you. You didn't see the truth because we didn't want you to. We're con men, Nemo," he tells me, stopping just a few feet before me. "Bad, bad men who lie and manipulate everyone around us." I can't stop my tears as I stare into his eyes, wondering if it was all a lie. If every touch, taste, and soft spoken word that helped put me back together was all a trick designed to destroy whatever was left of me.

"Fuck!" I don't even see him move but a second after a sob breaks free from my chest I find myself wrapped up in Fox's arms so tightly I can hardly breathe.

"I was the clichéd bad boy from the wrong side of the tracks who turned out exactly like everyone predicted. My whole life was a tainted mess, but now there's you. You are the only good thing in this place. I'm obsessed with you, Nemo, there is no way you haven't noticed that. It has nothing to do with me being an asshole and everything to do with you being the angel I never even knew I needed until you turned up here with your scared eyes and your scarred heart. You can be mad, you can be angry, you can yell and scream and hit me but you can't leave me, Nemo. I won't let you go. You changed everything. You made men of the boys that came here." I sob into his shoulder, feeling the other guys close in around us, stroking my hair or resting their hands on my back.

"Dylan and John were sick," I hear Nate say from behind me. I turn a little in Fox's arms so I can see him looking down at me with remorse.

"They were the reason we attracted the attention of the Phoenix Project and like Fox said, we had nothing left to lose."

"Except your life, Nate," I tell him.

He shrugs, nonchalantly, like his being in the world means so little.

"I didn't matter to anyone, I had nobody left to leave behind. But now, now there's you." The stark vulnerability on his face is my undoing. I pull free from Fox and wrap my arms around Nate, who wastes no time in picking me up and wrapping his arms around me.

Everyone is quiet for a moment, letting my mind settle and my heart calm.

"Okay, I'm sorry, Nate, I just—" Fox's voice cuts off as he snatches me from Nate and sits on my bed with me in his lap.

Instead of being upset, Nate laughs out loud. It's not something he does often but it should be the law that he makes that noise every single day because just hearing it wakes my body more than a shot of caffeine.

"Fuck you Nate," Fox, says, but there is no heat in the words as he nuzzles his nose against the back of my neck.

"I have to touch you, Nemo. When my hands are on you, I know you're safe," he whispers for my ears only, making me melt into him.

"I'm okay, Fox," I say softly, watching as the guys sit on the floor around us.

He takes a deep breath, trying to calm himself but when he speaks, I can tell he is far from calm.

"Tell me what happened." His tone is gentle but his words are sharp. Fox wants blood for what happened to me but he's too late for that.

"I... John happened." I jump when Levi stands up and walks over to the door, punching it hard enough to dent it. When he doesn't stop, I climb from Fox's lap, despite his protests, and walk slowly over to a visibly distraught Levi. I place my hand on his back, stumbling a little when he whips around wide-eyed. Taking me in, he pulls me against his chest, holding me tightly, just breathing me in much like Fox and Nate did before him. When Levi pulls back, I can see he has managed to get himself under control. He places a soft kiss to my forehead.

"Thank you, Nemo." He heads back to his spot on the floor. I study these guys, these big, bad scary motherfuckers that nobody in their right mind would mess with and see what I'm guessing nobody else does. Their fear and their loneliness.

"Does anyone else want a hug before I carry on?" I ask, making light of the situation. I laugh when AJ jumps up and hugs me, planting a kiss against my lips, which makes the territorial Fox growl.

"As if I would ever say no to you," AJ tells me before stepping back and making room for Jack.

"You scared the fuck out of me, you little shit," he admonishes me before squeezing me tight.

"I'm sorry," I say, squeezing him back.

"Don't do it again!" his words make me snort.

"No dying, check."

Now it's his turn to growl. "Not funny, Cam. I'll tell Fox that you think he has a tiny dick and let him tie you up and spank the shit out of you for that comment."

I choke in surprise. "Oh, like that, is it?" I smile sweetly at him.

"Fox, Jack said he wants to have sex with me." I shout making Jack's eyes widen. I really shouldn't poke the bear, I mean, Fox, given the mood he's in, but I can't resist.

He spins to face Fox who is prowling toward us. "She's joking, I like dick, remember?" I fight my smile as that penetrates Fox's brain and his steps slow.

"My mistake, Jack, I swear you said something about

fucking my ass." Fox swings for Jack but Jack ducks and heads in the other direction. Fox sweeps me up in his arms and stalks back to the bed, plonking me down in his lap.

"Not cool, Cameron!" Jack yells at me, making me laugh.

"Mine!" Fox grunts like a damn caveman behind me. "I decide who gets to fuck you and where and nobody is taking your ass before me." I squirm in his lap; now is not the time for my vagina to wake up.

"You are a walking contradiction, Valentine Fox." I kiss him softly, or try to, but he slides his tongue between my lips, leaving me a panting mess.

"Your fault, Nemo. You've ruined me," he admits, settling me comfortably so I can see each of the guys.

"Seems only fair, Fox, I'll be your ruin and you'll be my downfall."

"Tell us the rest, Nemo," he asks, so I do. I tell them everything John did and said to me right up until I killed him. That is just not something I'm ready to deal with yet.

"Something spooked him and he ran before I passed out." I shrug waiting for them to call me out on it but nobody does, thankfully.

The room is tense and filled with animosity.

"Guys, I'm okay, I really am." I try to reassure them.

"She is not to be left alone again." Fox speaks to the room at large.

"Fox..." The look he gives me has me shutting up. There is no arguing with him and being as I can't tell him John's dead, I let it go.

"What about at the clinic?" AJ asks.

"We won't be here much longer, but even so the walls are paper thin. With us not taking that pill anymore, Nemo only needs to scream and we will all hear her.

"I want to give you a few self-defense lessons, Nemo. You won't need them but it will make me feel better," Fox tells me.

I smile but shake my head.

"I'm good, Fox, but thank you."

"You're not, you need to know how to protect yourself."

"Fox, I have a black belt in Krav Maga and karate. It's not that I didn't have the skill, it's that I underestimated my opponent, which will never happen again."

"John isn't skilled—" I cut off Levi, knowing what he is going to say.

"John is a potential. He, for the want of a better word, has super strength. I've never seen anything like it. He threw me against the wall and I swear I felt my spine snap. Before I could recover, he was on me. Under his fists, my bones shattered like kindling. I know now to treat every threat as a person with potential."

"Fuck!" AJ curses.

"Thank god you can heal." Fox's words rush out.

"Now, that, we can both agree on."

# ELEVEN

After the heaviness of our conversation, I decide to go for a walk around the town. Of course, the boys have decided that going alone isn't an option, so after a riveting game of rock, paper, scissors, and agreeing to meet up with them at the store in a couple of hours, I find myself trying to keep up with Nate's long legged stride. It doesn't bother me though; I'd happily jog beside him if it meant getting out of the apartment for a little while and away from the flashes of what happened. This also gives the perfect opportunity for Nate to show me the best exit points, and where to meet up with them if we get separated.

The warm autumn days have given way to a crisp early winter which, thankfully, means that wearing a beanie doesn't draw any unwanted attention. Not that there is anyone around anymore to pass judgment.

"This place gives me the freaking creeps," I comment, making Nate turn to face me. When he sees me trying to keep up, he slows down.

I know it's never been full to capacity here, but thinking back to the bus loads of people that arrived with us just a few months ago makes me wonder how many of their ghosts walk these streets and how many are locked up in a secondary location waiting for their fate to be decided.

"It's just so sad when you think about it. All these people, just poof, gone, and the only time their family will know is when the check arrives at their door. A million dollar check, and yet, that price tag just seems to cheapen everything."

"As hard as it sounds, Cam, people knew what they were getting into when they signed up." We walk in silence for a while as I contemplate his words, each of us lost in our own thoughts until Nate stops me with a hand on my arm.

"Walking the perimeter is going to draw too much attention to us, so we won't go any closer than this towards the main exit. If you look left, you'll see the eight-foot fence is topped with barbed wire and that gate is never left unlocked. You can't see them from here, but there are two guards stationed on either side of the gate. From what I've seen, they change shifts every twelve hours. Beyond that, they do not leave their spots." He indicates with his head for us to go left so I turn and follow him. I notice that a lot of the places that were open for business, even if they were all mostly self-serve, are closed, not just deserted like I first thought.

Shutters are drawn on some buildings, lights are off in others. It almost makes me feel like I'm trespassing.

"The woods that run all down the right-hand side of this place and butt up to the back of our apartments are the best place to leave from. There is some fencing, but it's unguarded, and with bolt cutters we can move through it instead of over it. The forest will also provide us with some cover. The farther we can get from here undetected, the better." I nod in agreement.

"We have a little time before we have to meet the guys, want to sit down for a bit?" I ask him and point to the little grassy area and the lonely looking wooden bench in the middle of it.

"Sure." We make our way over and sit quietly beside one another. Unfortunately, for some reason, this silence doesn't feel as comfortable as normal.

"Are you mad at me?" I ask him and watch as he rears back in surprise.

"Fuck, no. Why would you think that?"

I move my hand between us as I talk. "You're just being really quiet, and I'm being ridiculous, huh?"

His lips twitch in response, which I take to mean yes. "I don't know if you've noticed, Cam, but I'm not a talkative guy."

I chuckle. "Yeah, okay, I get it, stop acting like a girl."

Nate's gaze turns from friendly to smoldering in an instant as his eyes move provocatively over my body. I'm almost betting he has x-ray vision if the look on his face is anything to go by.

"Definitely don't stop acting like a girl," he tells me, his voice taking on a husky tone. I flush as I remember Nate coming over my chest. He leans toward me and runs a fingertip over the apple of one of my cheeks.

"What are you thinking about that's got you so flustered?" he asks, intrigued.

"I... erm..."

"Are you thinking about what you did to me, Cam? Are you thinking about how you made me so fucking hot that I shot my load all over you like a teenage virgin after prom?" His words stir something in my stomach and I feel myself getting turned on.

"Are you thinking about how hard you made me? Or maybe you're imagining all the things I could do to you?"

I squeeze my thighs together and whimper, imagination providing me with pictures to go with his words. Nate with his mouth between my thighs. Nate looking down on me as he fucks me hard and deep. Nate as he takes my mouth while Fox fucks me from behind. Shit. Thinking about Fox is like a bucket of cold water being thrown over me. Not because I'm not turned on by the possibility of a Nate and Fox tag team but because Fox has skewed the lines which I normally color inside of, making it unclear to me what is and isn't okay.

Sure, he brought the guys into our room and let them participate, but that doesn't mean he would be okay with me fucking them. Would he?

"Earth to Cam? What are you thinking about so hard?"

"Cock!" I blurt out and then freeze with my mouth open in embarrassment. Nate blinks at me before dissolving into fits of laughter that I'm too embarrassed to appreciate.

"Oh my god! Can we please pretend I didn't just say that?" I can't tell if he agrees because he's still laughing. I look at my lap, positive I must be the color of a tomato while he gets his laughter under control.

"Hey." He lifts my chin with the tip of his finger and places a soft kiss against my lips. "Don't worry so much. We'll figure it out."

"I just... Fox and I are... but then you guys are... and I don't know what's expected of me." He cocks his head before nodding like my garbled gibberish makes complete sense to him.

"Valentine Fox is an enigma, Cam, but he will always be upfront with you. If you're worried, talk to him. What you need to know is Fox likes power and control. No, it's more than that, he needs it. I'm not a psychiatrist, but you don't need to be one to figure out that shit stems from his childhood." I open my mouth to ask him to explain but he places a finger over my lips, halting me.

"Not my story to tell. What I can say is he will always act like a bulldozer, pushing his way into your life and trampling over whoever he needs to stay there. AJ, Levi, and I are the only exceptions to that rule." I wonder if I look as confused as I feel.

"I can dominate, and I'll be honest, I can think of nothing

sexier right now than tying you to my bed and having my way with you, but I don't *need* that kind of control every time. Fox does. He lets us love on you, Cam, but your body, at least as far as he is concerned, is his to control. Your heart is and always will be yours to give away. Only you can decide if you want us to be occasional bedroom visitors or something more." I stare at him in shock, trying to make sense of what he's saying. He kisses me again, longer this time, slipping his tongue inside my mouth. My eyes flutter shut and I give in to the sensation. Oh yes, I want more Nathan Adler in my life. The question is, what does Fox want? Nathan pulls away, a sound of protest slipping from me that makes him smile. Damn ninjas and their stealthy kisses.

"Come on, let's go and meet the others. I'm sure Fox is having withdrawals by now." Nate smirks, holding out his hand to me. I slap him on his arm, hurting my palm far more than I hurt him, and huff.

"You make him sound like a junkie," I tell him, slipping my hand in his and letting him pull me toward the store.

"Isn't he? Tell me, Cam, can you think of anything more addictive than love, especially for a guy who has never experienced it at any level before?" My thoughts come to a crashing halt as I think about the fact that Fox has never known love. How is that possible? I vow, right then and there no matter what, I will love that boy wholeheartedly and make sure I tell him every single day.

When the supermarket comes into view, I spot the guys gathered out front waiting for us. Nate puts his fingers in his mouth and whistles stupidly loud in my ear to gain their attention. When they swing around to face us, I see Fox's whole body relax. Fuck it. I let go of Nate's hand and run, full out, toward him. When he sees I'm not going to stop, he braces himself, catching me with ease as I jump into his arms and wrap my legs around his waist. His hands grip my ass, pulling me as close as he can get me as I slip my lips over his. We make out like a couple of teenagers, ignoring everyone else around us for a few minutes until a pinch on the ass has me gasping and pulling back.

"Hey." I eye AJ and Levi who look around, trying to act naturally, while Nate laughs beside them.

"Junkie," he cough-snorts, making me scowl at him.

"Be nice or I won't make you any cookies," I tell him, fighting back my own laugh as his smile slips from his face.

"I've been good," Fox whispers in my ear. "Can I eat your cookie?" I try to hide my shiver but I know the smug bastard feels it when his cheeky smile turns smoldering. I wiggle until he puts me down. I lead the way up the steps to the double doors.

"So, cookies then?" I ask, making my way inside.

"I'll eat anything you bake," AJ assures me with a smile.

"What about brownies?" Levi asks, licking his lips.

"I can do that," I agree.

"No, do cookies," Nate grumbles.

"How about brookies?"

"Now you're just making shit up." Jack laughs.

"Am not. They're good, I swear. It's a layer of brownie

with a layer of cookie on top." I shrug and stop short when I almost run into the back of Nate. I look up and realize all the guys are staring at me like I just stripped naked and offered them all blowies.

"That's a real thing?" Jack asks in wonder.

I can't help but laugh at them all. "Come on, I'll grab the stuff and make you a batch."

We head inside, splitting up while the boys grab whatever crap they want and I head to the baking section with Fox. I grab all the stuff I need and load him up like a pack mule, making him curse about grabbing a basket. It's not until I head to the fridges that I realize they're off. That's when it clicks that the lighting above is the emergency lights.

"Did the power go out?" I ask Fox. He looks up at my words, frowning as he takes in the things I've already noticed. He whistles loudly, making the boys reappear laden down with bags of chips and salsa.

"The power's out. The lights must run off the backup generator but looking around, that's about all that does. Go take a look outside and see if it's just this store or if it's the whole town." Levi and Nate nod, tossing their stuff into AJ's and Jack's arms before heading outside.

"Don't look so worried, Cam, us big strong men will protect you from the dark." Jack winks at me.

I look at Fox and see him watching me. I move to the fridge and check the contents, confirming my suspicions before I say anything.

"Tell me what you're thinking, Nemo," Fox orders, not giving me time to second guess myself.

"All of this stuff is out-of-date. The milk is dated the same as the last lot I bought a few days ago. I don't think it's a power shortage so much as a power shutdown. The Phoenix Project is coming to an end and I'm kind of concerned that they don't seem worried about feeding us anymore."

Fox tosses the stuff he has in his hands at AJ before pulling open the refrigerator doors and checking the dates himself.

"Fuck!" He tugs his hair before facing us. "We need to move up the deadline. Jack, I want you to take Nemo back home with you. I need you on that laptop. Get everything you can off it, we are out of time. Nemo, make sure your shit is packed and don't leave Jack's side, got it?" I nod, knowing better than to argue with him.

"What about you?" I ask.

"AJ and I are going to do a little in-apartment snooping. We'll wait for Nate and Levi to return, then send them back with you. Go now, and stay safe." Fox kisses me hard before nudging me toward the door. Jack snags my hand and pulls me along with him, leading the way. I turn and look at Fox over my shoulder.

"Be careful," I yell, my voice cracking with worry. Fox flashes me his cocky trademark smirk that says he'll be anything but careful.

We don't waste any time after that, jogging toward our place, feeling exposed out in the open.

As soon as we get home, we split off to our separate rooms, Jack to hack into the Phoenix Project's mainframe and me to pack a bag. Talk about a difference between our skill sets. I don't bother to weigh up what to take and what to leave, wanting to erase any proof of my existence. It's on that note that I lift my head and glance at Fox's bed. I can see he's stripped the sheets, leaving his bed bare and the dirty sheets housing the evidence of our intimacy bundled in the corner, forgotten in the craziness that followed afterwards. I have an overwhelming need to burn them, the thought of leaving any trace of our DNA in this place sending terror through me. With everything going on, I can't say that it's unwarranted. I place my backpack on the floor and stand, quickly stripping the covers from my own bed. I snag the pillow, stopping when I hear something drop to the wooden floor. I search until I find it and frown, bending down to pick up the item I know damn fine isn't mine. A memory stick. Abandoning the sheets, I slip the memory stick in my back pocket and head over to Jack's room, knocking softly before entering.

"What's up, Cam?" Jack asks without looking up from the screen he's watching, his fingers moving so quickly over the keyboard I'm surprised I can't see smoke coming from it.

"Any chance I can borrow the laptop after you're done with it?" I ask him quietly, waiting for a barrage of questions. But Jack is too deep in the zone to ask.

"There's a spare under the bed. We grabbed two in case this one was corrupted. The internet is disabled on it though," he mumbles, his eyes darting back and forth over the material he's reading, reminding me he has an eidetic memory. My brain flashes briefly to the look of horror on John's face just before he burned to ash in my arms. I'm sure a lot of people would be jealous of Jack's gift, but I can't imagine the thought of not being able to forget anything. How can the passage of time soothe wounds if you always remember as if it happened only the day before?

"Thanks, Jack, that's perfect." I bend down and reach under his bed and feel around until I snag it and pull it out. "I'm going to sit up on the roof for a little while and wait for the guys to come back, okay?"

He mumbles his consent, his mind already back on the task at hand. I clutch the laptop to my chest and leave the room before Jack can ask me anything. Hurrying up the stairs to the roof, I sit in the corner farthest from the door, next to a huge planter filled with a variety of fragrant herbs, and lean my back against the wall. Crossing my legs, I prop the laptop on my knees, turn it on, and wait for it to boot up before sliding the memory stick in. Mixed feelings of hope and trepidation, as well as a burning need to know what's on this thing, burn within me as I click to open one of the three files on it. It's a video of a harried looking doc with her long dark hair pulled up into a messy bun and a tear stained face. I swallow and turn the volume up a little so I can hear her.

"Cam, god, I hope you find this. I have so much to tell you but no time left to do it. Do you hear me, Cam? It's time to leave, get out and get far, far away. I... I won't be coming. I'm sorry, I know that wasn't the plan but I'm being too closely watched. I... I won't lead them to you, Cam, I owe you more than that.

"There are three files on this hard drive; this one, the location and blueprints of the second facility, and your full medical history that I found hidden inside a dummy file. I destroyed everything I could find. What's in here should be the last remaining copy.

"God, Cam, I'm sorry, sorrier than you will ever know. Hear me when I say, nothing that happens from here on out or that has already happened is your fault. Please don't wear this on your shoulders.

"You mentioned your father briefly but not his name. I didn't know... fuck!" I watch her rub her fingers over her tired eyes in frustration.

"Cam, your father created the serum. From what intel I could gather, you were diagnosed with leukemia when you were two years old and despite treatment, you deteriorated rapidly. You were given less than a month to live. Your father, who had been working on targeted immunotherapy at the time, decided he had nothing left to lose by treating you himself.

"Shockingly, you stabilized, and within a month the cancer was gone. He then administered a shot of nanobots, something he absolutely did not have permission to do, but it does explain why I found existing nanos in your blood. Your story was a success, which spurred him to push for more test subjects, fifty-six in total. Only one survived. Horrified, he tried to shut his experiments down, but the government had already seen the potential. They ordered him to do another round of testing. Three hundred and twenty-two people took part. Only four survived. It was around this time that you started showing signs of other symptoms. Deadly high temperatures, so hot you would melt whatever you touched. It was at a routine checkup he was conducting with you when you apparently erupted into flames, which resulted in your father's lab burning to the ground along with his two assistants."

I hit pause on the video, my body shaking so badly I nearly drop the laptop. I try to calm myself by slowing my breathing but it wheezes in and out of me harshly, like a pack-a-day smoker. I count to ten in my head and when that doesn't work, I count to twenty. Finally, when I reach fifty, my heart's slowed enough that I don't think it's going to explode out of my chest.

I'm a killer, a murderer, a monster. I squeeze my eyes shut, my finger hovering over the play button while I stall for time, trying to build up the fortitude to hear the rest. For one brief second, I picture myself walking over the roof's edge and jumping. I could happily go to my grave without knowing that the one person who was meant to protect me, inadvertently set forth a chain reaction that would be my destruction. With shaking hands, I press play as if I'm pulling a pin from a grenade and try to prepare myself for what comes next.

"Because of your age, you had no control over your emotions, which seemed to govern your newfound powers.

Your father felt he had no choice but to give you an inhibitor. This blocked your ability, and all seemed to be okay again. The subjects that had survived the other testing were showing a variety of new traits themselves, so he went back to studying them as a way to find a cure for you and the problem he had accidentally created.

"The second issue arose when you ran into the road after a ball when you were five years old and got hit by a car. That accident stopped your heart for over a minute, broke your left arm, both legs, and your pelvis as well as left your body covered in scrapes and bruises. Three days later, you didn't have a mark on you and x-rays revealed a flawless skeleton beneath your skin. Your father fled with you and your mother and erased your medical files from the hospital that treated you. All that was left was an urban legend of a little girl who was blessed by the angels. A walking, talking, twenty-first century miracle. It wasn't enough for your father, who was right to be paranoid. He faked your death, even held a funeral for you. He then changed your name and began giving you a drug known as a mimic. It's mostly used by spies and its purpose is to make the person taking it appear to have symptoms of an illness they don't actually have. A popular version mimics a heart attack, but your version, Cam..." She pauses and lifts her hand to touch the screen as if trying to offer me a little comfort when inside I'm screaming for her to just say it.

"Your version mimicked leukemia. With your father now working in the oncology department at the hospital in your new city of residence, and you having a new identity, it was easy for you to become his patient without worrying about ethics. You would have your monthly sessions which would make you seem sick when you were actually the healthiest person in the hospital.

"After his death, and I'm sorry, Cam, but I don't believe for one second his death was an accident, your treatment fell to someone else who for whatever reason, kept your prescriptions the same. Laziness, probably, assuming you were being given a new cocktail of drugs as part of a drug trial. That I don't know. All I know is that while you moved in and out of foster care, your doctor and treatments stayed exactly the same. You were not getting any worse. In fact, it appeared for a time as if you were in remission. My guess is the nanos were finally adjusting to the mimic. The issue arose when a new doctor took over. I don't know if you remember, but he stopped prescribing the meds. Naturally, you got better. That should have been the end of it. But... you found a lump.

"There is no easy way to say this, Cam. I'm so sorry. The lump was benign, despite what you were told. It was just used as an excuse to put you on a new type of mimic, one that gave you all the symptoms of breast cancer. They said you would need a mastectomy and afterwards they told you the operation had failed and the cancer had spread. It wasn't true, Cameron; it was all a lie." Her voice is quiet, her face turning to the door as she tips her head and listens before turning back to the screen.

"Your doctor somehow knew who you were from the start, or at least he thought he did. What I found leads me to believe they hadn't quite figured it all out. Either way, he played you to get you here and, low and behold, as soon as you stopped taking your meds you started to get better again. You weren't sick when you arrived as I thought; you haven't had cancer since you were four years old. It's all in your original medical file I've attached." She looks at the door again.

"There's one more thing I need to mention. An x-ray showed a foreign body lodged in your spine at the base of your neck. As best I can tell it's some kind of kill switch, designed to knock you out cold and immobilize you. It's usually only used on supers. It's a precautionary measure in case a patient becomes hostile and loses control. I wanted to remove it but it's embedded so far I was worried about causing you additional harm. With the nanos in your system, your body will take care of this foreign object itself. I just don't know how long it will take. The kill switch works on a high-pitched frequency and isn't key specific, meaning if they hit it to calm a combative patient, it won't just drop them, it will drop everyone with a kill switch within a ten mile radius. It isn't fatal despite the awful name; it just renders the patients unconscious. Fighting it off, I'm not going to lie, will be painful. The pressure will build until there is nowhere else for it to go, causing hemorrhaging from the ears, eyes, and mouth. The best course of action for you until the nanos break the kill switch down is to block the noise. It's that simple and that hard." She shrugs helplessly.

"I have to go. I'm sorry, Cam, so goddamn sorry. I don't know if I will ever see you again. If I don't, it was an honor to meet you. I think you might just be the bravest person I've ever met and if my little girl had grown up to be half the person you are, I would have been the proudest mother in the world." The video cuts off, the screen goes black, showing the reflection of a heartbroken girl with tears running down her face.

"Cam," Jack calls me softly from the doorway. When I look up and see his wet eyes, I know he heard enough.

"They lied to me. Imbedded a kill switch inside me." I shake my head in disbelief. "They took my breasts, Jack, sliced them off with a scalpel without a care in the world for the small, scared girl they were doing it to. They left marks on my skin and scars on my already fragile heart and they didn't give one single fuck about the carnage they were leaving behind." He sits beside me and wraps his arms around me as tightly as he can, absorbing my pain as if it were his own.

"Shhh... I've got you, Cam. I've got you," Jack repeats over and over as I cry into the crook of his neck. I pull away when I can finally breathe without a painful hitch in my chest, and look up at him.

"Everything is such a mess, Jack. I don't know what to do," I whisper.

"You get up. You wipe away your tears, wash your pretty

face, and you stick your middle finger up at them all. They might think they have some kind of power over you but they've never met Valentine Fox."

I do a weird cry laugh and possibly get snot on him but he doesn't complain. He just wipes away my tears with the pads of his thumbs and offers me some of his strength.

I open my mouth to thank him when there is a loud knock at the door, making both Jack and me look up.

"It's okay, I'll go. I dead bolted the door to the apartment when I came up here to find you. I wanted to be on the safe side but I forgot the guys wouldn't be able to get in." He smiles. "I'll be right back. Take a minute, there's no rush." He stands and leaves as I take a look down at the other two files on the screen. Am I really ready to look at my medical file? Surely I know the worst of it now.

"Hey, what the fuck?" Jack's angry voice travels up the stairs and through the door he left ajar. I close the laptop and hide it behind the planter before standing up and making my way downstairs to our apartment. I walk into our living area just in time to watch a nightmare unfold in front of me. A man I vaguely recognize as the key speaker from the other day has a gun pointed at Jack.

"Where is my son?" he barks.

"Jesus, fuck. I don't even know who your son is," Jack tells him, his hands in the air.

The guy looks at me briefly before facing Jack again.

"He came for her. Now tell me, where is my son?" It takes

me a second to process but then it clicks into place. Mr. Davis, John Davis's father.

"You're John's dad?" I gasp, dismayed. Looks like the poisoned apple didn't fall far from the tree.

"Holy shit!" Jack yells out, making Mr. Davis sigh. I see the second he makes his decision. I scream Jack's name but it's too late. The explosive sound of the gun firing makes my ears ring as my eyes struggle to take in the scene of Jack's body crumpling to the floor.

# TWELVE

Mr. Davis swings the gun around and points it straight at me.

"Where is my son?" he screams.

I ignore him, running for Jack, throwing myself over his prone body even as I feel the heat of a bullet tearing through my shoulder and another through my calf. I scream in fear and anger and hopelessness.

"I killed him, you sick fuck! He tried to rape me; he beat me." I turn my head, keeping my body covering Jack's, offering myself as a shield. "But you know exactly what kind of monster your son is, don't you?" He aims the gun at my head but I watch his hand shake as tears run unchecked down his face. Where is the fucking fire when I need it? I thought the flames might be tied to my emotions but even as

I will my body to heat up, the only thing I can feel is an overwhelming sense of sorrow. I must still be drained from my fight with John. Fuck!

"He wasn't always bad, there was something wrong with his brain, an inoperable tumor, they said. He just needed help. The serum was supposed to help!" Mr. Davis yells at me, commanding me to believe him.

"It just made him stronger. It turned a very bad man into an unstoppable predator. You didn't fix him, you turned him into the ultimate weapon," I spit at him without a shred of remorse.

"You know nothing!" he screams, banging the gun against his head.

"I know enough. You brushed his problems under the carpet when you should have had the balls to get him the help he needed. You made him your dirty little secret."

"I was going to fix him, fix everything," he mumbles swinging the gun back toward me. "You killed him. You took him from me, all my hard work was for nothing!" Spittle flies from his mouth as the gun shakes in his hand.

"I might have killed him but your son was long gone before he ever met me. You let him hurt people and covered it up. He was sick, but you... you have no excuse for what you did."

"No, no, no! That's not right. I was a good father. You don't know what I did for him."

"I can guess. He should have been locked up somewhere

that kept him and everyone around him safe but you enabled him to turn into a monster. Tell me this—would the boy he was be proud of who he became? Would he have thanked you for what you did to him, for what you're doing right now?" His hand shakes rapidly now. Any second I'm going to get shot in the head but I'm too far gone to give a shit.

"No, that can't be right. He… oh god! He'd hate me. What have I done?" I don't answer him because there is nothing more to say.

"It's too late. I'm too late, too late, too late," he repeats over and over. I don't fully understand his words until he turns his gun on himself and, without any hesitation, pulls the trigger.

I don't give him a second thought as I awkwardly lift myself up on my uninjured arm and look down at the boy who took my hand that very first day we arrived here. I look at my friend who became like a brother and know he's gone. The damage is too extensive and Jack doesn't heal like I do. I know it's true, and yet I refuse to believe it. I won't accept that this is the end of his story. This beautiful, smart, and funny boy who had so much to offer the world can't be dead in my arms. Tears flow down my cheeks, blurring my vision, leaving the taste of sorrow upon my lips.

The pain that radiates through me is bitter and dark, twisted with anger and regret. The need for vengeance burns through me but disappears as fast as it arrives, leaving my body fatigued with unbridled sadness and memories tainted with the horror I've just witnessed. I dip my head, burrowing into him and squeeze him tightly to me, my heart shattering into a million pieces. A scream erupts from within me with a ferociousness that threatens to crack my ribs and strip the skin from the walls of my throat.

"No! Nooo!" I'm dimly aware of the sound of pounding feet and splintering wood before I feel hands on my body trying to pull me away from Jack.

"No! Get your fucking hands off me," I yell, my voice hoarse from screaming.

"Nemo, Nemo! Stop," Fox yells, picking me up and wrapping his arms around me, pinning me in place with my back against his chest.

"He's gone, Nemo. He's gone." I can hear the sorrow in his voice and it rips through my own pain, pulling me out of my grief-filled fog and slamming me back into the here and now. I let my body go slack and, sensing my acquiescence, Fox loosens his hold on me. I pull free and drop down to my knees once more beside Jack's prone body. I lift a shaky hand and touch his face that still feels warm against my fingers, smearing blood across his pale cheeks. The spark that usually fills his eyes is absent, leaving behind a hollow void of who my friend was. I fight back a sob even as the tears continue to course freely down my cheeks. They drip onto the ground beneath me, mixing with the crimson puddle that seeps from Jack, pooling underneath my knees.

"Come on, Cam, let's get you cleaned up." Nate reaches for me, his voice gentle like he's talking to a wounded animal.

Maybe he is. I shake him off with a shrug and continue stroking Jack's cheek.

"I'll never be clean again. I have Jack's blood on my hands. It stains my soul, Nate. No amount of washing will wipe that away. He died because of me and there isn't a damn thing any of you can say to change it."

"No, fuck that!" Nate drops to his knees behind me, wrapping one arm around my chest and one around my hips. "You are not responsible for this, Cam, and Jack would be pissed as fuck to find you blaming yourself."

"That's just it though, Nate, Jack isn't here to be pissed at me because he's fucking dead!" I shout before I collapse in Nate's arms. He curses and turns me around, tucking my head against his neck, holding me tightly, even as my tears soak through to his skin. I fist his T-shirt and cry until there is nothing left inside me to give.

"He's dead, Nate, he's dead," I whisper, saying it over and over in disbelief even though the proof is lying on the cold, unforgiving floor behind me with his heart a pulpy mess in his chest.

I feel myself being turned into someone else's arms before Nate presses a kiss against my temple.

"Get her out of here, Fox, we'll take care of Jack and the mess." I hear Nate speak but I don't have the energy to protest. Fox lifts me into his arms and carries me to the bathroom, gripping me tightly to him as he leans over to turn on the shower.

Slowly lowering me to the floor, he holds my hips,

making sure I have my balance before letting go. I watch robotically as Fox strips off his clothes, his eyes never leaving mine.

When he reaches over and snags the hem of my T-shirt, I lift my arms and let him pull my blood-soaked top over my head before he tosses it in the sink at my back. He eyes the faded pink circle on my skin where the bullet ripped itself free of my body, and shudders. A reminder of how close he came to losing me, or of how Jack could have been spared if I could have traded my healing ability with his.

I take a shuddering breath, pushing away my chaotic feelings of despair, hopelessness, and worst of all my inadequacies. Why couldn't I save him? What could I have done differently? Useless rhetorical questions that can't change the past or influence the future. There will still be no Jack here tomorrow.

With deft hands, Fox pops open the button on my jeans before sliding them down and off with my underwear, tossing those in the sink too. I close my eyes and let my head fall forward, bumping my nose hard against his collarbone, but I don't feel any pain. As numbness takes hold of my shaking body, I realize subconsciously I don't feel anything anymore.

Lifting me off my feet, Fox walks us into the shower, under the hot steamy water, cradling me against his chest as the hot spray beats down against my soiled skin.

I stand there in a daze as Fox washes my hair and then my body with surprising tenderness. When I look up at him,

I see his own grief-ravaged eyes staring back into mine, mirroring everything I'm feeling and more. Fox knew Jack longer than I did and, in my selfishness, I forgot how much this would be hurting him and the others. Jack loved Fox, in more ways than Fox was able to return, but it didn't mean that Fox didn't love him back.

"Oh, Fox, I'm sorry," I whisper, covering his cheeks with my hands, tipping his head down and pressing my lips against his. There is no reluctance on his part, in moments his tongue is in my mouth and his cock is sliding inside me as my back slams against the cold tiles. This isn't just fucking, it's a vicious union of two broken people. It's brutal and raw, making my already battered heart start to bleed all over again. I absorb his grief, letting his demons play with mine as we fuck our way into oblivion. Scratching, biting, and clawing, anything so as not to feel the harrowing sorrow that threatens to engulf us. He stills inside me, crushing my trembling body against the wall, pressing his head against my shoulder and the side of my neck. Our roles reverse as I try to pour all my love into him, offering what's left of my strength, even when my knees threaten to buckle as I feel his own hot tears against my skin.

"I love you," I tell him gently, feeling it with every ounce of my broken soul. This man, this beautiful and equally broken man, has managed to fuse his heart to mine so intricately that I don't know which of the shattered parts are his and which are mine.

"Mine." He breaths against my skin, licking up the column of my neck as he starts to harden again inside me.

I look over Fox's shoulder when the shower door opens and find a naked Levi watching me, stroking himself. Fox doesn't stop, he doesn't turn to see who entered, but I know he knows someone else is there. His movements pick up, his dick throbbing inside me before he pulls out. He spins us so his back is to the wall and my back is pressed against his chest. Bending a little, he nudges his cock at my entrance before sliding back inside my overheated core where he belongs.

I can't take my eyes away from Levi, who has stepped closer, the hand stroking his cock moving faster and faster. His eyes travel over my body, blazing a trail and making my pussy spasm around Fox's cock.

His eyes hold no disdain as he takes in my chest, but they also don't linger there for long. When he focuses on Fox pistoning in and out of me, his hand speeds up to mimic Fox's movements. I moan loudly as Fox rubs against something inside me, making my eyes close from the dual sensations of pleasure and pain. They quickly snap open though when a hot pair of lips kiss their way over my chest and down my stomach. When Levi licks me from one hip bone to the other, I arch back and force myself farther onto Fox's cock, taking him deeper, stretching my body to its limits.

"Levi," I whisper, sensations bombarding my body, threatening to break through my blessed numbness. I don't know what we're doing here, but whatever it is, Fox is comfortable with it.

Levi drops to his knees and fastens his mouth around my clit, sucking and nibbling until I'm delirious with need. The fact that Fox's cock is inches from Levi's lips pushes my arousal through the stratosphere. I scream out my release, making my already tender throat feel like I've swallowed razor blades. I'm thankful for Fox's tight grip on my hips when my legs lose their ability to hold me up any longer. Levi continues to suckle, letting me ride out the last of my orgasm before standing and stroking his cock again in sharp, rapid movements. His breathing turns erratic, his movements faltering for a second before his eyes close and a guttural groan escapes his lips just as ropes of cum shoot over my chest and stomach. Fox roars behind me, spilling his seed inside before biting my shoulder in a move that screams ownership. He gets off on the guys touching me, on them wanting me, but his mark on my skin is a not so subtle reminder of who I belong to.

Spent, I lean back against Fox as Levi washes his essence from my skin with his rough calloused hands.

"Thank you," he whispers before placing a feather light kiss against my lips, leaving me and Fox alone in the rapidly cooling water.

"Let's get you out and dried. We need to talk," Fox tells me, switching off the water and reaching for a towel to wrap me in. I let him help me out and dry me, feeling no shame at having him take the reins. It's been so long since I've had someone want to look after me that I can't help but become a sponge, absorbing each and every moment.

Once in the bedroom, he passes me to Levi, who is now shirtless in a pair of jeans. As Fox gets dressed in his standard issue black jeans and T-shirt, Levi bends to his knees, making me blush as I flash back to the shower. His mouth kicks up into a small smirk, likely knowing what I'm thinking about, but he doesn't say anything. He just helps me slide my legs into a pair of purple lace panties before helping me into a pair of jeans as I clutch his shoulders for balance, realizing belatedly that I'm still shaking like crazy.

"Thanks, man, I've got this," Fox tells him, walking over toward me with his massive black hoodie. He pulls the towel free before slipping the hoodie over my head. Instantly, I'm engulfed in the scent that's uniquely Fox and feel myself start to calm a little.

He holds my face with his large tattooed hands, tipping my head up to look into his eyes.

"We can't stay here, Nemo." I nod readily. No fucking way can I stay in this place anymore. It was bad enough being attacked by John, but after losing Jack here, I just can't. It would feel like I'm living with ghosts. Quite frankly, I'm haunted enough.

"Here at the apartment or here at the facility? I think the sooner we leave, the better. I'm sick of waiting around to see what their next move is going to be. They hold all the cards here. We need to get out, somewhere neutral, and even the score a little. Or maybe we would be better off disappearing.

I don't know anymore. At this point, I would take a zombie infested island over this circle of hell."

"Okay, Nemo, we'll figure it out. We're going to need to pick through whatever intel Jack gathered. No acting out of the ordinary, okay? We don't want to alert anyone to our movements." He sounds so clinical and cold it makes me shiver, but I get what he's doing—compartmentalizing so he can separate the pain from the plan. He has to focus because there is no way they're going to just let us walk out of here. At least not me.

"Where will we go?" I ask. He leans down and kisses my forehead before answering.

"Leave that to me and the guys. One thing's for sure, though, you'll be by my side the whole way." I look up at him, seeing my own feelings echoed back at me in his eyes.

"Promise? Promise me you won't let me go. I'm doing everything I can here to just hold on, but if they get me or do something to me that changes me mentally, please put me out of my misery. I don't want to spend the rest of my life in a cage," I tell him, my fears bleeding to the surface, mixing with guilt over the fact that I still haven't managed to find the right time to tell him about the fundamental changes my body has gone through. I just don't want him to ever look at me any differently than he is right now.

"I promise, Nemo, and if for some reason we end up separated, I will find you, even if I have to hunt you to the edges of the world."

In real life, where I would be just a normal girl who goes

to college and dates the boy from the wrong side of the tracks, this would be a blazing red flag illuminating the night like a flashing neon sign. But here, in this fucked-up crazy place, after seeing what I've seen, after becoming something... different than I was, his words bring me nothing but comfort.

"Thank you," I whisper.

"I'll do anything for you, Nemo." I let him guide me out of the room with my head turned into his chest so I can avoid looking at the bodies. It might make me a coward but the Jack I cared about was full of life. His eyes would sparkle with laughter, his smile always a touch too mischievous, and he wore every emotion he felt unashamedly for the world to see. I want to remember him as the gorgeous boy who held a piece of my heart. The body on the floor is nothing more than the shell that housed his beautiful soul.

Fox leads me down a flight of stairs and into one of the now empty apartments below ours. They're void of life, the last person having never returned over two weeks ago.

This place is an exact replica of ours. Minus the memories and the carnage that desecrates it.

Fox maneuvers me to the sofa and pushes me down onto the soft cushions. He sits on the arm and we wait in companionable silence until, one by one, fresh from the shower, the others make their way down to us. Nate sits beside me, sliding his arm around my shoulder, hauling me toward him until I face-plant against his chest. I breathe him in, the fresh, citrusy scent of his body wash, and swallow down the ball of fear over losing anyone else.

"We still need to head back to the clinic," Fox speaks, holding up his hand when AJ tries to protest.

"We need answers that are there. We aren't staying, we know it's not safe here anymore, but knowledge is power and I won't let Jack's death be in vain. I don't know what he found and what he didn't, and we don't have the time to sift through and decode the data he has right now. Our objective now is to seek out any and all information you think might be relevant and then destroy everything. Retrieve what you can and head back here where we can go over it." He turns to face Levi and AJ who are on the sofa to his left.

"I need the two of you to head back to the market first. Use the list you made to fill a pack for each of us with whatever necessities you think you might need. We don't know how far we're going to need to travel before we can arrange a pickup."

A pickup? Shit, I forgot about the world at large and the fact that there are people in it other than us. Like Charlie. A calm washes over me at the thought of seeing my baby brother again. I can't wait to wrap my arms around him and hold him tightly and breathe in the scent that never fails to make me feel like I'm home. Even if I have to leave him and go into hiding again afterwards, I want just one more hug, one kiss, to carry me on.

The guys all nod at Fox in agreement.

"Jack?" I ask quietly. AJ looks over at me sadly.

"He's been taken care of," he tells me quietly, evasively not answering my question. I open my mouth, but he shakes his head.

"You don't need to know, Cam, just let it go, okay? Focus on getting through the rest of the day."

I drop it. I suspect their reluctance to tell me has less to do with me knowing and more to do with their worry about me looking at them differently.

"We need to get some serum," Nate tells us quietly.

"Why?" I answer before anyone else. I knew I wanted it when I thought the guys would die without it but now knowing the guys don't need it is a blessing in disguise.

"Ah, shit. You think I need the serum? That I'll get sick again without it? Fuck. I have so much to tell you and like Fox pointed out, no time to do it. Can you guys trust me to tell you I don't need the serum anymore if I promise that when we are far away from this hellhole I'll explain everything to you?"

"Swear to me that you're not just saying this to get us out of here. I'll never forgive you, Nemo, if you die. I'll climb back down into hell and drag you out myself," Fox growls, making me look away from Nate to him.

"I swear, although I feel like it's important to point out at this juncture that I was planning on going up to live in a big, fluffy castle in the sky." He slips his fingers between mine and grins like he knows something I don't.

"I hate to break it to you, Nemo, but that ship sailed the first time you let me slide my cock inside you. There isn't enough light within me for them to let me inside the gates upstairs, so it looks like you'll be spending eternity somewhere more tropical than you had planned."

I snort at him. His hand grips the back of my neck, tilting my face up toward his so his next words are said against my lips.

"You can laugh now but know this, Nemo. I won't let something as simple as death keep us apart, even if I have to become a reaper and steal your soul myself." He kisses me hard and fast before pulling away.

"I don't know whether to hand you my panties or a restraining order."

"Doesn't matter which you give me, Nemo, both will still result in you getting fucked hard." I wrap my arms around his neck and breathe him in, basking in the comfort this man brings me.

"So, are we staying here tonight?" I ask, looking around.

"Yeah, I think that's best. I'll go and grab our bags and stuff and bring them down. Nate, you come with me and see what food we have that we can scrounge up a meal with. AJ and Levi can figure out the sleeping arrangements. I personally don't care where we all sleep as long as Nemo is beside me." Valentine Fox, everyone, melter of panties and hearts.

He presses a quick kiss to my lips and untangles himself from me. Nate leans over and kisses my temple, leaving me with AJ and Levi, who sit staring at me.

"What?"

“We don’t want to be away from you tonight either,” AJ says quietly. I get that. Night times are the worst, especially when your brain refuses to switch off.

“How about we move the sofas back and put the coffee table over there against the wall? Then we can spread all the mattresses on the floor, toss on a pile of pillows and quilts and hey, presto, we have a fort.” I like the idea of us all camped in here together. Safety in numbers and all that.

“Not quite but...” Levi looks up at the ceiling fan and over to the curtain poles before turning back to me with a smile.

“I’m pretty sure I can rig something up to make a canopy of sorts. Then it really will be like sleeping in a giant fort.”

“I love that idea, Levi, it’s perfect,” I tell him with a smile.

“Excellent, come and show me how much you like it by giving me one of your hugs.” Normally, I would assume Levi was being his usual flirty self, but I don’t miss the tightness around his eyes or the tension in his shoulders. I stand and walk over to them both and wedge myself between the two of them on the sofa. I wrap an arm around each of their shoulders and tug lightly until they each rest their heads against either side of my chest. We sit there in the quiet, drawing strength and comfort from each other, without judgment.

“I’m sorry about Jack. I keep thinking about what I could have done differently. I should have thrown myself in front of him because I’m a stronger healer or pushed him away or something, but I just kind of froze.”

AJ lifts up his head and cups my cheek.

"That's just not true, Cam. When we came upon you guys, you were acting as a shield for Jack even after you knew he was already gone. Hell, you took two bullets as you fought your way to get to him. Don't take the blame, leave it at the door of the madman with the gun. You do Jack's memory a disservice by blaming yourself." A tear slips free, which he wipes away with the pad of his thumb.

"He's right, Cam. Jack would kick your ass if he thought you were blaming yourself right now." I nod, not shaking off the feelings of guilt entirely but enough to know they're right.

"Thank you, both of you." I place a kiss on Levi's lips before pulling away and placing one on AJ's mouth too. When I start to pull back, AJ's hand tangles in my hair, halting my movements. He slides his tongue against the seam of my lips, asking me for entry. I part my lips and let him inside. He kisses me reverently, gripping my hair tightly as if he's worried I'll pull away, but I won't. I feel a warm hand slide under the material of Fox's hoodie to rest on the bare skin of my back and know it's Levi. I squeeze AJ's arm a little as I pull back, making him groan, but he lets me go even if it is under protest. I turn back to Levi, who wastes no time in taking over where AJ left off. His hands roam a little more freely, sliding further under my top to graze over the ridges of my spine before I pull back.

I climb into his lap sideways and rest my head against his shoulder as AJ lies down with his head in my lap. I close my eyes and run my fingers through AJ's hair as Levi holds me tight and feel myself start to drift off to sleep.

I rouse a little while later when I hear whispered voices and hands under my legs lifting me gently before laying me down onto the sofa. Someone covers me with a blanket but I'm too tired to open my eyes and thank them. The day from hell has taken its toll on me, so I drift back to sleep, hoping when I wake up everything will magically go back to the way things were before.

I sleep fitfully. I'm not burdened with the scenes of Jack's death, thankfully, but my mind plays on a loop all the memories I have of him. I replay his laugh, his smile, and even his frown, all things that eventually I won't be able to remember anymore. When I wake up sometime later, my body feels a little more rested, but my heart feels a little heavier for all it has lost.

I sit up and swing my legs around, confused for a second when I realize the sofa I was sleeping on has moved, but then I see the giant fort built in the middle of the room and remember. I can't believe they moved the sofa with me sleeping on it and I never woke up, even once. I suspect that healing takes a lot out of a person. Sleep is probably the best way to recharge.

I stand and stretch my arms above my head, feeling a satisfying click in my back as I work out the kinks.

"Where the heck is everyone?" I mutter to myself when my brain finally comes online enough for me to notice that the living area and kitchen area are empty. I'm surprised they left me alone after everything. I try to keep the feeling of panic from welling up inside me as I head toward the bedrooms, but finding they are all empty too does nothing to alleviate my fears. They wouldn't leave without me, right? Maybe they really do blame me for Jack. Oh god! I run to the door and pull it open only to collide with a familiar wall of muscle.

"Hey, what's wrong?" Nate scoops me up and I proceed to wrap my arms and legs tightly around him and bury my head against his neck.

"I... I thought you'd left me. Don't leave me, Nate, please don't go. I'm so tired of being lonely," I tell him.

"Hey, hey." He sits on the sofa with me in his lap before tipping my head back so I can see him. He frowns at my tears, wiping them away, but it's a pointless endeavor as more replace them.

"I'm not going anywhere, Cameron. If you think I drive you nuts now with my ninja moves, as you call them, then be prepared to lose your mind because I'm going to be your shadow. Every time I leave you alone, something happens. I... I can't save you if I'm not with you." He appears equal parts angry with himself and worried for me.

"I don't need you to save me, Nate. I need you to love me," I say, surprising myself.

"I've loved you from the beginning. I'll be honest, you had me questioning my sexuality there for a while," he admits, making me chuckle. I remember the confused looks he kept giving me that day in the kitchen when we were making pancakes.

"But boy or girl, I always knew you were going to change my world." I pull his face down toward mine and kiss him. It's not hard and consuming like Fox's kisses; it's soft and seductive, teasing and comforting all in one. Nate's kisses feel like home.

I hear the door open behind us. I ignore it in favor of Nate but smile against his lips when I hear Fox's grumpy voice.

"Why is everyone always kissing my girl?" he complains.

"Maybe because she's not just your girl, caveman," AJ tells him, flopping down beside us with a bundle of quilts.

"Fox always did hate sharing his toys," Levi comments from somewhere behind me, making Fox growl.

"She's not a fucking toy."

"I know that, dickhead. I'm just talking about your, mine, mine, mine attitude."

I turn my head and lay it against Nate's chest, facing Fox. He looks at me and frowns.

"You've been crying. Who do I need to kill?" He glares up at Nate.

"Nobody. I had a wobble, that's all. I woke up and you were all gone. I thought you guys had left me."

"How many times do I have to tell you that you're stuck with me for you to get it?"

"Stuck with *us*," AJ corrects, making me smile

Fox rolls his eyes but doesn't say anything.

"You should probably tell me every day. I'm gonna be one of those needy chicks that wants you to tell me nice things and call me pretty."

"I'm not good at nice, and you're not pretty." He scowls. "You're fucking beautiful." I beam at him.

"You're nice to me," I point out.

"Only you, Nemo." He reaches over and steals me from Nate who doesn't put up too much of a fight, used to Fox's antics.

"Maybe I should just handcuff you to me." His voice drifts off, making me look up at him. My smile fades when I realize he's not joking.

"Valentine Fox! You can't handcuff me to you." He looks down at me with something of a challenge in his eyes, making me gulp.

"Nope. Don't even look at me like that." He says nothing but keeps staring at me with that infuriating smirk of his.

"Handcuffs are for the bedroom only, Fox, I mean it." That makes his dark look smolder. His hands slip to the edge of my hoodie, which he starts to pull up but he stops when my stomach choses that moment to let out a loud growl. With a sigh, he pulls away.

"Food first, Nemo, come on. Nate made up a bunch of sandwiches while you were asleep." He tugs me into the kitchen area and pulls a plate filled with sandwiches from the fridge. I grab a stack of plates and walk back over to the guys, handing them each one. We sit and eat as the sun sets, keeping the conversation light and inconsequential as the day turns to night, but after a while, it starts to feel strained.

"Guys, I know you're trying to make this easier for me but I don't want Jack to become the elephant in the room. He was a good guy, the best. He deserves to be remembered."

I collect their dirty plates and toss them in the sink. Gazing out the window at the night sky brings a sense of peace. I stand there and appreciate it for a moment, remembering how small and insignificant we are in the universe and yet these boys have become my world.

# THIRTEEN

After a quick shower, I brush my teeth and slip into a T-shirt Nate had laid out for me, along with a pair of baby blue lace panties. The guys are in various stages of undress when I walk back out into the main room, all stopping to stare at me when I enter. Fox looks up, and his eyes flare when he sees the T-shirt I'm wearing. He stomps over and rips it over my head, tossing it on the floor behind him. Before I can come out of my shocked stupor to say anything, he pulls off his own shirt and drags it over my head.

I gape at him, opening and closing my mouth as he pulls my arms through and tucks me against him, pulling me toward the fort.

"That's five bags of M&M's you owe me, AJ." Levi laughs.

"She was wearing a shirt? I only saw a scrap of blue lace," AJ groans.

"You owe me five too," Nate adds, making Levi laugh even harder and AJ curse.

"I'll add it to my tab, assholes. I really did think he was getting better," AJ points out.

Fox ignores them, pulls me into the makeshift tent, and leads us to the center of the lined up mattresses. He nudges me to lie down before he does the same beside me, linking our hands together.

"Now!" Fox yells, causing me to look up, but the lights cut out, making it difficult to see him.

"Fox," I question warily.

"Just wait, Nemo." I stay quiet for a moment as I hear the other guys enter and then, all of a sudden, the sheets above us light up with dozens of tiny fairy lights.

"Oh, wow!" I exclaim as the guys find spots around me. Nate is on my left but at an angle so there is space for AJ, who has his hand wrapped around my calf. Levi lies next to him in-between my slightly parted legs because, let's be honest here, Fox is never going to make space on his side. They all lie on their backs to look up at the lights too.

"We remembered what you said about looking up at the stars with your little brother. How you always felt a little less alone gazing up at them, knowing everyone else was under the same sky as you," AJ tells me softly, his fingers trailing over my skin in a figure eight pattern.

"We can't give you the stars Cam, but we promise you'll never be lonely again," Levi adds, melting my heart.

"Guys." I sniffle, feeling choked up.

"You're our home now, Cam," Nate whispers from beside me.

"I love you. All of you. Thank you for this. I'll remember this moment always." Everyone is quiet for a while, making me wonder if they fell asleep when Fox pulls his hand from mine and starts trailing his fingers up my thigh.

"You love me most, though, right?" It's completely quiet for a beat before everyone starts cracking up. I laugh so hard I have tears in my eyes. It isn't until I've calmed down a little that I realize Fox isn't laughing. He's just watching me with a look on his face that I can't read.

"Hey, what's going on?" I roll and slide my hand over his jaw. He cups my hand with his own. The guys go quiet around me, sensing something is up, waiting to see how it's going to play out.

"Doesn't matter, let's just get some sleep." He starts to pull away but I don't let him.

"Please don't do this." He goes still. "Don't ask me to quantify how much I love them against how much I love you. Since coming here, I have found that I have the capacity to love multiple people in many different ways. Love is love, no matter what type or how brightly it glows. Don't put me in a position where I end up hurting the people I care about, because that will hurt me too. What I feel for you, for all of you, is new." I look around at everyone briefly before focusing back on Fox. "It will take time to nurture it and help it grow. Either this thing between us all will work out and our love will blossom, or we'll let jealousy poison it, and watch it wither and die. You need to be really sure this is what you want because right now if I had to, I could walk away from them and give them a chance to find happiness with some other girl. I'd do that for you, Fox, to explore the possibility of us. Losing them would break my heart, but losing you would destroy me.

"So, I'm begging you, for me, please be honest with yourself about whatever this is, about what you want, because a year from now I won't be able to walk away, not even for you, Fox." My heart pounds, waiting for him to speak, to say something, anything, but he just watches me.

"Fox, please talk to me." My eyes widen as guilt crashes over me. "Shit. I'm sorry. I'm so, so sorry. God, I'm an idiot. I read the signs all wrong, I thought I was just playing the hand you dealt. I should have asked you to be clearer. Jesus, fuck!" I put my hands over my face to hide my shame and embarrassment, but also to hide my tears. I might not feel for the guys what I feel for Fox *yet,* but the potential is there. I feel it growing every day.

"What the fuck?" Fox sounds confused, but it's Nate who answers.

"We're fucking with her head. She thought you wanted to share her with us, and now I think she has come to the conclusion that she read you wrong and has fucked everything up. She's obviously forgetting all the times we've instigated shit and crossed lines that would not be cool, that is if she was with anyone other than you. Just tell her this isn't about her, it's about your messed up insecurities, before she runs."

Fox takes both my wrists and pulls my hands away from my face, but I refuse to look up at him.

"Nemo." Fox says my name softly, a caress intended to coax me.

Nope, not happening.

"Nemo, look at me!" His voice is firmer now and I hate how my body naturally responds to his command. It makes hiding next to impossible.

"I'm fucked-up. I try to pull it in a little around you, but you cloud my brain. I don't always have the clearest sense of what's right and wrong and I don't want to mess this thing up, for you, for me, or for any of us." I blink at him, worried that if I speak he'll stop talking.

"I'm a possessive bastard, Nemo. Levi is right about me usually not wanting to share, but If something happens to me, they will keep you safe. They will make you happy." He drifts off for a second, as if he's gathering his thoughts.

"Nothing is going to happen to you!" I snap, making him smile as he smooths my hair back from my forehead.

"It's not just that. If a stranger were to put his hands on you, I would remove every offending digit that touched you, finger by finger. But when Nate touches you..." Fox pauses, looking over my shoulder at Nate, communicating with him silently the way they seem to be able to do.

Suddenly, I feel Nate's warm hand on my hip before it slides up under the edge of my T-shirt, resting on the bare skin of my stomach. Heat rolls through me from his touch and from the way Fox's eyes follow his movements.

"Or AJ—" Again his voice cuts off before a set of fingers start to trail up the inside of my leg.

"Or Levi touches you." I watch as Levi moves to kneel between my legs, shifting my T-shirt up a little to place a kiss at the apex of my thighs.

"It makes me as hard as steel. It's fucked-up and hard to explain but—" I gasp as Levi places a kiss against my lace-covered mound.

"I don't consider you theirs. I'll never share you equally. You're mine, only mine." We all freeze and look at Fox, waiting for his next words, knowing they'll change everything between us.

"The difference is, they're mine too." Everyone becomes unstuck but me. There's a flurry of movement as Levi and AJ pull my underwear down my legs but I don't take my eyes away from Fox.

"They are my brothers in every way but blood. I wouldn't trust you with anyone other than them." He leans down and licks my lip.

"I like that they covet what's mine, that they want to put their fingers and tongues inside a pussy that belongs to me. They get to touch you because I allow it. This is my body, Nemo," he tells me, yanking his T-shirt over my head before pressing his lips to my skin.

"My heart, my soul," he continues, kissing from my chest to my stomach as his hands head south. I arch up in surprise when he roughly pushes two fingers inside me.

"This is my pussy, Nemo. I say who gets entry to it, understood?" he tells me, thrusting his fingers in and out of me rapidly. I thrash my head side to side, his words warring with the feminist inside me.

"Nobody touches you without my permission, Nemo, not even you." He pulls his fingers free and sucks them clean.

"AJ, I think she deserves a little tongue fucking for being such a good girl, don't you think?" AJ's answer is to move between my legs and spread them wide. Nate holds one while Levi grips the other, holding me open and exposed, which AJ takes full advantage of.

"Oh god!" I gasp as his hot tongue slides through my folds and dips inside me.

Nate turns into me and sucks and bites his way over my shoulder and up my neck to that spot behind my ear that makes my eyes cross, before retracing his movement.

AJ stiffens his tongue and fucks me with it in short, shallow thrusts, making my juices run down his chin.

"How does she taste, AJ?" Fox asks, watching my face, taking his enjoyment from the pleasure he's allowing them to give me.

"Like fucking heaven," AJ answers, pulling away a little, making me reach for him. I grip his hair and pull him back to where I want him most, feeling him chuckle against me.

"So greedy. What about you, Levi? Do you wanna taste

my girl?" Fox offers up my body and Levi hungrily accepts, swapping places with AJ before diving in and feasting on me like a starving man.

"Mmm, delicious," Levi murmurs before returning to the task at hand.

"Fuck, fuckfuckfuck!" I babble as Levi flicks over my clit before sucking hard. "Levi," I beg. Whether I'm begging for more or less, I don't know. I don't know what I need, but I need something. Now.

"You want to come, Nemo?" Fox whispers in my ear, biting down on the lobe while Nate sucks my neck hard enough to leave a mark.

"Yes! Please, Fox. I wanna come so bad," I plead, my pride having left me when my panties did.

"You want to come all over Levi's face, huh? He wants you to, you know? I bet he's dying for another taste. I know how addicting you can be."

I pant, remembering the shower scene with the three of us.

"Please, goddamn it," I all but sob.

"Do it, Levi," Fox orders. Levi swirls his tongue over my clit, applying more and more pressure before biting down lightly. It's enough, though.

"*Now*, Nemo. Come," Fox roars, and I do, forcing my pelvis up and pushing as close to Levi as I can get. He takes the hint and grips my ass, tilting it completely off the bed as I explode in his mouth and he drinks me down.

Finally, when I can't handle any more, he lowers me back

down, flashes me his panty-melting smile and wipes the back of his hand across his mouth lasciviously.

"Even better than your cookies, Cam." He winks at me, making me blush.

"Eyes on me, Nemo." I snap my attention back to Fox. He slips his two fingers back inside me, fucking me with them once more, the walls of my pussy feeling snugger thanks to my orgasm. I can hear how wet I am as he crooks his fingers against a spot that has me cursing out loud. I just came and already I can feel another orgasm closing in. He pulls free from me and raises his cum-coated fingers to my face. He uses his fingers to paint my lips with my own essence, before sliding them into my mouth to lick clean.

"Kiss her, Nate." Fox moves back as Nate leans over and swipes his tongue over my painted lips. A rush of wetness runs from me from the carnal act. I open up and slide my tongue out to play with his. I taste myself on him and when he leans farther over me, I can feel exactly what this is doing to him.

"Well, now I think it's only fair that you should taste Nate, don't you think, Nemo?" I groan into Nate's mouth, agreeing wholeheartedly.

"Such a dirty girl, up on your hands and knees for me, Nemo," Fox tells me, helping me up and into position as Nate pulls back and kneels, freeing his large cock from the confines of his boxers.

Nate moves in front of me with his cock in his hand. He grips my chin, tipping my head up a little to look in my eyes.

He must see what he's searching for. He smiles like a kid in a candy shop for a moment before letting go and grabbing my hair with his free hand, holding me in place as he uses the tip of his cock to trace my lips much like Fox did with his fingers. This time, though, I taste pre-cum when I slip my tongue out for a taste. I swirl it around the head of his cock before opening wide and welcoming him in. I feel hands on my hips, sliding down to cup my ass, then they move down a little farther, pushing my thighs wider apart. I jolt when I feel a tongue on my pussy again. I realize when hands slide back around my ass and pull me down a little that someone is lying on their back with their head between my legs.

When Nate starts thrusting I have to focus on him or risk gagging.

"I want you to sit on my face, Nemo. Let me fuck this pretty pussy with my tongue while Nate fucks your pretty little mouth."

"Fucking hell," I hear someone say but I'm too far gone to figure out who it is. I do as Fox asks, letting Nate slip free as I get into a sitting position that's supported by Fox's hands. I'm a little concerned that I might suffocate him, but I don't have time to worry about that as Nate's cock demands entry to my mouth.

I let them take control of my body, handing the reins to them as my body becomes overrun with pleasure. They take and give; Fox teases and Nate thrusts into my mouth at a steady pace.

Finally, after what could have been minutes or hours, I

notice that Nate's movements are becoming erratic and more forceful, pushing farther and farther, making me gag.

"Fox," Nate warns him, making Fox pull his mouth from me.

"You want to swallow Nate's cum, Nemo?" I groan in response, mainly because it's hard to talk with a dick in your mouth.

"If you don't want this, pinch Nate's leg now." Nate's movements slow for a second, waiting for a response. I slide my hands around his ass and pull him farther into me, effectively giving him the green light. It's like something snaps in him then and he starts thrusting into me hard and fast. I try my best to keep up with him but it's impossible. I feel him stiffen and tighten his grip in my hair a moment before he calls my name and spills himself down my throat. He pulls away and places a tender kiss on my forehead, making me smile.

Only Nate could go from throat fucking to tender kisses in the blink of an eye. He collapses on the mattresses beside AJ and Levi, who are both naked and stroking themselves to the live porn show we are entertaining them with.

"My turn," Fox tells me, letting a little of his dark side bleed into his voice. He crawls behind me as I stay kneeling, watching AJ and Levi stroke themselves. Fox matches my position, slotting himself behind me, arranging himself until his cock finds my entrance, then he drives himself inside me. He pulls me back so I'm pretty much sitting on his lap and bands one hand tight around my chest and wraps the other one around my throat.

"Look at them, Nemo, they can't get enough of you. They want to fuck you so bad right now," he grits out into my ear, his words punctuated with the thrust of his cock. "But they can't because you're mine, Nemo, mine." He thrusts harder into me, making me cry out.

"Tell them who's fucking you, Nemo."

"You are."

"Say my name, baby, scream it as you come all over my cock. Tell them who you belong to, Nemo." He's hammering into me now, squeezing my throat a little tighter. Not enough to hurt but enough to remind me who's the boss.

"Fox," I sob, needing relief so bad, "I belong to Fox." Fox doesn't make me wait.

"Such a good fucking girl." He thrusts up hard inside me as the hand around my torso moves down to strum my clit. Fox doesn't do gentle; he does hard and all-consuming. When I scream out his name seconds later as he spills himself inside me, I'm reminded of the French saying la petite mort—*the little death*. Having sex with Valentine Fox might just kill me, but what a way to go.

"Shit, shit, shit." AJ breaks the spell I'm under, his voice thick with lust. I snap my eyes open and realize he's going to come. He leans back, I'm guessing so he can finish himself on his stomach. I reach out and grab his leg.

I turn my head and look over my shoulder at Fox and ask,

"Can I?" His dick throbs inside of me, happy that I asked permission.

"AJ, it seems Nemo is still feeling a little cock hungry. If you—"

He's cut off by AJ, who jumps to his feet comically fast while holding his dick up for me. "Thank fuck, I'm gonna blow."

I snicker as Fox rolls his eyes, but bend forward and wrap my lips around AJ. He wasn't kidding, I barely have time to suck before he erupts all over my tongue, a little of his salty goodness leaking from the corner of my mouth.

"Holy mother fucking god." AJ falls down on his ass and lays back with his eyes closed.

"What about me, Nemo? Fox, can I?"

Fox nods.

I don't answer with words, I just open my mouth and let Levi in. It's fascinating to me how different they all taste. I mean, it's not like any of them taste of strawberries, but the subtle differences are enough for me to be able to pick them out if I was blindfolded. Hm... maybe that's a possible game for the future.

"Here it comes, Cam. Oh god, that's it." Levi pushes forward, forcing his cum down my throat before pulling away.

Levi plonks himself down next to AJ and Nate, who look happy and content sprawled on the floor. I wait for the awkwardness and the embarrassment to come rushing in but all I feel is a kind of empowerment. I mean, Fox calls all the shots, which, to be fair, we all seem to get off on, but it's my body, my pussy, and my mouth that put those dreamy looks on the guys' faces.

"Can I grab a T-shirt?" I ask, stepping out of the fort and moving to the pile of clothes on the sofa. I'm feeling a little self-conscious after the fact, but Fox follows me out and stops me.

"Not done with you yet, Nemo. Rest for now but I'm going to be sliding back inside your slick, wet heat before the night is over and clothing will just get in my way.

"Well... okay then." I shake my head and grin. "If I can't walk tomorrow, you'll have to carry me everywhere."

"That's fine by me, Nemo." Why am I not surprised? The guys make space for me when we reenter the fort, letting me lie back down in my original spot as they resume theirs.

"You okay?" Nate asks, linking his fingers through mine. "You need anything? Hungry?" It kind of melts my heart how nervous he sounds.

"I'm wonderful, thank you. Plus, I've kinda consumed enough protein to keep me full for a while."

The guys laugh around me, making me blush, but I did what I set out to do, which was to make sure everyone was at ease.

We chat into the early hours about our random likes and dislikes. Getting to know the basics about each other until we all fall asleep.

I wake up to darkness a little while later with a mouth between my legs and hands all over my body. This time, nobody speaks, Fox's approval clearly already having been given.

Not knowing who is touching me, tasting me, or inside me only heightens my pleasure as all of my other senses sort to overcompensate for my lack of sight.

After a night of limitless pleasure spent in the fort, I worry I'll never want to sleep alone again.

# FOURTEEN

"Hey," I look over my shoulder, pulling my gaze from the brisk morning outside the window, and smile at a sleep-rumpled Fox.

"Hey yourself." He slips his hands around my waist and rests his head on my shoulder, taking a moment to enjoy the silence with me.

"How you feeling this morning?"

"Pretty good, actually. About last night—" He doesn't let me finish, anticipating what I'm about to say.

"I always want you to call me on my bullshit, Nemo. Never censor yourself around me. I want this with you, with them, I just needed you to know that."

I pull free from Fox with a wince.

"You couldn't have a small dick, could you?" I grumble,

making him laugh as he scoops me up and carries me into the bathroom. Sex without a condom is freaking messy.

"You love my big dick." I don't argue because we both know he's right. I stand in the shower boneless as he washes me from head to toe.

"You are so good at this."

"I like taking care of you, Nemo." He helps me out, dries me off, and helps me dress before trudging me back out to the others.

"You know our little group dynamic is always gonna be tipped in my favor. I can't change who I am, Nemo," he tells me, looking down at me.

"I got that, Fox. I mean, it's not like dating four guys is in any way conventional. I just don't want to unexpectedly step on a mine that I didn't know was there. I meant what I said last night, given time, I could quite easily love them as much as I love you. You need to prepare for that."

"I am. I want you to love them and have them love you back, but Nemo," he slides his hand over my cheek, "it will be my ring on your finger when you're ready to take that step."

"I will never be able to have kids, Fox," I remind him quietly. He shrugs.

"As long as I have you, Nemo, I will always have everything I need." I lay my head against his chest and breath him in.

"You're stuck with me now, Fox. I just want to make sure everyone is on the same page. Be upfront and honest with the guys and then, if they still want to tie themselves to us, they can do it with their eyes and hearts wide open.

"We've already talked about it, Cam." I still in Fox's arms and turn to face AJ, Levi, and Nate who have emerged from the fort.

"Come sit." AJ waves us over. I grab Fox's hand and pull him behind me toward the sofa. When he sits, he pulls me onto his lap and rests his head on my shoulder, waiting for the guys to speak.

"None of us have family anymore," AJ explains, leaning down with his forearms resting against his thighs. "Some of us, like Fox, never had any to begin with and some of us, like me, lost them when we got sent down that last time. Prison is brutal, even for guys that can handle themselves. Unless, of course, your name is Valentine Fox and you just don't give a fuck." I smile widely at him. That sounds like the psycho I know and love.

"Nobody messed with him and survived so when he took each of us under his wing and offered us his protection, it was a really big deal."

"Jesus, do you remember when Jack first got there and that Johnson guy started on him? Fox cut off his—" Levi freezes for a second, remembering who he's talking to. I stare at him with wide eyes as he hurries to carry on, shaking my head in amusement. Nothing about Fox surprises me anymore.

"Anyway," AJ continues, "we became family, much to Fox's annoyance." Fox snorts out a laugh behind me.

"Oh, he tried to shake us, but we can be persistent little shits when we want to be. My point is, even without you, Cam, we would have followed Fox anywhere. He means something to us." I nod. I understand what he's saying, and I love that they have that with each other.

"Then there's you, smart, strong and fearless. We couldn't have picked a better person for Fox if we had molded you ourselves. The fact that he's willing to share you, the one person he truly loves wholeheartedly, with our group of misfits and fuck-ups, blows our minds. It makes us feel worthy like he has placed a precious gem in our hands to guard. It's both an honor and a privilege."

"And the sex is spectacular." Levi winks at me, making me giggle.

"We all love you, Cam, maybe not the way Fox does, but it's still there growing and evolving. None of us knows what the future holds. It could all end tomorrow, you know that better than anyone, but we would all like a shot to see where this thing goes," Nate adds, looking at me. I can see in his eyes that he really does want this. Butterflies swarm in my stomach. If they can be brave enough to put their hearts on the line, so can I. I look from Nate to AJ and Levi, their eyes filled with the stars they hung for me, and feel a sense of rightness click into place.

"And everything Fox said about marriage?" Would they really be okay with this?

"You'll be Fox's wife, Cam, but you'll still be our girl," AJ confirms.

"I have a billion questions, but I think I just need to let everything soak in for a little while first," I tell them, knowing I have shit they need to know before any of them can truly commit to me. I open my mouth to tell them what's been going on with me when Fox speaks.

"You don't need to process it all today, Nemo. Besides, we need to get moving. We have shit to do. I need to go over the files Jack was working through. Levi and AJ, I want you to finish collecting what we'll need. Nate? You good?"

"Yeah, there are a couple of places I want to get a second look at."

Fox nods. "Okay, everyone has their jobs. Nemo, think you could rustle up some food? You drained me dry, woman." I shove him lightly but nod in agreement.

"Yeah, don't worry guys, I'll figure something out. How long until we leave?" I'm so ready to get out of this place and the awful sense of foreboding that's been wearing on me.

"If we can get everything done that we need to today, then I say we leave tomorrow after our daily clinic appointments."

"Why not sneak out before then? Why put yourselves through that at all?" I don't understand.

"I want to wipe out our existence from the server. I can't do it remotely like Jack could have. I'll need to be onsite for that." I sigh but don't argue. He's right. It's a risk worth taking if it gets rid of any samples pertaining to any of us.

"Okay, boss man, I can't argue with you when you use common sense and logic." He barks out a laugh.

"I won't make a habit of it," he tells me, lowering his voice a little. "Boss man? Hmm... I like it." I roll my eyes and stand up, squealing when he slaps my ass.

"You shithead." I ignore the laughter and head off to get ready. I dress in the usual dark jeans but opt for one of Fox's black T-shirts, knotting it at my stomach and showing of just a sliver of skin.

Back in the living area, everyone else is heading off to do their own thing so I head into the kitchen and see what I can make us. Nothing exciting by the looks of it. I end up making a big batch of oatmeal with water since we have no milk and sweeten it up with some cinnamon and brown sugar. The boys don't complain, food is food at the end of the day. It's only going to get worse before it gets better, especially if we have to hike our way out of here on foot and stay hidden for a while.

"I'm going to go up and work in Jack's old room," Fox tells me quietly. "He has everything set up in there and notes spread out around the room, which I'm sure are in some kind of order." Yeah, that sounds like Jack.

"AJ and Levi will stay down here with you though. I don't want you to come with me, Nemo, there is nothing in that apartment you need to see." He's not going to get any kind of argument from me. But that does give me an idea.

"Can I go up to the roof by myself for a little while if we leave all the doors open? Nobody is going to get past you guys and I really need to get some air." He looks at me for a moment and I see that he wants to say no. I can't say I blame him. Eventually, he concedes and agrees, shocking me.

"I can be reasonable, Nemo."

"Thank you."

"You ready to go now? You can walk up with me." I stand and put our dirty dishes in the sink before grabbing Fox's hoodie off the back of the sofa.

"I'm ready." He snags my hand, pulling me out into the corridor.

"Guys, wedge the door open and keep an ear out," Fox yells out. He walks me up to our old apartment door and stops me. Sliding his hands into my hair, he kisses me. It's soft at first but this is Fox we're talking about and it quickly becomes heated. One minute his hands are in my hair, the next my legs are around his waist and his hands are on my ass. He pulls away, breathing as heavily as I am. I love that I affect him as much as he affects me.

"As much as I would love to slip inside your hot little body, Nemo, I have shit to do."

"Urgh, fine. Go do your thing now, then do me later," I tell him with a wink, sliding my legs back to the ground.

"Careful, Nemo, or I'll bend you over right here in the corridor." And he would, I know it.

"Go. Find me when you've finished."

"Yes, ma'am. Yell if you need me, Nemo" He kisses me one last time before letting me go.

I nod and head up to the roof, feeling Fox's eyes on my

ass as I walk away. Heading over to the planter, I sit down next to it, and reach around for the hidden laptop.

Thankfully it hasn't rained and when I turn it on, I'm happy to see that the battery is almost full. I click on the file with the blueprints first, needing to prepare myself to look at my medical one.

The facility is huge, almost twice the size of this one. The medical wing takes up the largest portion. It doesn't say if it's a town like this place or something else, but I guess it doesn't really matter.

The schematics are hard to read and the location is a set of coordinates that mean nothing to me but if anyone can figure it out, it will be my guys downstairs. I study it the best I can, filing away the things I think might be important, like the area marked containment cells. Fuck, it's like something out of a sci-fi movie. Shit like this doesn't happen in real life or, at least, it shouldn't.

The fact that it all started because of my father, even if his intentions were honorable, knocks him firmly off the pedestal I had once placed him upon. Nobody should have the right to play god with the lives of others.

I close the file and sit for a moment wondering what the best course of action will be. Running and hiding might keep the monsters at bay, but what about everyone else? If we don't help them, who will?

I run my finger over the mouse pad, bringing the screen back to life, and hover over my medical file for a second before clicking on it. I start to read it, taking in everything it says, which just confirms what the doc had already told me. As I scroll down, I notice the amendment at the bottom of the file in red ink, a copy of a death certificate, which I assume doc added herself. I click on it to see what my name was before I became Cameron James Miller. If it's freaking Apple I will—

The laptop slips off my leg as my brain tries to make sense of the words on the screen. *Phoenix Callahan*. My name is Phoenix and these sick motherfuckers named this whole thing after me.

But if they knew who I was when I got here, then why all the subterfuge? Sure, most people seem oblivious to who I really am. Hell, I was just another sick person in the crowd of many others, but someone behind the curtain knew, or I would have had a kill switch implanted long before I arrived here. Maybe they've been waiting to see if I showed any cool new gifts. If they knew I was the little girl who survived a car crash and burned a building to the ground, then they already knew I was a super so—

"Fuck." They weren't testing me for mutations, they already know I have the capacity for that. They are using me to test the inhibitors. I've been taking the inhibitors longer than anyone else, so I'm guessing they wanted to see if any long-term damage had been done and if without them my gift would return. Well, they can just keep on guessing. If I never use my gifts, they'll assume the inhibitors erased them and the target on my back will become a little smaller.

Plus, I really don't want to accidentally hurt anyone. I

know I was a little girl last time my abilities spiraled out of control, but people still died because of me and my inability to control them.

I pull the memory stick free and slide it into my pocket before slipping the laptop behind the planter once more. I don't make a move to go back downstairs, needing some time to gather my thoughts. How are the guys going to react when I tell them? Will they blame me? I rub my hand over my face, sick of second guessing everything. I climb to my feet and walk over to the edge of the building and look down at the deserted town below, feeling an overwhelming sense of hopelessness. I sit down, swing my legs over, and lean back on my hands to stare up at the sky.

I think of Charlie and wonder how he's doing. They'll know I'm still alive because they haven't received my death check, as I like to call it, yet. They're caught in limbo, just waiting around for the money that will change their lives, waiting for their daughter and sister to die.

There is a selfish part of me, a tiny little piece, that feels resentful that I know my mother will be okay. She'll cry, be sad for a little while but then she'll move on with her new husband and son and I'll just be a distant memory. She fell apart when my father died, barely having the strength to make it through the day as her life spiraled out of control. Her daughter's death though, she'll recover from. Surviving the loss of me will be easier for her to cope with than losing the love of her life. How tragic is it that her little girl could never quite measure up. I try to shove it aside, compartmentalize my conflicting feelings, knowing that Charlie at least won't have to live through the aftermath of her grief. He'll never feel unwanted or unloved for a single second because although she might mourn me, she won't let her sorrow drown her this time.

A large body sits behind me, legs outside of mine, feet bumping into my own as they hang over the edge. He doesn't speak but he doesn't need to; I can feel Fox from a mile away. I lean back into him, drawing comfort from the one person who would spiral out of control if something happened to me.

"I have so many things to say to you." I turn to look at his handsome face over my shoulder.

"I know you've spent a lifetime being written off as nothing more than a bad boy who was too rough around the edges. But the boy they said would never amount to anything grew up to be the man who is perfect for me. I'll take all your rough and broken edges, Valentine Fox. I'll take you just the way you are. I need you to know that no matter what happens, thanks to you and the guys, I've been happier here than I have ever been in my entire life.

"If these were my final moments on earth, I would use my last breath to tell you just how much I love you."

He kisses me, pouring what he feels for me into every touch and taste. I lose myself in his arms, ready to leave this place behind and yet at the same time hoping to stay right here in this moment forever.

He pulls away and lifts me, turning me around so I'm

straddling him. Behind me is a sheer drop to the unforgiving concrete and yet I've never felt safer. Fox would never let me fall.

"Did you get what you needed from Jack's computer?" He wraps his arms even tighter around me but even so I feel him emotionally pull away.

"Fox?" I question, sliding my palm over his cheek.

"When we are free of this place, we need to talk. I have things I need to tell you, things that will change how you look at me." I nod, knowing I have things I have to say too, things I have been keeping from him and the others. I guess we're not so different after all.

"I have things I have to talk to you about too, but not here, not now. I want to spend my last night here in your arms, in the little fort we built. All the other bullshit will still be there to wade through in a few days." He leans his forehead against mine, his hand sneaking up under my top to rest on the bare skin of my back just above my ass.

"I wish I could promise you a lifetime of happiness, but I'm not that guy. I'll hurt you, break you and make you cry. I'm not the hero of your story, Nemo. I've done bad, unforgivable things, but I will never let you go and I'll kill anyone who tries to keep you from me," my dark knight tells me and I know he's right.

"There's beauty to be found in broken things. They have stories to tell, histories to unravel and truths to reveal. They can be rebuilt, forged into something stronger. Maybe they'll never be the same as they were before but sometimes what emerges is something far more formidable." I press a kiss against his lips and continue to speak so he doesn't just hear me, he feels me.

"You'll be the dark to my light. We'll find our happy in the gray."

"Fuck," he whispers against me.

"Mmm... yes, please."

"I've created a monster." He laughs but his words grate against my skin. If only he knew.

"I... um actually would like to do something tonight but I don't know what the guys will think," I tell him, biting my lip.

"Doesn't matter what they think. If you want to do it, then we'll do it." I smile, not my hero my ass.

"I want to do a little memorial up here for Jack. I know in the grand scheme of things he was just one person out of thousands who lost their lives here but he was important to us. I hate that he's not leaving with us tomorrow. I want to say goodbye."

"Nemo, he's already free." I bury my head against his shoulder and sniff back the tears.

"If a memorial is what you want, then a memorial is what you'll get. You tell me what you need and the guys and I will get it for you."

AND THEY DID.

. . .

Hours later we stand together as a unit, a family united in grief over their fallen friend, along the edge of the roof with candles flickering gently in the rapidly cooling evening air.

"We'll carry you with us always." I speak into the quiet, looking over the town that houses all my memories of the dimpled boy who offered me his hand the first day I arrived here and his shoulder the day he left.

One by one, we share our memories, the good, the funny, the poignant. Although the evening is cloaked in sadness, there is something cathartic about it too. Jack would lose his shit if we didn't pull ourselves together. This place has taken so much from us we can't afford to give it any more. Tomorrow we need to be ready for anything. Despite the fact that the city is filled with nothing more than ghosts, I doubt very much they will let us leave out the front gate with a handshake and a smile.

# FIFTEEN

We never did make it back to the fort last night. We slept up on the roof, under the stars. It made me feel closer to Jack and somehow closer to Charlie, the little boy I so desperately wanted to get home to.

Hours later I wake up to a tongue flicking over my clit. My eyes spring open, taking in the still violet streaked sky as the sun starts to rise. The sleep quickly recedes from my brain, making me realize belatedly that I'm naked from the waist down.

"Sleeping beauty awakens," Fox murmurs. Drawing my attention to him, I notice it's still dark. When I open my mouth to speak, he takes advantage and presses his lips against mine, sliding his tongue inside my mouth. I sigh in contentment. When a finger slips inside my pussy, I make a strangled noise that Fox captures and swallows down. I pull away, gasping for breath as one finger becomes two. I look down and see it's Nate between my legs. It figures the stealthy ninja would be able to strip me half naked and go down on me without disturbing me until he was ready.

He scissors his fingers before sliding a third finger inside me. The stretch makes me burn a little but that only heightens my arousal.

"He's getting you ready for me. You might feel like those three fingers are pushing you to your limits but we both know my cock's bigger. You can take it, Nemo, you're my good girl."

"I can handle it," I moan in agreement.

"Oh, I know you can. AJ and Levi are doing a little recon so while they do that Nate and I are gonna love on you a little."

"I like this plan but I feel bad for AJ and Levi. You guys got the better end of the bargain," I manage to get out.

"Oh don't you worry about that. I've made a little deal with them to make it worth their while."

"Deal?" I question but it comes out high-pitched when Nate sucks hard on my clit as he starts to move his fingers inside me faster.

"They want to take you together, Nemo, one in your pussy, one in your ass," Fox tells me, his voice rough, letting me know he very much wants to watch this. A rush of wetness flows from me into Nate's mouth. His groan of approval echoes through my pussy, making my back arch off the ground.

"Oh, she likes that idea, Fox," Nate says as he lifts his head to look at me, licking his lips.

"Hm... Nemo, you really are perfect for us. Of course, I'm going to have to stretch out your tightest hole before I let them near you. Nobody is getting in there before me. Now I want you on your hands and knees," Fox orders, letting me know this is not a request. "I want to watch you suck Nate's cock again, being as you enjoyed it so much last time. Then I'm going to fuck you so hard you'll feel me inside you for the rest of the day."

Nate grabs my hips and helps turn me over, repositioning himself near my head after I rise onto my shaking knees. Fox moves behind me, leaving nothing for me to focus on but Nate's calloused hands sliding up and down his hard length.

I glance over my shoulder with a glare when Fox directs a sharp slap to my ass.

"Take him in your mouth, Nemo." Fox's voice is deep and filled with need.

Nate rubs his cock over my lips, waiting for me to open up. When I do, he slides right in.

"That's it, Nemo, just like that."

"Fuck," Nate grunts out, reaching out to grab my hair in his hand. I take him as far as I can, relishing the velvety feel of him sliding over my tongue until he comes to a stop at the back of my throat. I swallow, making Nate curse just as Fox nudges his cock into the entrance of my pussy. It's the only warning I get before he surges inside, pushing me farther onto Nate's cock and making me gag a little.

"Such a good girl, Nemo, taking our cocks like that." I hum at his praise, feeling powerful at the pure unadulterated need I bring out in them. He only gives me moments to adjust before he pulls back and slams himself inside me once more, thrusting forward until his thighs are flush with mine. Nate moves his hands to my jaw, holding my head steady as he fucks his cock in and out of my mouth. I let them take control, focusing on the taste of Nate and the feel of Fox as they push and pull me between them. All my senses feel heightened as it chases the high I know they can both give me. They move in tandem, a rhythm that speaks of familiarity and trust, showing the strength of the connection between them.

They pick up speed, one thrusting in as the other retreats, until finally, my world explodes into a kaleidoscope of colors.

They don't relent though. Finding my release gives them the green light to find theirs, fucking me hard and fast. Instead of my pleasure fading, a second orgasm approaches on the heels of the first, threatening to steal the breath from my lungs. I scream out an unintelligible sound, beyond words, or even coherent thoughts at this point.

Nate comes first, shouting my name hoarsely as he pumps his cum down my throat. It triggers my own release, making my pussy clamp down tightly around Fox's cock.

As Nate pulls back, Fox wraps his hand in my ponytail,

making my back arch as he pulls my head back. He thrusts into me forcefully, riding the edge of pleasure and pain before I feel a rush of warmth inside me and my name escapes his lips on a whispered plea.

"You just get better and better, Nemo," Fox tells me, placing a soft kiss at the base of my spine after he pulls himself free.

"Shower?" Nate asks me with a soft smile. I can feel the evidence of Fox's and my lovemaking running down my thigh and nod quickly. He scoops me up into his arms, clearly not worried about coming into contact with bodily fluids that aren't his.

"I'm stealing our girl," Nate informs Fox, standing with me in his arms. I wait for Fox to protest but he nods, standing and placing a kiss on my head. There is something off, something on his face that he's trying to keep hidden from me.

"Keep her safe. I'll join you guys in a few." I want to ask him if he's okay. I want to reach out and grab him and pull him to me and hold him tight, but something is telling me to give him a moment, so that's what I do. I rest my head on Nate's shoulder and let him lead me away.

When we reach the doorway, I call over my shoulder, "I love you, Valentine Fox."

"I know," he calls after me, making me smile but when he adds in a quiet voice, "I just hope it's enough," the smile slips off my face. Something is wrong, I feel it, that ominous shadow of foreboding that I felt yesterday, only now it's more prominent. As much as I'm praying that everything is going to be okay, I already know it won't be.

WE'RE ALL PACKED, our bags full of necessities for our escape, all trace of us eradicated from both apartments. It's like we were never here.

"Nemo?" I turn to face Fox after Nate pulls the strap of my pack tight for me. It's heavy but I can manage. There is no alternative and I don't want the guys to have to carry my load.

"Yeah, what's up?" His dark eyes stare into mine. I have to bite my lip to stop from losing myself in them.

"When Jack pulled everything he could find from the clinic, he didn't find your file." Shit, I have to tell them.

"I... I have my medical file on a hard drive in my bag. The doc wanted me to have it before I left. She said she wiped the rest," I tell him, waiting for his anger.

"Okay, Nemo." He strokes his hands up and down my arms to calm me. "It's fine, Nemo, deep breaths."

I do as he asks and suck in a lungful of air.

"The problem is, she left a footprint, an echo if you like. Sometimes the absence of information is more of a red flag than the information itself. Do you understand what I'm saying?" I nod slowly, clarity dawning.

"We need to head over to the clinic before we leave and wipe the whole system. Every hard drive and every backup. I don't want to leave anything to chance. Nemo, is there anything in that file that would make you a target? Well, more of a target than the rest of us. Is there something in there that would mark you as a person of interest?" I stare at him and feel a tear roll down the side of my face as I nod slowly.

"Fuck!" he roars, making me jump. He curses before pulling me into his arms and holding me tight. "Don't worry about that now, Nemo, there will be time later for you to tell me why you didn't feel you could come to me with this. For now, we need to move." I nod against his shoulder and pull away. None of the other guys say anything. They look at me like they want to ask a dozen questions but as Fox said, now isn't the time.

We head out into the surprisingly mild morning air. It's still early but we've been up for hours preparing everything. It's now or never. We jog toward the clinic, which looks empty, if the lack of lighting is anything to go by. We move silently, nothing needs to be said that hasn't already been covered. We all know the plan: stay together, destroy all the evidence, and then make our way over to the woods behind grid sector G.

I watch the guys pull open the double doors and tear their way through the clinic as I follow along behind them at a much slower pace. I look around the waiting area at the stark white walls and the hard, blue plastic chairs and flash back to the robotic faces on the mass of people there the first time we arrived here. I knew even then, subconsciously at least, that the fucked-up story they sold us was just the tip of the iceberg.

Death comes for us all. Coming here messed everything up and now we have to deal with the consequences.

"Stay within shouting distance, Nemo," Fox yells, his voice echoing off the silent walls that saw too much.

I head to the treatment room I always used and cautiously open the door. I'm so surprised when I see the doc in her chair hunched over her laptop that I stumble. I thought she would be long gone by now.

"Jesus, doc, you scared the shit out of me. What the hell are you doing sitting here in the dark? We need to go. Take whatever you can carry and leave everything else." I walk toward her and place my hand on her shoulder and turn her chair to face me when she doesn't answer. A startled scream escapes when her glassy dead eyes stare back at me completely void of life. The small gunshot wound at her temple provides the answer of how, but not the why.

The door swings open and smacks against the wall, letting me know Fox heard me cry out. He takes me in from head to toe to make sure I'm okay before walking over to see what startled me.

When he sees the very dead doc looking back at me, he lets out a string of creative profanities before pulling me against his chest.

"Why would they do this, Fox? She didn't deserve this, she was trying to make a difference," I cry out into his shoulder.

"I don't think anyone did this to her, Nemo," he says

softly, turning me and pointing at the gun on her desk that I failed to notice before now.

I sniff into his shoulder at the unfairness of it all.

"She found her own way out after all," I tell him quietly, which earns me a squeeze.

"Fox!" I hear Nate yell from another room. Fox looks down at me, torn about leaving. I lift up onto my tiptoes and place a light kiss on his lips to let him know I'm okay and pull away from him.

"Go, Fox, it's fine. I'm ready to get the fuck out of this place. I just want to say goodbye, 'kay?"

He nods once, already slipping back into the role of leader of our ragtag group and heads out the door leaving it ajar.

I bend and place my hand against her cool cheek.

"I hate that you couldn't see another way out. I hate that you left this world wearing a cape of guilt and regrets but I'm glad you're finally free. Say thank you to your husband and baby girl for letting me borrow you for a little while. I'm still standing, and I won't go down without a fight, I promise you that. Thank you for saving me."

I swallow and stand ready to leave when the notebook on her desk catches my attention. Ignoring the blood splattered across the page, I lift the book and try to make sense of the odd words.

*Fly away, firebird,*

*The hunters are coming.*

It sounds like a line from a children's book, but the words feel ominous, making the hairs on my arms stand on end.

Firebird? *Phoenix.*

Shit. They've sent someone to wipe us out. I run to the door with the notebook in my hand, stopping when I hear a voice that doesn't belong to one of my guys. It's oddly familiar but I can't place it. As far as I'm concerned, everyone here other than my guys and me is a potential threat.

I run back to the desk and swipe up the gun before stepping back behind the door. I listen quietly through the crack, wondering who this person is talking to and how many of them there are.

"Where is it? I'm sick to fucking death of waiting around. We're leaving today with or without it." I don't know what it is they're looking for but I'm pretty sure if it's that important they won't think twice about going through the guys and me to get it. I know the guys are capable of taking care of themselves but I refuse to let them be blindsided. I wait for the voice to drift away a little before quietly sliding up the large window and climbing out. My ankles jar as my feet make contact with the hard ground. I don't waste time worrying about minor injuries I know will heal, and I make my way around the edge of the building toward the next window. A quick look inside shows the room is empty, so I move on to the next. When I find that one empty too, worry worms its way through me. Where the fuck is everyone?

I stop and strain my ears when I realize I can hear faint voices. I follow the sound to the edge of the building and peer around the side, careful to remain hidden from sight. I sigh in relief when I spot AJ, Levi, and Nate talking. I tuck the gun into the pocket of my hoodie and take a step towards them but freeze when I realize that it's not Fox they're talking to like I thought, it's the man from inside. And just like that, I remember where I've heard his voice before.

*"I would like you to administer a second dose of the serum, doctor, and observe the patient closely. Keep them here for monitoring for the next twenty-four hours if necessary."*

*"But sir, that much is likely to be lethal."*

*"Might I remind you that we are running out of time? Do it, that's a direct order."*

He's the doctor that nearly killed me. What the fuck is he doing here and how does he know my guys?

"I didn't bring you guys here to pity fuck some cancer ridden chick. I'm sick of this shithole, I'd have thought you lot would have been too." I watch Nate step toward him, his anger palpable, but AJ and Levi hold him back.

"Watch your fucking mouth, Keets. We came here to do your dirty work but we don't answer to you. I've given two months of my time to you for this cause, to help you and your fucking team find the answers you're looking for, watching on as everyone around me died. So don't fucking preach to me about being stuck in this shithole. You have no fucking clue."

I push my fist into my mouth and bite down hard to stop myself from screaming.

Keets stands tall and throws Nate a superior look.

"You might be our first wave success story but you won't be the last. You are stronger and faster than the average regular Joe, I'll give you that, but you are nothing compared to the soldiers this batch of serum is producing. They are fucking mutants with powers beyond your wildest dreams and we'll either harness it or eradicate it," he tells him, unaware his words are leaving my insides shredded.

"I don't want or need mutant fucking powers, Keets. I'm as fucked-up as I am because of you and your goddamn group of wannabe gods."

"Fuck you. I took you from a cage—" he yells, but Nate cuts him off.

"And swapped it for a gilded one."

"Oh, cry me a fucking river. Where's Fox?"

"Here." Fox's voice sounds from behind me, making me spin around. All eyes fall on me, making me back myself up into the wall.

My heart threatens to punch its way out of my chest as Fox stalks toward me, bracing his arms above my head and pinning me in.

"Nemo." His voice is guttural and thick with a plea of some kind but I can't decode it, my head spinning with all the new information it has just been bombarded with.

I look up into the eyes of the man I love and let him see the damage he's done.

"This changes nothing, Nemo."

"This changes everything," I whisper, my voice thick with tears.

"Shit, we wanted to tell you," AJ adds as the others finally close in on us.

"Were you ever in prison?" I ask, not knowing what's true or false anymore.

"Yes. All of that is true, even the part about being recruited. It's just that it was two years ago for us. There was a security breach so we were placed back into the prison undercover when we found out John had been preselected for this project." AJ answers.

"You all acted like I was crazy when I said we could heal." The hurt is clear in my voice.

"I know," Levi agrees, not offering me any excuses.

"Why though? Why make me feel like an idiot? You could have told me the truth."

"We were ordered to maintain our cover no matter what," Nate tells me with regret in his voice.

"And was I part of your cover? Or was I just something of a team building exercise for you guys to pass your time with? Was that your idea of doing a good deed, give the poor little sick girl a good dicking before she kicked the bucket?" I yell turning back from Nate to Fox.

"No, Nemo. Fuck, no. You were never part of our mission; we were woefully unprepared for you."

"As touching as this is, you four still have a job to do. Get rid of her or I will," the asshole barks at Fox, making him stiffen.

"If you touch her, Keets, you will die." Fox's voice is lethal.

"Remember who supplies you with your serum, Fox," Keets warns him.

"What?" I gasp. Fox pulls back a little, cupping my jaw so I can't turn away.

"We were criminals, Nemo. We had no one at home and nothing to lose. We were approached by the Phoenix Corporation with an offer that seemed too good to be true. A year of our lives being tested on like lab rats and if we survived, we would be given new identities and our freedom. We started taking the serum and instead of killing us, it made us better. Phoenix Corps made us a counter offer, a second chance if you like, to be better men than we had started as. We became soldiers, Nemo, and we're damn good at it. We even train the new recruits. There are fifteen groups of us at the moment and we trained them all."

All the times I thought they worked like a team and how Fox acted as their leader wasn't just my imagination. My subconscious figured out what I refused to see.

"Was there anything I told you that you didn't already know?" I laugh self-deprecatingly, all the easiness between us disappearing.

"We couldn't tell you anything. And we really didn't know about the little white zombifying tablets." Fox glares, stepping away from me, taking an aggressive step toward Keets. Nate stops him before he can grab him.

"But why are you even still taking the serum after all this time?" I'm so fucking confused.

"We're soldiers, Cam. The best of the best. We keep everyone safe and the serum allows us a better chance to come home afterwards by giving us an edge," Nate tells me.

"But you don't need the serum with the nanobots," I point out. My words are met with silence before it's shattered by the unmistakable sound of a gun firing. Searing pain in the side of my head, a second before I drop to the floor, makes me gasp in disbelief. *I've been shot.* Dimly, I'm aware of Fox's roar of anger and the sound of flesh hitting flesh.

The feel of my body being moved and my head being lifted into someone's lap has my brain exploding with searing pain as agony ripples through me.

"Cam. Cam?" I manage to peel my eyes open but everything is red like someone has put a filter over the world.

"Holy fuck! Fox. *Fox*!" Nate shouts at the top of his voice. "She's alive." It must be Nate's lap I'm lying in as I can see his haunted face looking down at me before Fox is there too, his hands hovering over me like he doesn't know where to touch me. He looks ravaged with pain himself.

"Fuck! Fuck! Don't you fucking dare leave me, Nemo. Someone give me something to clean up this blood. I can't see jackshit," he yells, but I can hear the panic clear in his voice.

"'Soookay," I slur, my tongue feeling too big for my mouth.

I see Levi step up and whip his T-shirt over his head before tossing it to Fox. He catches it one handed and with shaky hands, uses it to wipe the blood from my face. Huh, so that's what the red film was. Why am I always getting hurt? Fuck's sakes it's getting really old.

"I got shot again?" I don't know if it's a statement or if I'm asking for clarification because the shock refuses to wear off. *Someone pointed a gun at me and pulled the trigger yet a-fucking-gain.*

"Bring her back to the treatment rooms if you want her to live," I hear Keets rasp out from somewhere to my left, but I can't turn my head to locate him.

"I'll never let her anywhere near you. If you even speak her name, I'll break more than just your legs," Fox tells him, his voice as lethal as a whip.

"She'll die without the serum." He laughs but a smack of flesh against flesh leaves him moaning again.

"Don't listen to him, Nemo. I'm going to find you some serum and you'll be good as new. Just hold on for me, okay?" Fox tells me softly but when he tries to stand, I grip his leg.

"I don't need it. Self-healing, remember?" I tell him with a grimace.

He swallows hard before speaking.

"You've been shot in the fucking head, Nemo. You can't heal from that, not without a little help."

"I'm a class four healer, Fox," I tell him something I suspected that was confirmed in my medical file.

"What?" Levi asks in wonder from beside Nate and I realize all my guys are gathered around me.

"I can heal from all non-fatal injuries," I explain quietly, feeling the bullet begin to expel itself from my body.

"This *is* a lethal injury, Cam," Levi points out.

"And yet here I am. It's not a lethal injury for me. I'm pretty sure nothing short of a beheading or having my heart removed will kill me. Let's just not test that theory yet." The silence around me is broken only by everyone's harried breathing.

"You promise?" Fox asks, his shoulders rigid with tension.

"Well, I've never been shot in the head before but..." Fox's creative curse words cut me off from speaking. Right, too soon for jokes.

"Fox! Calm down right this second." I raise my voice, hoping my head doesn't explode. Surprisingly, he does as I say just in time to hear the click of metal dropping to the asphalt beneath me.

Fox sifts through my hair until he finds the flattened bullet, lifting it into the air for everyone to stare at in disbelief. It always amazes me how something so tiny and innocuous can cause so much damage.

"Amazing," the dickhead who shot me observes. Feeling stronger now, I look over to where he lies on the floor with his legs bent at unnatural angles.

"That's twice you've tried to kill me." I pull on Fox and

despite everyone's protests I use him as leverage and pull myself into a sitting position.

"What are you talking about?" Levi asks me.

"Your good friend Keets over here double dosed me with serum, boiling me from the inside out, until eventually, my heart gave out. Doc saved me," I tell them with a shrug. They all have matching expressions of anger and horror across their faces. After experiencing what that stuff feels like racing through their veins, I'm sure they can appreciate the absolute agony I had been in.

"You were causing a distraction. They had a mission; you were fucking with it. You had proven useless other than providing us with the knowledge that prolonged use of inhibitors will eradicate any new powers the serum bestows upon a person. Thinking about it, that might become handy in producing a vaccine. You never know when one of these mutations will be an evolutionary step too far." He chuckles like we're old friends and not like he's a psychotic asshole who just shot me in the head.

"When you didn't show any signs of mutation or any healing abilities beyond a class one, your usefulness had come to an end. I pushed the double dose of serum in the hopes of forcing a reaction or disposing of you once and for all. You didn't gain any powers and you didn't fucking die like you were meant to."

"It wasn't an accident I was placed in that apartment with these guys, was it?" Please be wrong, I beg. He rolls his eyes at me like I'm dumb.

"No, of course not, although the whole you pretending to be a boy thing threw me for a while." I turn back to face Fox and the guys ready to rip them a new asshole when I see them staring at Keets and me in shock.

"You didn't know?" How can that be? I turn back to Keets.

"Why would you put me with them and yet not tell them about me?" That doesn't make any sense.

"I knew they would keep an eye on you if you lived with them regardless of them knowing who you were and, frankly, beyond that, I didn't care. You might be a person of interest to one of the bigwigs further up the Phoenix Project chain but I have far more pressing things to figure out than you. When I realized you were compromising them, I sent that idiot John after you. As soon as I told him you were a girl putting out for all his housemates bar him, he was eager to help. Now he's unaccounted for and I have his father asking questions. Care to shed some light on that?"

"John's father was the leak. We followed the trail and it led back to him," AJ tells him.

"John had spiraled and he was getting sloppy at covering up his crimes. Daddy dearest had put all his faith in this project working and, well, if it failed he was going to use it as a scapegoat. I can just imagine the newspaper's front page now, 'Prominent judge's son retreats to a mental health facility after the government funded Phoenix Project caused him irreversible brain damage thanks to the administration of prohibited drugs,'" Levi points out.

"Luckily for you, John and his father are dead, dickhead,"

I say. "Thanks to you, though, so is Jack." He looks around as if just now noticing Jack's absence and shrugs like it's nothing of importance, like forgetting to pick up milk from the store.

I climb to my feet and walk over to this sorry excuse of a man and stomp on one of his broken legs. He squeals loudly but something is off. I have learned to trust my instincts, so I take a step back and look him over.

His skin is a little pale but apart from the obvious injuries he doesn't look too bad.

"You're a super," I whisper. The guys are at my back in an instant.

"You're delusional."

"No, I don't think I am." I look at him and tip my head curiously.

"Both your legs are broken and yet you haven't even broken a sweat. Your moans and groans feel fake and practiced and you shot me knowing Fox would beat you almost to death... You can't feel pain," I conclude. He looks at me for a second as if he's about to deny it but then thinks better of it, his superiority rising to the surface.

"There is nothing he can do to me that I can't handle," Keets spits out.

"Yeah, try and tell me that when he rips your head off."

"Listen here, you whore-" Fox has his hand around Keets's neck and his body inches off the ground before he can even finish his sentence.

"*Don't speak to her,*" Fox grits out through his teeth before tossing him to the ground like a rag doll.

"Fox will kill you. How can you not see that?" I'm severely questioning this guy's sanity.

"Fox needs me, they all do, and their need for the little boost the serum gives them will override whatever he thinks he sees in you."

I hold my finger up and turn my back on him to face the guys.

"Are you guys supers or potentials?"

"We are the Phoenix Project's first-generation potentials. We heal, as you know, and we're stronger, faster, and smarter than the average person but none of us has developed any fantastical powers," Nate answers with a shrug.

With a frown, I consider his words and think back to the last time I wondered about coincidences. I was right then. And something is nagging at me now too.

"That just doesn't seem right, Nate." I look up at them all frowning down at me.

"What are the odds that none of you are supers when dickhead over there is? And why are you still getting the serum shots? You were never sick to begin with, so you didn't need them to repair anything." I'm missing something but the headache from getting a bullet to the skull is messing with my thought pattern.

"We're soldiers, Cam. We get injured. We take the serum to give us a boost and to heal any damage caused on a mission.

"But that's what the nanos are for."

"No, shut your whore mouth," screams Keets, only

shutting up when Nate kicks him in the head with his booted foot, knocking him out. I remember doc's words about how none of the soldiers would know about the nanos and swallow hard.

"Nanos? Explain," Levi demands, sounding like Fox at this moment.

"Stage two is the administration of nanobots into the bloodstream. They take over from the serum. The serum repairs any damage, that's true, but once your body is as good as it's going to get, the nanos take over that role. Kind of like a maintenance crew, keeping everything in check. The serum has already changed your physiology, the nanos just maintain it. You don't need the serum because the changes won't wear off. So, either you haven't been given the nanos or..." Fuck!

"Or? Cam, just spit it out!" AJ yells.

"Or they've been injecting you with an inhibitor," I tell them quietly.

"No, that can't be right, Cam." Levi shakes his head, clenching his fists at his side.

"You would need to receive the inhibitor weekly for them to counteract the nanos because they'll work to get rid of it. So I could be wrong. When you're off on missions, you don't go for shots, right? So maybe it's something else. Maybe you were never given the nanos—" Fox cuts me off.

"We travel with a member of the medical team. They administer our dose before we go to bed." And that explains why they never noticed the loss of time before.

“I still don’t get it. After all this time, the serum would have done all it could do. I understand them using the sedatives because I don’t think I could handle two years of having lava pumped into my veins every day, but the question remains, why?”

“Lava? What are you talking about? The serum feels uncomfortable, granted, but it’s more like ice water being pumped into you then lava,” Levi points out, confused.

"Oh, shit.” I snap my mouth shut, understanding what’s happened.

“What?” AJ asks.

“The serum feels like fire racing through your veins. I have, however, experienced the icy cold feeling you’re talking about. That’s what the inhibitors feel like.” I’m silent for a beat, letting them absorb that blow.

“This means you might all be supers. You just won’t know it until the inhibitor is worked out of your system completely.”

AJ walks over to an unconscious Keets and starts kicking him over and over. Fox grabs him, holding him back as AJ struggles in his arms.

“Get it together, AJ. I get it, man, I get it, but now isn’t the time.”

I look down and notice Keets is awake and watching us all. “Why?” I ask him. “Why would you lie to them about this? You could have had four more super soldiers to add to your collection so why would you use inhibitors on them?”

“It was unauthorized. They work for us, yes, but we also

send them out as soldiers for hire. We needed to see if these powers could be controlled first and, let's be honest, they are fucking criminals. We gave them a second chance but the rest had to be earned. If they remained loyal, they would be taken off the inhibitors much like you were— "

"And that's why you wanted me here so you could see firsthand what the side effects are from being inhibited for so long." I shake my head at the irony.

"You fucking prick!" Fox spits at him.

"Why are you doing this?" I question Keets, suddenly feeling tired of all of it "What was in it for you?"

He looks up at me with a sneer. "I was part of the second test trial run by Doctor Callahan." I flinch, hearing my father's name but Keets is too caught up in the sound of his own voice to notice.

"Three hundred and twenty-two people walked into the lab that day. I was one of only four who walked out. I was the leading heart surgeon in my field at the time, helping to heal patients and send them back home to their loved ones, until I got sick. A brain tumor, they said. It affected my speech, my thought process, and my ability to hold a scalpel. All my years of studying and working my fingers to the bone to become the best of the best were for nothing. It was all gone in the blink of an eye. I went from a man who was known for saving the unsaveable to the man who couldn't even save myself. I heard about the trial through a friend who worked at the same hospital and added myself to the list of candidates. I was one of the lucky ones selected and it worked. A true fucking miracle. But the good doctor decided the reward wasn't worth the cost.

"I was so angry. He had a fucking cure that could change the world but he was too much of a fucking coward to utilize it. I was living proof it worked, I felt amazing, better than I ever had before, but nobody wanted to listen. When I stopped responding to pain stimuli, everyone put it down to the side effects of the treatment but I knew it was more than that. I concealed my involvement as a patient and went back to work until I was approached by Phoenix Corps who were looking for someone with my skill set and my unique experience. Phoenix was more than happy to take all the risks needed. In the end, it didn't matter, we couldn't achieve the same results Dr. Callahan had. He could heal the body completely like it was never sick to begin with, while all we can do is freeze the diseases' progression. He had something we didn't, I just couldn't figure out what it was. Then I found out that the whole company was named after encryption that was found in one of Callahan's old research papers. He mentioned a Phoenix on dozens of occasions, but it was always in some kind of code that obviously only made sense to him. Somehow, though, I just knew that whatever this Phoenix was, it was the key to everything. Tony, John's father, was brought in as a consultant because once upon a time before he became a judge, he was a soldier who was somewhat of an expert at breaking codes. That's how he got John into this project; you scratch my back I'll scratch yours kind of thing. Should have realized he was a two-faced asshole. He spent months looking and still couldn't tell me one fucking concrete thing about the Phoenix." He turns from me to the guys who look at him in disgust.

"You guys think you're strong now, faster than ever, but just you wait. If I can find the Phoenix, I can give you new gifts beyond your wildest dreams." His eyes are wild with insanity. I step back, his words twisting my insides apart, making me turn around and vomit all over the floor.

All of this over me. All these people gone. Wait—

"Where are the rest of the staff members?"

Keets smiles like the murderer he is.

"They all went on with the new batch of mutants to the secondary location, leaving behind me and Cameron's doctor friend over there. She was dead when I found her, which was handy as it saved me a job.

"You're psychotic!" I spit.

"I'm a hero! I will save lives. While you only see this place as a factory to create human weapons, I see it as a place that makes our soldiers stronger on the frontline. I'm not the bad guy here, I just have to make the hard decisions. It's a tough world out there, little girl, one you just aren't equipped to deal with." he yells, clearly believing his own delusions.

"Oh, don't give me that. You're purposely misleading people, taking innocent lives and believing your own bullshit. I'll happily watch you burn for what you've done."

He laughs maniacally, looking at the guys around me.

Enough of this bullshit.

"Your soul might be glacial Keets," I tell him, lifting my

hand and holding it palm up, concentrating on the sensation of heat licking over my skin, "but I have fire burning in mine. You won't be walking away from here today even as you run your mouth to buy yourself time for your legs to heal."

"You *are* a super," he whispers in awe as a flame sparks in my hand.

"Nemo, what the fuck is going on?" Fox questions but I don't take my eyes off Keets.

"Do you even know who I am?" I question him, knowing he has no fucking clue.

"You're the only remaining subject from the original drug trial." Is that what they think? "You presented as a potential, but it didn't say what your gifts were. The Phoenix Corp found you through the inhibitors you were being prescribed. They wanted to see if you would gain your powers back or if the inhibitors had killed them off completely. I can't believe you're a super." His greedy eyes light up. I bend forward a little, needing him to hear my words.

"I'm so much more than a super, Keets. *I am Phoenix*." I watch his eyes widen in shock like it never occurred to him the Phoenix might be a person.

"How?" he croaks out

"My father was Dr. Callahan, the one who created the serum. I'm not a patient from the original test trial. I am the original patient." He shakes his head in denial, but I step closer to him, not giving him an inch. "You tried to kill me more than once. You kept my guys prisoner with your lies and Jack is dead as a result of your actions. I won't let you walk away just to hurt someone else."

"You'll forgive them for their sins but not me for mine when my intentions were pure?" he asks, shocked and confused, fiddling with a silver cross around his neck with a red gem in the center. I twist my head slightly as a low hum fills the air.

"You think you're a man of god because you wear an effigy around your neck. What you did goes against everything he stands for. Do not talk to me about forgiveness, I don't buy into that bullshit. I love them, so even though I'm mad as hell at them right now, we'll get past it. They don't really need my forgiveness, which is just as well, I'm not really the forgiving kind. All forgiveness does is absolve the culpable party of their guilt. Fuck that and fuck you."

The noise gets louder but instead of dropping to my knees, I'm subjected to nothing more than a dull ache and a trickle of blood leaking from my nose that I swipe away with the back of my hand. I stomp over to him and snap the chain away from his neck and see the little red gem is actually a button. *A kill switch.* Son of a bitch. I heat the offending cross before pressing it against Keets's forehead, burning an imprint of it into his skin. Without pain receptors, he can't feel a thing, but I know he can smell the charring of his skin.

"Where's your god now, Keets?" I mock him.

"Where's yours?" He laughs, his next words collapsing the foundations of my world upon me, leaving nothing but ash in its wake.

"Perhaps he's at Wembley Avenue."

I see Fox stiffen next to me and turn to face him, but my words are for Keets.

"How do you know where my family lives?" Doc wiped my file so he must have known from the start. I watch Fox freeze and all the color drain from his face.

"Fox?" I whisper. Something is wrong, very, very wrong.

"She hasn't figured it out yet?" Keets laughs uproariously. "Let's see if she still thinks you don't need her forgiveness."

"We didn't know. It was mixed in with the information Jack found the day he and I came to the clinic for answers," Fox tells me, taking a step forward but I take one back.

"The records we found showed that some of the missions we were contracted to do or that our teams were contracted to do were bogus, nothing more than a smokescreen to further their agenda. It's one of the reasons we were so ready to leave with you. They used us. We thought getting out of jail meant freedom, but it was an illusion. We were being manipulated; we were never free." He takes another step toward me and I mirror the movement, taking a step back.

"We were serious about leaving. You, me, and the guys. We can make a life for ourselves far away from here," he implores as AJ, Nate, and Levi step up beside him, looking at me with varying degrees of guilt and fear.

"Tell me what's going on, Fox," I order him quietly, my voice making him flinch.

"They lied to us, Nemo. They instructed us to take out a terrorist cell that was ready to strike. We were given specific orders. We're soldiers, we don't question orders, that's what gets you killed. We do what we're told, but I swear to god we didn't know." Fox begs me to believe him but the fact that Fox is begging me at all makes my head spin. Fox doesn't beg, Fox takes what he wants unapologetically.

"Oh, Cameron. You poor, naïve girl. Did you honestly think the Phoenix Corporation was going to pay out a million dollars to all of those families? Don't be so fucking ridiculous," Keets scoffs. "Why do you think we chose people from all over the world with small family units?"

"What is he talking about, Fox?" My voice is scarcely above a whisper, my whole body vibrating as my core temperature begins to rise. The flames from my hand slowly ascend their way up my arm.

"We were ordered to take out a terrorist cell at zero-twenty hours, then three hours later we were ordered onto a bus that brought us here." He tells me irrelevant shit that doesn't answer my question. "We rigged it to look like a gas explosion—"

"Where?" I whisper, but I get it now. I fucking know exactly where.

"*Say it!*" I scream at him when he doesn't speak.

"846 Wembley Avenue," he answers, dropping a bomb on my world, a second bomb to be precise.

"No. No, nononnono. No, Fox, please, please, please no." He moves forward but I step back, pushing myself up against the wall of the clinic, fire now burning up both arms and over my chest.

"We didn't know. I'm sorry, baby, I'm so fucking sorry," he whispers.

I scream, the pain inside me needing an outlet. I scream and scream until I taste blood in my throat and my voice gives out. I had experienced grief before, more than anyone my age should have, but nothing could have prepared me for this. Before I had hope, just a flicker of it, but it was enough to guide me through the insanity and now it was gone. Snuffed out along with everything I loved.

"You killed my family," I breathe out, my voice jagged and painful to hear, like broken glass being dragged over an exposed wound.

Fox looks into my eyes, his wet with grief and filled with shame and guilt.

I stare at him blankly, the wreckage of our relationship lying in ruins at our feet. He told me he would break me and he was right.

My voice comes out cold, void of all emotion. I feel as if all life within me has bled out, leaving me a shell of the girl I was before. Is this how Charlie felt before his eyes slipped closed for the last time? A wave of despair threatens to cripple me but I fight against the onslaught. I will never leave myself vulnerable again. I mentally flood my veins with concrete and encase my heart in fortified steel, preparing to protect myself as I flay myself open one last time for all to see.

"You carved your name into my heart but before you came along, I gave a piece of it away to another. You wrapped my heart in barbed spikes, each one making me bleed a little with every breath I took. I told myself that was okay because you reminded me that I was alive. But Charlie," my voice breaks completely on his name, "he wrapped my heart in ribbons and bows, treating it as the most precious gift he had been given. Then you took your knives and shredded his ribbons and my heart right along with it. My brother is gone, and now so, too, is my reason to live." And with that, I shut off all my emotions and let the flames twist themselves around my body.

"No, you have us, we can—"

"You are dead to me." My voice is empty, sounding nothing like me at all. I walk backward through the open door into the clinic and push the fire outward, watching it spread along the walls and floors, over my face and over my hair. My mind and body are on emotional lockdown, but I understand all that rage and hopelessness has to go somewhere. I use it to fuel the inferno around me, relishing the heat as it licks over my skin.

"No, fuck, no, Nemo. NEMO!" I can see Fox screaming and fighting to get to me as Nate, AJ, and Levi struggle to hold him back. I push more and more energy out, feeding the flames, draining myself before I fall to my knees and weep scalding hot tears that drip into the flames with a hiss. The whole building is now engulfed in a storm of fire, impenetrable to anyone but me. I can just make out Keets's body burning on the ground outside and the surge of fire that makes its way toward the men I once loved, the men who finally succeeded where everything else in my life had failed. They managed to kill me.

## Fox

I watch from the open chopper door as the town is ravaged and destroyed by an unrelenting fire. A fire born of pain, misery, and hate. A fire I started.

"I'm sorry, Fox," AJ says from beside me. I turn to look at him, taking in his split lip and the black eye I gave him in my struggle to get to Nemo. I turn away without saying anything. I feel nothing. I am nothing without my Nemo.

She can hate me, she can try to kill me, she can even try to kill herself but I still won't let her go, never. Nemo is mine whether she wants to be or not. I told her I would drag her out of the fires of hell, I just didn't know how literal that was going to be.

We pull away as the fire continues to sweep through the town, turning everything to rubble and ash.

"How do we know she's still alive down there?" Levi asks from in front of me.

"Because I'd feel it if she were gone." I say it with a certainty born of instinct.

"She'll never forgive us," Nate tells me something I already know.

"I know, nor should she." I look over at them, the people who are as close to me as brothers and tell them my truth.

"I don't need her to forgive me, I just need her to love me.

I'm done trying to protect her from my darkness for fear of snuffing out her light. I've already fucked that up. I broke her just like I knew I would. It's time to bring her over to the shadows and together we can make everyone pay for the roles they played in this."

"What are we going to do?" AJ asks, using *we* instead of *you,* making me nod my head in gratitude.

"We're going to play with fire, whatever it takes to get Nemo back. I'll watch the whole world burn if necessary."

"She won't be the same girl, Fox," Nate warns me.

"I know, but she will rise up again. She doesn't know how not to. After all, she's a motherfucking Phoenix."

* * * * * ★ ★ ★ * * * * *



Turn the page for an excerpt of From the Fire

# EXCERPT: FROM THE FIRE

## ONE

It might have been the hand around my throat that woke me. But it's the pulling of my clothes by determined hands that has me snapping out of my sleep-filled haze and slipping into defensive mode. I lift my hand and gouge my thumb into my assailant's eye socket, reveling in his cry of pain. I use this distraction to hook my leg over his and flip him onto his back before straddling his chest, pinning his arms beneath my thighs.

I look down in disgust at the dirty, disheveled man as he glares up at me.

"What, isn't this what you imagined? You between my spread thighs?" I taunt as he tries to buck me off, but I'm stronger than he is, and he doesn't have the element of surprise on his side anymore.

"Fuck you, whore," he yells, spittle flying out of his mouth.

"Yeah, that's not gonna happen. Want to know what happened to the last guy that put his hands on me without permission?" I ask as he writhes and curses beneath me. I lean down and whisper into his ear.

"I killed him with my bare hands." I smile as my hands heat up, and I reach to cup his face. His eyes widen in fear as the color bleeds from his skin, leaving me feeling vindicated and powerful. I pull back before I burn him alive, smiling when I see two scorched handprints on either side of his face.

"Every time you look in the mirror, you'll think of me and the time you paid the price for trying to take something that wasn't yours." I stand up, ignoring his crying just as he would have ignored mine.

"Next time, I'd think carefully about the easy mark you plan to target. They might just surprise you."

Grabbing my backpack off the floor, I slide it over my shoulder and head out of the deserted building I've casually called home for the last month. I wince as the early morning sunshine momentarily blinds me before I glance down at my watch. Jesus, it's not even eight o'clock yet, and it's already threatening to be a scorcher. Not that I mind. I found I quite like the heat after all.

Walking around the block, I join the crowd of people heading off to start their day. Bankers and teachers, doctors, and accountants, mixed in with parents doing the school run, all oblivious that a fire starter walked among them. That's what I am now, thanks to the Phoenix Project and my father. They decided to play god and ended up creating a monster.

A year ago, I was dying. I traded what was left of my time to the Phoenix Project in the naive belief that they would provide for my little brother after I was gone.

But they lied to me. They lied to us all and now my little brother's body is nothing more than ashes in the wind, his life cut short by the very men I loved. I swallow hard and cut off that train of thought. It has taken me all this time to get my powers under complete control, but if anything were to set them off, it would be thoughts of my little brother Charlie and the guys that haunt my dreams.

I head towards the gym two blocks away, knowing it will already be open. When I get there, the little bell above the door signals my arrival and makes Victor, a hulk of a man with a shock of red hair, look up from the magazine he's reading at the desk.

"Hey, Ro," he greets me. "Gus is in the back." I nod my head and make my way down the dimly-lit corridor towards the main brightly-lit room at the back. I spot Gus in the far corner talking to a newbie so I leave him to it for a moment and look around to see if there is anyone else I recognize.

I spot Tom and Jason sparing in the boxing ring, talking about who did what to each other's mother the night before when both know that neither has been laid in months. There's a skinny kid with an attitude punching the fuck out of one of the bags, taking out his aggression on the leather that can handle what someone's face might not. He kind of reminds me of me when I first arrived here. I was like a powder keg of emotions threatening to explode at any moment, literally, and Gus helped me channel it.

The other guys that train here took a little convincing, telling me there was a ladies gym down the road. But Gus saw something in my eyes. He recognized the darkness in me and agreed to train me and give me an outlet for it. He is also one of the few people in the world who knows my secret.

Any sane man would have freaked the fuck out when I accidentally set the ring on fire with nothing but my body, but not Gus. No, it turns out Gus is quite possibly crazier than me. His only comment was to ask if I could heat up his coffee for him before holding his cup out toward me. I hadn't even realized I was crying until he was awkwardly patting me on the back. I ended up spilling my story. It's the first and last time I've told someone what happened, but he deserved to know what hollowed out the girl that stood before him.

"Ro!" I turn towards the voice and see Gus walking towards me. I don't say anything or even change the expression, but somehow I know he knows.

"You're leaving?" he asks.

"It's time," I tell him softly. I spent a year coming here, fighting, learning and training to be the best I could be, but that wasn't all. I somehow managed to pick up the pieces of my fractured soul and rearrange the broken parts into who I am now. It's not much, but the fact I'm still breathing and not staring into the bottom of an empty whiskey glass is a testament to how brightly my need for vengeance burns.

He looks at me, his dark shrewd eyes staring into mine. He doesn't try to talk me out of it, knowing it would be pointless. He just watches me, gauging my readiness before finally nodding.

"Run through everything you've learned. I'll be watching you. I want to see you for a few minutes before you go. It's important, okay?"

I nod and agree. Gus never asks me for anything, so this is the least I can do.

"Now go. I don't have time to stand around chatting with you. I have a gym to run, don't you know?"

I roll my eyes, my lips quirking up a little at his abrasiveness. Gus can act like a grumpy asshole for the world to see, but I know damn fine that beneath his prickly layer, there runs a heart made of marshmallow.

I change into one of the two spare outfits I have in my bag, swapping out my gray skinny jeans and black hoodie for a stretchy pair of black yoga pants and a cobalt blue racerback tank top. I don't really give a toss what I wear, but the yoga pants give me the freedom to move that skinny jeans don't.

I make my way over to the large leather bags in the corner, stepping over to the one beside the skinny dude with the anger issues.

His speed has slowed, his breathing becoming rapid, and each punch that hits the bag becomes less and less forceful.

Yes, it seems the bag was successful at absorbing his aggression today. A part of me envies him, knowing he will walk out those doors feeling lighter than when he entered, but then I remember how much my anger fuels what I need to do next and shake it off.

For the most part, I ignore him, focusing only on the task at hand. Jab, Jab, cross. Jab, Jab, cross. I zone out, concentrating on each movement I make, pulling my punches a little at the last minute, so I don't give these guys a display of my true strength.

I spend the next six hours working my way around the gym, dividing my time between each piece of available equipment and sparing in the ring with whoever is feeling cocky enough. In the end, it doesn't matter; they don't come out of the ring with anywhere near as much swagger as when they entered it.

I might not have any boobs, thanks to an unnecessary mastectomy, but it doesn't change that I am indeed a girl and most men's egos can't cope with having their asses kicked by someone who they believe to be the weaker sex.

When I'm finally spent, I head to the showers and stand under the scalding water, letting it wash away the day's grime and sweat.

Climbing out, I swipe my hand over the steamy mirror and stare at the reflection of my face. My once chocolate eyes are now an amber color that flash like fire when I'm angry or agitated, or at least they used to until I had gotten better at controlling it. My skin is blemish-free and smooth, any bruising or cuts disappear almost immediately now, depending on the severity of the injury. The lack of marks on my skin bugs me the most. It's like a shiny coat of paint over a rusted broken-down car. Both deceptive and untrue. The lack of bags under my eyes implies I'm well-rested when I haven't slept properly for a year.

I look down at my hands and see nothing but soft, smooth skin. After six hours of punching things without gloves, I should have broken skin and bloody knuckles, but no, nothing. It's all smoke and mirrors. The face staring back at me might be considered flawless to some, but beneath that layer of false perfection is nothing more than a chasm of emptiness. Everything inside me has been hollowed out to avoid feeling anything except this bone-deep anger. If I switched my emotions back on now, I'd bleed to death under the onslaught of pain and despair I had barely managed to keep at bay to function.

I was broken, scarred, bruised, and bleeding. I just refused to feel it, and nobody looked beneath the surface long enough to see it.

I take a deep breath and remind myself that it's only going to be an asset to be able to heal this quickly when I'm about to go to war with a company that is bigger, stronger, and has far more resources than me but it's still a bitter pill to swallow.

I slip on my last outfit of black skinny jeans, long-sleeved black Henley, and my knee-high black combat boots. I redo the two Viking braids on either side of my head and shove everything back into my backpack before heading out to find Gus.

He's waiting for me in the small dimly-lit room at the back of the building. He sits behind his large desk that is cluttered with — well, everything by the looks of it— and watches me enter and close the door. I take in his off-white walls mostly hidden beneath a layer of newspaper cuttings. Some recent, providing accounts of champions from this gym, some were much older, but the yellowing and fading of time didn't take away from this man's pride in the people who came through these doors over the years and went on to discover their inner greatness.

"Sit," Gus orders, nodding to the empty chair in front of the desk.

I drop my bag to the floor and sit like he asked and wait for him to continue.

"You have a plan?" he questions, the faint traces of Russian accent slipping through even though Gus has been a New Yorker for forty years.

"Locate and kill mostly," I answer with a nonchalant shrug.

"Simple but effective." He nods. "I have two stipulations before you leave." He raises his hand, stopping me from arguing with him.

"Did I give you the impression this was negotiable? Nyet, you will give this old man peace of mind or I will tie you up and gag you," he tells me, his face set in a determined scowl.

"Tie me up and gag me? I mean I like you Gus, and I'm

not one to kink shame, but you're old enough to be my grandfather," I say with a shake of my head, making him roll his eyes at me while muttering what I'm sure is a multitude of Russian curses under his breath.

"You are a pain in my ass," he tells me, making me smile because he's not wrong.

"Stipulations?" I prompt.

"You check in regularly. Just one text is enough to know you are alive, but if I don't hear from you, I will assume you're dead. This means not only will I find your body and kick your ass for dying, I will blow the lid off of this fucking Phoenix Project. I will take it to every single news outlet in the world."

Again I open my mouth to tell him that is a very bad idea, but he glares at me. I sigh and give in. I guess I'd better not die then.

"And the second thing?"

He grins then and if I didn't know him, I'm pretty sure I would have just crossed the street to avoid him.

"Come." He stands and heads out of the office, not bothering to wait for me as I trail behind him out of the gym and across the walkway that leads to the two-story nondescript house Gus lives in.

I've been here a few times, mainly for dinner when Gus wouldn't let me refuse, but I've never stayed, despite Gus's insistence and him having a spare room. The thought of living with anyone again—I shut it down. Those thoughts have no place here.

He leads me through his small kitchen, into the utility room, and finally into a darkened garage, which I actually hadn't been inside before. When he flicks on the overhead fluorescent lighting strip, I can see why.

Sitting proudly in the middle of the room is a fully restored 1982 F-150 truck in blue and white. She's so pretty to look at, she almost distracts me from the rest of the room but only almost.

I'm thinking it would take a classic Shelby at least to distract me from the row upon row of guns, knives and other weapon paraphernalia lining the walls.

I turn to face Gus, who is beaming from ear to ear like he's showing off his grandchildren and not an arsenal of weapons, and cock an eyebrow in question.

"Why, Gus, I do believe you have some explaining to do."

# ACKNOWLEDGMENTS

Jay Aheer – Designer magician. Thank you for weaving your magic into my beautiful cover.

Tanya Oemig – My incredible editor - AKA miracle worker - who goes above and beyond.

Missy Stewart – Proofreader, lifesaver, and the nicest person on the planet.

Gina Wynn - Formatting Queen. Nobody does it better than you.

Sosha Ann – My amazing PA and friend.

The Parents of Aspen Marks, AC Wilds, and Isobelle Carmichael – Thank you for having sex with each other and creating the most awesome women on the face of the planet.

When I started out on this crazy journey, I had no idea I was going to be lucky enough to find not just one, but three of the best friends a girl could ask for. You ladies have walked beside me every step of the way. I adore each of you and can't imagine my life without you in it.

Julie Melton, Rachel Bowen, Sue Ryan - My Beta Angels. You ladies are the bee's knees. I will never be able to tell you how much I love and appreciate everything you do for me.

Thais Neves – My geeky t-shirt wearing, afternoon napping, kebab obsessed, pineapple on pizza hater, sprinkler of commas, coffee drinking, science nerd. You are my favourite human on the planet. If friends were noses, I'd pick you over and over again. My life is a thousand times better because you are in it. #youcanneverleave.

My readers – You guys are everything to me. I am in awe of the love and support I have received. You are the reason I keep going even on my darkest days.

Thank you for taking a chance on my book. If you enjoy it, please leave a review.

# ABOUT THE AUTHOR

Candice is a romance writer who lives in the UK with her long-suffering partner and her three slightly unhinged children. As an avid reader herself, you will often find her curled up with a book from one of her favourite authors, drinking her body weight in coffee. If you would like to find out more, here are her stalker links:

FB Group https://www.facebook.com/groups/949889858546168/

Amazon amazon.com/author/candicewrightauthor

Instagram https://www.instagram.com/authorcandicewright/?hl=en

FB Page https://www.facebook.com/candicewrightauthor/?modal=admin_todo_tour

Twitter https://twitter.com/Candice47749980

BookBub https://www.bookbub.com/profile/candice-wright

Goodreads https://www.goodreads.com/author/show/18582893.Candice_M_Wright

Printed in Great Britain
by Amazon

36499586R00180